LooseId

ISBN 10: 1-59632-128-8
ISBN 13: 978-1-59632-128-1
HARD CANDY
Copyright © 2005 by Loose Id, LLC
Cover Art by April Martinez
Edited by: Linda Kusiolek, Maryam Salim, and Erin Mullarkey

Publisher acknowledges the authors and copyright holders of the individual works, as follows:
HERO SANDWICH
Copyright © January 2005 by Angela Knight
CANDY FOR HER SOUL
Copyright © January 2005 by Sheri Gilmore
FORTUNE'S STAR
Copyright © January 2005 by Morgan Hawke

This book is an original publication of Loose Id. Each individual story herein was previously published in e-book format only by Loose Id and is a work of fiction. Any similarity to actual persons, events or existing locations is entirely coincidental.

Printed in the U.S.A. by
Lightning Source, Inc.
1246 Heil Quaker Blvd
La Vergne TN 37086
www.lightningsource.com

Contents

Hero Sandwich

Angela Knight

Meg Jennings stepped out onto the roof of her apartment building, her boots scraping on the concrete. Below, horns honked and an eighteen-wheeler growled in acceleration as a fire truck wailed its way down the street.

Restless, she strode to the roof's edge. All around her, the lights of Manhattan glittered in the darkness as if the stars had showered down to earth. Meg stared downward, brooding.

She'd had no choice except to break it off with Richard tonight. Much as she loved him, she couldn't keep tolerating his secrecy, his habit of disappearing, his evasiveness. She couldn't even remember the last time they'd actually ended a date without him being called off by some mysterious phone call. Any explanation he'd bothered to give afterward always had the ring of a lie.

Meg had lived a double life long enough to recognize the signs in somebody else. She knew what she was doing in hers. She wasn't at all sure she wanted to know what Richard was doing with his.

Maybe he was a hero, risking his life in the pursuit of justice. But there was something about Richard, something just a little bit dark, a little bit ruthless. That sounded more like villain than hero to Meg—and she wasn't willing to go down that particular road again. She didn't like where it led.

Even so, the expression on his handsome face when she'd told him it was over had stabbed into her soul. Pain and vulnerability were not emotions she associated with Richard Drake, billionaire captain of industry.

She'd found herself explaining. "I just can't live with the lies anymore, Richard."

A cool gleam of determination replaced the pain in those wolf-pale eyes. "We all have our secrets, Meg. And we all tell lies." Then he'd walked out.

Now she glowered at the city below. *We all have our secrets.* What the hell did that mean?

With a huff, Meg stepped off the edge of the roof and into empty air. For an instant, she fell like a rock. Then the generators in her suit started pumping out lev-fields, and she rose slowly skyward like a soap bubble on the breeze.

Absently, she watched the traffic stream below her boots in a river of headlights. Was this what Richard meant? Did he know what she was? And would he tell anyone in that other life she suspected he led?

If he did, he might as well paint a target on her chest and declare open season. Too many pissed-off villains—and even a few heroes—had sworn to take revenge on Paparazzi for the photos she'd taken. If any of them ever found out who she was, she wouldn't have a prayer.

It was hard to believe Richard would deliberately endanger her that way. But then, she didn't really know him, did she? That was the whole problem.

Frowning, Meg stretched her body out in the air, letting the lev-fields cradle her in invisible lines of force. With one hand, she checked the bag attached to her equipment belt. Her camera gear was safely stowed, ready for the night's adventures. Taking a deep breath, she slowly flexed her toes, triggering the acceleration controls in her boots. Instantly, she shot forward, propelled by the levitation fields rippling around her.

It was ironic, really. If her father hadn't been such an adrenaline junkie, he could have been pulling in billions in patent proceeds. The American military would have paid a great deal for a suit that could both levitate its wearer and turn him invisible.

Unfortunately, exploiting his inventions had always held less appeal for Gerald Jennings than committing crimes as the supervillain Bankbuster. He and his partner Nightwolf had terrorized New York together, in between battles with superheroes like Cougar and Lynx. Which was why Gerald was doing fifty in Attica now instead of living the high life in Acapulco.

Meg was lucky she hadn't gone down with him. When she'd turned fifteen, Nightwolf had lost a fight with Cougar and gone to jail. Her father hated working alone, so he gave her a lev-suit and forced her to become his sidekick, Sneak Thief. For the next two years, she'd lived in a constant state of terror as they used their suits in nighttime bank robberies.

Finally, Meg could take no more. She told her father she'd robbed her last bank. Enraged, Gerald beat her so badly, he had to take her to the hospital before he robbed the bank he'd targeted. Cougar and Lynx caught him that very night.

Bankbuster's conviction freed Meg from her life of crime, but it also left her with a very big problem. Her mother was dead, and the money Gerald had left in an offshore bank wouldn't last long. Though she was old enough to go out on her own by then, she had no way to support herself except minimum-wage jobs.

Meg briefly considered selling her own suit to the Army, but she didn't know how it worked. Besides, admitting she had Sneak Thief's costume wasn't exactly a good move, given the charges hanging over her head. She had to find another way to make a living.

* * *

Meg had been at a loss until the night she decided to take a camera along on one of her flights through the city. She'd always loved shooting the New York skyline from the air, but her subject that night proved a lot more exciting.

She was just about to snap a shot of the Empire State Building when a flash of fire in the night sky caught her attention. When she flew over to investigate, it turned out to be Megaman locked in battle with the Crimson Scorpion. Invisible, Meg zipped around them, snapping pictures of their combat.

As soon as the fight was over, she made a beeline for one of the city's newspapers. The night editor bought the photos on the spot, despite his doubts about the masked woman who'd taken them.

And so Paparazzi was born.

The question was, did Richard know her other identity—
and would he tell anybody?

* * *

Cougar had chosen his vantage point carefully, right on the
edge of the rooftop. He figured he'd be silhouetted against the
streetlights below.

Easy for anybody flying overhead to spot.

"Think she'll show?" Lynx asked. The communications unit
in Cougar's mask was so good, it sounded as if his brother was
whispering right in his ear.

"Tonight?" Cougar shrugged. "Who knows? Eventually?
Yeah, eventually."

Lynx grunted. "Hope she doesn't take too long. We've got
more important things to do."

"Patience, Grasshopper. She's had this coming for a while.
And I mean to make sure she gets it."

There was no sound for a moment except the roar of traffic
from below. A jet screamed by overhead. Finally, Lynx asked,
"Isn't that a little extreme? I mean, it's not like she's Nightwolf.
She's just a photographer."

"What, you *enjoy* being a joke on Leno?" The photo in the
New York Daily Journal had been taken immediately after last
night's brawl with Battle Ax. Unfortunately, the brotherly arm
Cougar had thrown around Lynx's shoulders had looked like
something entirely different to people who'd been speculating
about their sexual preferences for years. Everybody from Jon
Stewart to Conan O'Brien had riffed on it.

In the shadows of the building's rooftop elevator, Lynx shifted his weight, boots scraping on the cement roof. Cougar's animal-acute hearing picked up the sound clearly. "People have been making those jokes since we started out. Like you always say, that's what happens when you run around in leather. Paparazzi was only doing her job."

"That's not what you said when Jay said we make a cute couple."

"I was ticked. Look, Cougar, pissing us off isn't against the law, so we can't take her to jail. What the hell are we going to do with her once we do catch her?"

Cougar smiled slowly. "I'll think of something."

* * *

Years of experience had taught Meg the perfect flying height if she wanted to spot supers in action. Even so, sometimes she circled the city for hours without seeing anything worth shooting. It was the luck of the...

What was that?

She braked into a hover, attention caught by a human shape standing on a rooftop, silhouetted against the lights. The guy was so broad-shouldered he just had to be superpowered. Meg shot down for an invisible fly-by.

He stood with one leg bent, bracing a boot against the low rooftop wall. Soft brown leather armor emphasized his narrow waist and the contrasting width of powerful shoulders. A leather helmet in the shape of a cat's head covered his face. The cat's roaring jaws framed his lower face and the grim line of his mouth. She'd always found that mouth perversely sexy.

Cougar.

Meg's heart began to pound as her instinct to run like hell battled her need for a closer look. New York's premier hero had fascinated her since she was a scared fifteen-year-old watching him battle her father. Every time Gerald had reeled under one of those powerful punches, guilt, terror, and hope had warred in her soul. Secretly, she'd dreamed Cougar would rescue her.

And in the end, he'd done just that.

Meg was twenty-three now, and Cougar still starred in her fantasies, though her dreams had taken a distinctly adult turn these days. He was just so...*male,* so dominant, so hard-edged and grimly handsome. You just knew he'd be the type to go for handcuffs and kinky sex.

She'd even told Richard about those fantasies one night after three glasses of really good champagne. Richard being Richard, he'd offered to rent a costume, but she hadn't been quite *that* drunk.

Now there he stood in the flesh. Cougar. All by himself. Not fighting anybody. She could actually get close and just look at him, instead of snapping a shot and fleeing for her life.

Meg drifted down to hover ten feet away. Taking her time, she floated closer, slow enough to avoid creating a rush of air that would betray her to Cougar's hyperhuman senses. He didn't seem aware of her presence. He just stared down at the street below as though watching something, still as a hunting cat.

Damn, he was big. Had to be six-four at least. Meg was willing to bet his armor wasn't padded, either. It exposed his arms from shoulders down to the beginning of his clawed gauntlets, and those biceps were mouth-watering. Eyeing the elegant curve of hard, tanned skin, Meg imagined what he'd look like naked, all that glorious brawn on display. His body must be as delicious as Richard's.

Except Cougar was a good guy. She wasn't so sure about Richard.

* * *

She was right in front of him. He could smell her. The hint of jasmine in her floral shampoo blended with the rich, complex scent of woman.

Aroused woman.

But good as his feline senses were, Cougar couldn't see her. She was completely invisible.

Wait for it, he told himself. *Let her get closer.* He had only one shot at this. If he blew it, she'd make damn sure he never got close again. And he wanted to get very, very close. It was a good thing he wore armor over his groin, or she'd have seen his hungry erection.

Cougar spared a thought for Lynx, ready to pounce from the shadows. They hadn't dreamed she'd be brazen enough to approach him head-on. He doubted his brother was even aware she was here. The serum they'd taken as teenagers had given Lynx speed and agility instead of acute senses and superstrength.

Cougar breathed in slowly. The light breeze brought more of that wonderful female scent, as though she was coming closer, flying right up to the edge of the roof he stood on.

Wait for it.

* * *

Meg wondered what color his eyes were behind his mask's opaque eye slits. The only thing she could really see of him was the lower half of his face.

She'd always thought Cougar had a grim, hard mouth, but now she realized his upper lip had a deliciously sensual curve, while the lower pouted ever so slightly. God, she wanted to kiss him.

Why not?

Why not just zip in, steal a kiss, and zoom off before he could grab her? He'd never know who it was. Hell, he might not even be sure what happened.

Her heart thudded an eager adrenalin beat. It was so risky. If he got those big hands on her…

She'd love it.

No, Meg, you would not, she told herself sternly. *You'd go to jail.*

Well, probably not. It wasn't against the law to steal a kiss, and he didn't know she'd been Sneak Thief. Where was the harm? Besides, Cougar might be big and strong, but speed was Lynx's talent. She was pretty sure she could fly off before he could catch her.

Meg floated closer. One inch. Two. Sloooowly. Holding her breath. She could smell him now, leather and man. His armor was exquisitely made in contrasting shades of warm brown, trimmed in metallic gold. It looked faintly Roman and extremely butch, unlike the spandex many heroes wore. She'd seen it stop bullets, so it had to be made of something more than just leather.

Her gaze focused on his seductive mouth. She licked her lips. Her heartbeat thundered. She was close enough now to reach out and kiss him. Tensing, ready to fly, Meg leaned forward the few inches she'd need to make contact with those velvet lips…

Powerful arms snapped around her like the jaws of a trap springing shut. She slammed against Cougar's chest so hard the breath left her in a stunned *whoof.*

As Meg gasped, a white grin spread across the mouth she'd wanted so badly to taste. "You've been a bad, bad girl, Paparazzi."

* * *

She went nuts in his arms, shrieking and bucking against him. Cougar held on, though his eyes insisted he had an armful of nothing.

"Jesus, you got her?" Lynx leaped from his hiding place and ran to help.

"She…" Cougar almost lost his grip when invisible teeth fastened on his lower lip. He squeezed once, just hard enough to make her let go. Glaring at what his eyes insisted was empty air, he snarled, "Don't do that again!"

"Fuck you!" she screamed in his face. "Let me go! I haven't done anything wrong!"

"I wouldn't go that far—" He bared his teeth. "—Sneaky." At the nickname, she froze against him. "Oh, yeah, I know who you are. It's been six years, but I still recognize that scent."

"Whose scent?" Lynx stared at him and his invisible prisoner as if trying to decide how to help restrain her.

"Sneak Thief's." Cougar backed away from the roof edge and turned to face his partner, holding his captive tight as she started squirming again. "Grab her shoulders. We need to get her out of this suit so we can see what the hell we're doing."

"Wait, Paparazzi is Sneak Thief?" Lynx grimaced, belatedly putting two and two together as he groped for the girl. "Flies, invisible—oh, hell, you're right. Why didn't you tell me?"

"I'll explain later." She was beginning to panic—he could smell it in her scent. He bared his teeth at her in his most savage expression. "Give it up, Sneaky. Even if you get away, I'll just hunt you down. And by the time I find you, I'll be pissed off."

She went warily still, obviously intimidated. Being a good guy had never stopped him from cultivating a nasty reputation. "OK, try it now," he told Lynx.

His brother slid an arm down, worked it between him and his prisoner, and coiled tight around what seemed to be her waist. The other hand found a grip around what was probably her shoulders, judging from the position. "Got her."

Cougar grinned wickedly. "Good. Let's get her out of this suit." Slowly, taking his time, he started searching for the zipper.

* * *

Panic beat at her like huge, battering wings until Meg wanted to throw up. She was going to jail. Never mind that she'd been a kid afraid of her father, they were going to charge her as an accessory to his crimes. Fifty years in prison... Christ! There had to be a way out of this. She...

A big, male hand brushed over her nipple, then returned to stroke.

Startled, she looked up into Cougar's face to see a wicked smile spreading under his mask. The caressing hand closed around her, brazenly cupping her breast. "What the hell are you *doing?*"

"Looking for the zipper," he purred.

Unzipping the costume would break the invisibility field. "It's down the front." Hell, he'd find it eventually.

He slowly trailed a hand down her torso, then brazenly slid two fingers between her legs, along the crotch seam of her costume. "Here?"

"Try the neck, asshole." She couldn't believe he was actually feeling her up. Despite her more lurid fantasies, the Defender of New York didn't grope prisoners.

"Cougar, what are you doing?" Lynx said in her ear, his tone uneasy. She could feel every inch of his muscular body pressed against her back. He was a hell of a lot bigger than he'd been the last time they'd fought as teenage sidekicks.

Smoothly, Cougar slid a hand from her crotch to her belly, found the line of her zipper, and followed it to the high collar of the suit. His leather gauntlet brushed her chin as he caught the metal tag and began to pull downward. The hiss of the zipper was loud, even over the blare of the traffic. Luckily, it was dark up here; she'd hate all of New York to get a good look of Paparazzi being ceremoniously stripped of her costume.

As the zipper parted, the invisibility field around her body collapsed, and she popped into view. "Well, hello there," Cougar said, his deep voice rumbling in a distinct purr.

Meg swallowed, staring up at him in hypnotized fascination. Her mask still hid her face, but she figured they'd get around to taking that off, too. "Look, um… I'm not wearing anything under the suit…"

His grin broadened as his gaze dropped to her breasts. "I noticed. You haven't been anybody's kid sidekick in a long time, have you?" That gloved hand continued tugging the zipper downward all the way to the edge of her pubic hair.

Meg froze, distinctly aware of Lynx's hard body at her back even as Cougar crowded against her from the front. She had the humiliating suspicion she was getting wet.

"Cougar, cut it out," Lynx snapped, outrage sizzling in his voice.

"Just satisfying my curiosity." He pulled back the edges of her costume, exposing the tight pink crowns of her nipples. "Very pretty."

Lynx jerked her away. "What are you, an evil clone? Since when do we fondle suspects?" Still glaring at his partner, he twitched the edges of the suit back into place. His determined gaze met Meg's. "I don't know what the hell's gotten into him, but nobody's going to hurt you."

Cougar's smile was dark and knowing. "She's not even remotely afraid of being hurt. In fact, if you probe between those pretty thighs, you'll find she's slick and hot. Sneaky's had fantasies about us for years, haven't you, Sneaky?"

"Don't call me that!" As humiliated as she was aroused, Meg glared. "My name is Paparazzi. I've gone straight."

He moved closer, crowding her again. "I'm delighted to hear it. But you still haven't paid for the crimes you committed six years ago."

Lynx backed away, pulling her with him. "Hey, you told me you suspected Bankbuster beat her, because you smelled her blood on both of them. If he was forcing her…"

"A mitigating factor, but no excuse." Cougar followed them, menacingly seductive. He had a good three inches on his partner, and at least six on her. "That's your cue, Sneaky."

Her nipples had hardened to tight little points. Meg hoped they'd think it was the breeze. She forced herself to sneer. "For what?"

"To say all those pretty, dick-hardening pleas on the tip of your tongue. 'Please don't send me to jail, Cougar.'" His voice dropped to a mocking, suggestive groan. "'I'll do anything.'" Behind her, her defender stiffened. "See? Even the Boy Scout just got a hard-on."

Lynx shot out a palm and hit Cougar's chest hard enough to knock him back a pace. "That's *not* the way we fuckin' play!"

"No, but Sneaky wishes it was. Don't you, sweetheart? Admit it—you'd just love to be the meat in a hero sandwich." He crowded in on them again.

Lynx's grip on her arm tightened convulsively. All three of them knew that if Cougar decided to take her, there wasn't a damn thing he could do about it. Lynx was fast, agile, and considerably stronger than a normal man, but Meg had seen Cougar rip a three-foot-thick steel door off a bank vault.

"Back off!" Lynx snarled.

"I will—if she asks." Cougar's full attention was focused on Meg. He was so close now her breasts brushed the hard leather plates of his armor. "Despite my idiot partner's taste for melodrama, I'm not a rapist. Tell me no, and we'll turn you loose. I won't even chase you." He gave her a slow, wicked smile. "Unless you want me to."

Meg stared up at him in shocked arousal. His mouth framed by that snarling cat mask looked astonishingly seductive. Despite the way he scared the daylights out of her, she was still dying to taste him. His shoulders seemed to fill her vision, while behind her she could feel the rasp of leather at her back as Lynx held her protectively close.

"Tick tock," Cougar breathed, lowering his head toward hers. "Say yes, or we'll be good little heroes and go away."

She licked her lips, staring helplessly at his mouth. "Why? Why would you catch me and then just let me go?"

One corner of his mouth twitched up. "Because I want to fuck you. If all I wanted was to send you to jail, I'd have done it after we caught Bankbuster." His breath puffed against her mouth as he spoke. Helplessly seduced, she started to rise on her toes.

Cougar straightened and looked at the man behind her. "I'm not hearing a yes. Call the car, Lynx. Looks like the lady doesn't want to play."

"No!" Meg's deprived libido went into instant revolt. Reaching up, she grabbed one ear of his mask and pulled his head down for the hungry kiss she'd been dying for. Cougar growled softly in satisfaction as he slid those muscular arms around her, hauling her off her feet and against his big body.

He tasted like sin and brandy, smelled like aroused male and skin-warmed leather. His hands felt hot and strong as one palm cradled her backside while the other cupped her shoulder. The hard plate over his groin pressed against the crotch seam of her suit. Maddened, Meg rolled her hips against him. She wanted to feel her naked breasts pressing into his armor.

Distantly, she heard the scrape of boots on tar as Lynx turned away. Cougar pulled away from the kiss and looked over at him. "You're going to disappoint the lady, pard. I promised her a hero sandwich. Can't deliver if you leave."

Lynx stopped and looked at them. Even with the mask, he looked a little wild-eyed. "You do realize this is fuckin' kinky."

Cougar grinned. "Oh, yeah."

Clinging to his broad shoulders, Meg panted. Both of them. She could have both of them. It was wrong, but God, she'd never been so hot in her life. "Don't leave," she rasped. "I want you."

Lynx's smile was slow, wolfish, and hot. "You don't have to ask twice."

He was on them in one long stride, his gloved hand tunneling through her hair where it escaped her hood. Roughly, he tugged her head back and swooped down for a long, slick kiss. Meg moaned as his tongue swirled around hers, then thrust suggestively deep between her lips. With his free hand, Lynx jerked the edge of her suit back to claim one fat cherry nipple. She moaned as he rolled and pinched it between leather-clad fingers.

Cougar laughed as he pulled the suit off her other shoulder, freeing her breast completely. "I'd better call the car. I guess we really shouldn't bang her in front of half of New York. Somebody'll take a picture, and we'll end up on the cover of the *National Enquirer.*"

Meg broke the kiss to grin at him. "That's one way to put the gay rumors to rest."

He lowered his head to her aching, ready breast. "Good point." His tongue lapped, circled. "Very good point."

Lynx moved to the side, bending her back into another bone-melting kiss as he kneaded her right nipple. Cougar raked his teeth over the left, sending a liquid shiver through her body. She was panting by the time she heard the whoosh of their aircar swooping down to land on the roof.

Dazed, Meg lifted her head as its wheels touched down. The vehicle looked a little like a streamlined van, painted in the same browns as its owners' costumes. They started guiding her toward it. "What's it use to fly, lev-fields?" she managed, as the big side door slid open, sending bright light flooding out. There didn't seem to be a driver; presumably it had some kind of computerized autopilot.

Cougar flashed a grin in the light from the interior. "Do you care?"

She laughed. "Not really."

"I didn't think so." To the car he added, "Back seats down."

With a hum, the seats folded up and sank down into wells in the floor, leaving a flat surface in the back. Meg crawled inside, feeling the thick padding yield like a mattress under her hands and knees. It seemed tailor-made for sex. "Do you guys pick up women often?"

"You're the first." The men got in after her as Cougar explained, "Sometimes we do transport people who are too big for the seats, though." To jail, he meant. Some of their villains were so dangerous, even the cops weren't equipped to handle them.

Meg eyed the thick metal rings that had popped out when the seats sank. They were obviously designed as anchor points for restraints. "Guess that explains the bondage gear."

"Now, there's a thought," Lynx said wickedly, as the door closed behind them with an expensive *thunk,* leaving them surrounded by the scent of leather and arousal. The lights faded to a gentle glow. "I've always had fantasies about bad girls and handcuffs." He scooted over to join her, his expression distinctly predatory behind the mask.

"I thought you were supposed to be the Boy Scout." Meg sat back on her heels, acutely conscious of the way the suit lay open over her breasts.

Cougar snorted. "That's an act."

Lynx flipped him the finger and reached for her. Heart pounding, she went into his arms.

"I feel like I've died and gone to a porn movie," she confessed, as Lynx pulled the suit off her shoulders and down her arms. Cougar caught one leg and sought out the zipper of her boot. "I've had a whole lot of fantasies that started just like this."

"Oddly enough, so have I." Lynx dragged the suit down past her hips, exposing soft copper curls. "Ooh. I do love a natural redhead."

Cougar laughed. "That makes two of us." The zipper hissed and he started dragging the boot off.

His partner reached a gloved hand between her thighs. Meg caught her breath as one armored finger slid into her core.

"Oh, God." Lynx drew in a hard breath. "She's so wet I can feel it even with the glove."

"I thought as much." Cougar threw the boot aside. "I could smell her. Sweet, hot cream." He grabbed her other ankle and jerked the zipper down. Panting, Meg lay back and let them strip her.

She thought of Richard. Guilt stirred. What the hell was she doing?

Then she pushed the remorse away. Kinky as this was, Cougar and Lynx were the good guys. She had her doubts about Richard, or she wouldn't be doing this now.

Before her guilt could break the mood, Lynx caught her by one ankle and lifted it high as he sank that gloved finger inside her again in a slow pump. She groaned in pleasure as the leather raked gently over delicate flesh.

"Like that?" Cougar asked roughly, stripping off one of his gloves. Both men watched her face with matching expressions of predatory hunger. They were still fully armored, making her feel even more deliciously naked.

"Oh, God, yes." Meg licked her lips, staring helplessly up at them as Lynx pumped slowly. When he flicked a thumb over her clit, she groaned.

"Good," Cougar said, grabbing the other ankle and lifting it high. "Try this."

Meg gasped in shock as he found her anus with one long finger. Before she could muster more than a whimper, he started working it up her backside. "She's tight," Cougar said roughly. He rotated it in and out. That finger felt huge as it slid past the one Lynx had buried in her cunt. "Really tight. You ever taken it up the ass, Sneaky?"

She swallowed, her eyes wide behind her mask. "No." Richard had wanted to, but he was hung like a horse, and she'd been afraid.

There was that dark, predatory grin again. "Good."

"I thought..." Meg had to lick her dry lips before she could continue. "...I thought I'd take one of you in my mouth."

"Oh, you'll do that, too." Another breath-stealing thrust, blending both pleasure and discomfort. "But I want this ass." She couldn't see his eyes behind his mask, but she could feel his hard stare. "And I'm going to get it, aren't I?"

Meg shuddered. "Yes." Her voice sounded faint.

Cougar looked at Lynx. "Get the restraints."

His partner grinned and withdrew the finger he'd buried in her twat. Dazed, Meg watched him move to an equipment locker that stood along the back of the vehicle. "Restraints?" She could hear her own pulse in her ears.

Cougar showed his teeth. "I've always had this fantasy about capturing and ass-fucking a pretty supervillain." He caught the set of cuffs Lynx tossed him. "We got anything I could use as lube?"

Lynx lifted a lid. Something metallic rattled as he dug around. "There's some antibiotic ointment in the First Aid kit."

"That'll do." He grabbed Meg's left wrist and clapped on one of the bracelets.

Good guys or not, Meg wasn't sure she wanted to be that helpless. "Now, look, nobody said anything about bondage!" She tried to pull free, but couldn't break his superhuman grip.

"Oh, come on, Sneaky, I know you've fantasized about doing it in handcuffs." Despite her struggles, he snapped on the other bracelet, leaving her wrists cuffed in front of her.

Lynx tossed him the tube. "Speaking of fantasies, I still owe Sneaky one for that sucker punch a few years back."

Cougar looked up, interested. "What have you got in mind?"

He crawled toward them, unable to stand up because of the van's low roof. It put her in mind of a tom creeping up on a fat canary. And she was the canary. "I'm thinking a nice, hard spanking would even the score. Fourth seat, down." As it obediently lowered, Lynx threw himself into it.

"Hey!" Before she could do much more than sputter, Cougar scooped her up and handed her over.

Cursing, Meg struggled, but it did her absolutely no good as the two men arranged her butt-up across Lynx's lap. "Cut that out, you big jerks!" To her shame, she felt her pussy grow even wetter. "Whatever happened to foreplay?"

"You'll get that, too." Cougar sat down and captured both her kicking feet, spreading them wide. "Eventually."

Helplessly, Meg twisted around to watch as Lynx lifted a big, broad hand over her butt. He gave her an evil grin and brought it smacking down.

The first loud swat made her jump. A sharp sting radiated through her bare flesh. "Owww! You bastard!"

Both men stared at her ass, wearing matching expressions of predatory hunger. She almost groaned at the stark heat that rolled over her.

* * *

Her butt was absolutely perfect, tight and round and muscular. With her legs spread, Cougar could see her pink pussy, glistening with arousal. Her anus was concealed by her pose, but he knew he'd soon have the chance to spread that sweet little backside for a deep, plunging fuck. His dick twitched behind the armored cup that was nowhere near big enough to accommodate it. "That's a really luscious ass."

"I noticed." Lynx lifted one hand for his next smack.

Paparazzi glared at them both over her shoulder. Despite the mask that hid the upper half of her face, Cougar could tell her high, pretty cheeks were flushed. Her sensuous mouth drew into a pout he badly wanted to kiss. "This was *not* what I had in mind."

Lynx grinned. "Too bad." His hand flashed down.

Smack! Cougar watched with lustful appreciation as she bucked across his brother's knees. Her long legs flexed, trying to kick, but he held on to her ankles as her skin flushed in a cherry outline of Lynx's hand. *Smack!* Her ass squirmed deliciously. "Bastard!"

"Now, that's no way to talk," Lynx said, laughing.

Smack followed smack as he laid down a pattern of swats over her creamy ass, making her writhe and yelp. With every bounce, Cougar felt his dick get harder as he imagined pumping into her virgin backside.

He'd always known he had a sadistic streak, but Paparazzi had a talent for bringing it to the surface.

The metal edge of the cup was digging into his cock. With a groan, Cougar rose onto his knees and reached for the buckle tucked under his groin armor. He found it and worked the strap free, sighing in relief when it finally released.

Lynx had broken off his spanking to caress the rosy flesh of Paparazzi's ass. She looked back just in time to see Cougar's cock spring free. Her mouth drew into a shocked little O that instantly made his erection throb and lengthen even more.

It was definitely his turn to play.

Picking up the lube with one hand, he reached for her ass with the other. Lynx gave him a questioning look. "I do believe it's time to get her asshole ready," Cougar drawled. "I'm not sure how much longer my patience is going to last."

His brother grinned back. Apparently Paparazzi brought out his sadistic streak, too. "Good idea."

"Now, wait one..." she began.

They ignored her, Lynx parting her ass cheeks as Cougar squirted a healthy dollop of gel over his fingers. She squirmed, but his brother pressed an elbow into the small of her back, pinning her in place.

Her anus was a tempting little rosette between the pale curves of her butt. Cougar presented a well-greased finger to the little pucker and started forcing his way inside. The snug little hole parted reluctantly, gripping his finger in slick, tight heat that made his cock ache.

"Pervert!" Paparazzi spat, and tried to kick him.

He caught her ankle with his free hand and gave it a warning squeeze. "The outraged act would be a lot more convincing if I couldn't smell how wet you are." Adding a second finger, he groaned as her tight flesh seemed to milk him. "God, I'm going to love fucking this ass."

"I don't know, Cougar," Lynx drawled. "She's pretty tiny. Sure you can get the whole thing in there?"

"I'll find a way."

* * *

Meg stifled a groan of mingled discomfort and lust as Cougar finger-fucked her butt, first one finger and then two, stroking deep and hard. When she turned her head, she could see his cock jutting from his armor, thick and flushed almost purple. It looked huge, as big as Richard's, and she wondered how the hell she was going to take the whole thing.

She was more than ready to make the attempt, though. That spanking had done a good job of bringing every nerve ending she had to pulsing attention.

And then there was the sheer dark eroticism of being naked while Cougar and Lynx were fully armored. Add the cuffs around her wrists, and it was no wonder her libido was doing a rumba of kinky anticipation.

"You know," Cougar said, "if I'm going to take her anal virginity, the least I should do is make sure she's good and hot." Damn, if she got any hotter, she'd go into meltdown. "Time to eat a little pussy."

On the other hand, who was she to stand in his way?

Cougar scooped her up like a rag doll. Mouth dry, she watched Lynx move out of the way so his partner could lay her back on the seat. The soft leather cradled her stinging ass as Cougar draped both her thighs across his broad, armored shoulders.

As he bent over her cunt, Lynx went for her full breasts, cupping and caressing. When she felt twin hot tongues begin to lick, she damn near exploded on the spot.

Cougar spread her lips and gave her clit a tongue flick that made her every nerve sizzle. Lynx raked one hard nipple with his teeth before settling down to suck. Pleasure swirled along her body like a swarm of fireflies.

In five minutes, Meg was quivering on the edge of orgasm. And Cougar knew it, damn him. He drew back just slightly and let the pleasure die. Dazed, she looked over Lynx's broad shoulder to see him watching her, his expression darkly sensual despite the feral lines of his mask.

Then he lowered his head again.

Licks. Gentle bites. Long, slow tongue strokes. Fingers pinching aching flesh, penetrating ass and pussy. Every move one man made, the other countered with a wet caress. Cougar sucked her clit as Lynx strung a trail of tiny bites over her hard nipples. Lynx kneaded and suckled one breast while Cougar finger-fucked pussy and ass simultaneously. She was so close to coming, her every nerve and muscle vibrated. But each time the hot swell of climax would rise, they'd stop until it died.

It didn't take them long to have her begging. "Fuck me!" Meg gasped. "God, I can't stand this. Let me come!"

With a soft growl, Lynx lunged to his feet and reached under the armor of his hip. He struggled with something a moment, and then his cock sprang free. "I've got to have her, Coug. Now."

"Take her mouth," Cougar growled. "I don't want her coming yet."

With a low growl of hunger, Lynx straddled her, one foot on the floor, the other knee bent and braced on the seat. Propping one palm beside her head, he used the other to aim his cock at her mouth. "Suck!" he ordered. His voice was low and rough with lust.

Too hot to even consider rebelling, Meg raised her head and closed her mouth around the thick, flushed head. Lynx groaned as she began to suckle. As if maddened, he pumped his hips, thrusting the big, smooth shaft into her mouth until she gagged. He rasped a hasty apology and moderated the depth of his thrusts.

Between her thighs, Cougar's tongue flicked over her clit, slow and hot and teasing. Meg moaned.

Her head was spinning. She felt utterly surrounded by aroused male, bound and turned on and so close to coming she wanted to scream. Lynx's thick cock felt deliciously smooth in her mouth, like one of those enormous candy canes she'd enjoyed as a child. She tightened her lips around it and sucked hard, enjoying his deep male groan of pleasure.

As if to remind her he was there, Cougar chose that moment to work three fingers into her ass, stretching her so wide she gasped.

Shuddering, wildly turned on, she suckled and nibbled and licked, until Lynx finally groaned and stiffened. His cock pulsed against her tongue. He threw back his handsome head and shouted as a spurt of cum flooded her mouth, salty and hot. Meg swallowed greedily, milking him as Cougar slowly finger-fucked her ass.

Finally Lynx rolled off her and collapsed on the floor, panting. Gasping, Meg lay still, lust sizzling her nerves in an erotic storm. Cougar withdrew those skillful fingers, and she groaned in disappointed hunger. The seat gave under her as he sat down.

Then he whispered, "My turn, Sneaky." He scooped her off the seat and across his lap. "Up on your knees," he ordered.

Bracing her cuffed hands against his chest, Meg licked her lips and obeyed. Was he going to fuck her now?

Where was he going to fuck her?

She got her answer when he pressed his cockhead against her anus. Before she could even think of drawing back, he caught her under both knees and lifted, tipping her back onto his shaft.

"God!" Meg sucked in a hard breath as the massive organ touched her rectum and began to press inside. Cougar controlled her descent with those strong hands, gripping her knees and lowering her slowly. She groaned as her ass began to stretch painfully around his width. Bracing her bound hands on his armored belly, she looked down at his face in alarm. "It hurts!"

He gave her a dark, cruel smile. "I was just thinking how good it feels. Brace yourself, baby; that was just the first inch."

His cock felt huge as it tunneled relentlessly up her ass, setting off a blazing ache.

"Oh, God!" she gasped.

He just grinned. "Consider this your debt to society..." Lowering her that last agonizing fraction, he added, "...getting paid."

Meg groaned. He was all the way in, buried to her bellybutton. "I never knew you were such a sadistic bastard."

"You just weren't paying attention." Effortlessly, he lifted her.

She gasped in startled pleasure as the thick cock teased her ass. As painful as the entry was, the exit felt dark and wickedly delicious.

"That any better?" Cougar purred.

She could only whimper.

He lowered her again, faster this time. The sensation of being stretched open was still hot and painful, but as he lifted her again, pleasure flooded in to join it. Then Cougar started fucking her in earnest, shuttling her up and down on that big cock while she writhed in his arms on the knife-edge between agony and delight.

"Damn," Lynx rasped from behind her, "that's the hottest thing I've ever seen in my life."

Meg looked over her shoulder. Despite his recent climax, he was rock-hard again, stroking his cock as he knelt on the floor behind her. His grin was as dark and nasty as Cougar's. "Didn't we promise you a hero sandwich?"

Her eyes widened. "Eeep."

"We did, didn't we?" Cougar purred.

Before she could babble a protest, he lifted her off his thick cock and slid to the floor on his knees, handing her into his partner's arms.

Lynx lifted and arranged her as easily as Cougar had, spreading her wide over his cock.

Then he impaled her pussy in a long, delicious glide that made Meg groan in delight. More than willing, she wrapped her legs around his waist and looped her bound arms around his neck.

Cougar moved up behind her. Meg stiffened in instinctive alarm as one armored hand grabbed her ass. The smooth, well-greased head of his cock touched her anus again. "Here we go," he rumbled.

She yowled as Cougar started working back inside her. As big as he was, he felt even thicker and harder sliding in against Lynx's cock. The entry went on and on, red-hot with blended pain and arousal, until both of them were all the way in.

Meg had never felt so impossibly stuffed in her life—crammed with dick in a ruthless double impalement. Cougar's hands slid around her ribs to find her breasts, capturing and teasing her nipples as he pulled her back against his chest. Lynx's hands caught her thighs, lifting her as both men began to thrust. First Cougar, then Lynx, so one man slid out as the other slid in, rolling and grinding.

The sensation was indescribably rich and darkly kinky. Meg rested her head back on Cougar's shoulder and moaned as they fucked her in long, slow strokes.

"Like that, Sneaky?" Cougar purred in her ear from behind. "All that dick in such tight little holes?"

She could only shudder.

"I sure as hell like it," Lynx growled through gritted teeth, his expression feral as he pumped deep in her twat. "I've never fucked anything this damn tight."

"Lift her a little more," Cougar ordered. "I'm in the mood to ream."

His partner tightened his grip, pulling her thighs even further apart. Meg groaned helplessly as the two men began to thrust harder, faster, slamming in and out of her tight channels, twisting and tormenting her delicate flesh. The savage blend of heat and pleasure tore a yowl from her mouth.

Somebody's pelvis ground over her clit as a dick pounded just the right spot, detonating her orgasm in a long, pulsing wave of fire. Meg screamed in ecstasy, barely aware as first Lynx and then Cougar stiffened, coming, pumping her twin channels full of slick, hot cream.

* * *

When it was over at last, they collapsed in a hot, sweaty pile on the floor of the car. Megan, panting, ass and cunt aching, stared blindly up at the roof overhead. Two sets of powerful arms clasped loosely around her.

She'd just had the most searing erotic experience of her life. Every kinky fantasy come true.

Why was she suddenly thinking of Richard?

Probably because, hot as it was, she knew neither man really gave a damn about her. She was just a former supervillain turned pain-in-the-ass shutterbug they'd just fucked blind.

Despite his secrets, despite his lies, Richard had loved her. And she'd ended it anyway. What had she done? Tears prickled at her lids. Even as she fought them down, her body began to yield to exhaustion. In moments, she was asleep.

But as her eyes slid closed, her drowsy mind betrayed her. "Richard," she whimpered.

Lynx, startled, met Cougar's gaze over her shoulder.

* * *

She dreamed she was in Richard's bed again. Her cheek rested on those familiar silk sheets, lightly scented with his cologne.

But behind her, she felt the ridges of studded leather armor. Somehow, Cougar was in bed with her.

Richard's voice whispered in her ear. "God, Meg, please don't leave me."

With a soft groan, she rolled over, eyes still closed. His mouth took hers, gently persuasive. "Richard," she whispered in welcome.

Then she opened her eyes and looked up into Cougar's face. And she knew.

"You son of a bitch!" Furious, she rolled naked out of the bed.

Richard's bed.

Cougar looked up at her, sprawled across those silk sheets in his leather and studs, fully armored now, the impressive cock tucked away. The cock she suddenly realized was a dead ringer for Richard's.

Outraged, Meg stared into his masked face, focusing on that seductive mouth she'd kissed so many times before. "I fucking cannot believe I didn't recognize you!" It was like the vase/face illusion she'd seen as a child, a shape that shifted from being a face to a vase depending on how you looked at it. Now that she'd seen the resemblance, it was obvious.

The secret identity Richard had been hiding was Cougar.

"You were a kid the first time you met me as Cougar," Richard said quietly, reaching up to pull off his mask. "You were an adult when you met me as Richard. Last night, you saw what you expected to see."

Quivering with anger, Meg stared into that handsome, familiar face with its broad cheekbones, square chin, and wolf-pale eyes. His dark hair had been mashed into sweaty, disordered curls by the mask. "You knew all along," she realized. "You knew who I was when we met at that gallery show a year ago!"

He nodded, meeting her gaze levelly as he rolled off the bed. "I recognized your scent."

"Was this some kind of *game* to you?" Angry tears stung her eyes. "Making your arch enemy's kid fall in love with you? Why? So you could break my heart?"

Richard winced, taking a step toward her. She backed warily away. "No. It wasn't like that. I just wanted to get to know you. It always bothered me that I wasn't able to save you from Bankbuster, and..."

"This was *pity?*" God, that was even worse. "I was a pity fuck?"

"Dammit, Meg, would you calm down? I asked you out because it was good to see somebody I fought actually go straight. Then I realized how much I liked you. I didn't expect that."

"You *liked* me?" She should have known. He'd been playing with her. Why else would he want anything to do with Meg Jennings?

Those cool wolf eyes heated. "It hasn't been 'like' in months, Meg, and you know it. I love you. It ripped my heart out when you told me it was over. You demanded my secret. Well, you know it now."

"But why the game? Why play kinky, dominant stud? Why bring Lynx into it, for God's sake?" Her eyes widened. "He's Adam, isn't he? You banged me with your *brother?*"

He braced both fists on his hips. "Did you or did you not tell me you had a fantasy about sleeping with both of us?"

"I was drunk! For God's sake, I never expected to actually end up in a hero sandwich with Cougar and Lynx. It's like a threesome with George Clooney and Russell Crowe. Something to dream about in a cold bed with a warm vibrator."

He grinned, visibly enjoying the comparison. "And you loved every minute of it."

Meg glowered at him. "My asshole still hurts."

Richard smirked. "It was my pleasure."

"I'm sure it was, you big prick." She remembered Lynx's outrage when Cougar first started feeling her up. "Did Adam know what you were up to?"

"He had no idea."

"Because he wouldn't have gone along with it if he had. Adam is a *nice* man." Her outrage was beginning to fade as her wicked sense of humor came to the surface.

It *had* been delicious.

"I'm a nice man." His expression was vaguely insulted.

"Yeah, I could tell when you started reaming my ass. Which, as I recall, I refused to allow you to do when you asked me the first time. No fair using Cougar to intimidate me into it."

He smirked as he stepped up to her. "Oh, you wanted it. You just needed to be persuaded."

"I did not." Meg glowered as he tugged her into his arms. "Cut that out. I'm still pissed off at you."

"No, you're not." He lowered his head. "You want to kiss Cougar again."

"No." He was right, of course, but she stubbornly turned her head anyway, pouting. "I'm sticky and I haven't brushed my teeth."

"We can fix that." He gave her that roguish smile and swept her into his arms, then carried her toward the bathroom as if she weighed no more than a kitten. He'd done it before as Richard, but she'd never noticed how easy it was for him. She should have realized he had far more than normal strength.

Meg decided to drop even the pretense of irritation in favor of satisfying her curiosity. "How did you and Adam get your powers?"

Richard set her on her feet beside his huge whirlpool bath and turned to busy himself with the taps. Water began gushing into the tub. "That's a long, ugly story." He stood and started stripping out of his armor as she watched with absorbed interest. With each piece of armor he dropped, more and more delicious muscle was revealed—shoulders to die for, a set of abdominal muscles that flexed and rippled as he moved, bunching brawn in calves and thighs. And the most delicious ass she'd ever wanted to bite. "You know my dad was a geneticist, right?"

"Yeah, I think you mentioned that."

"Well, he'd invented a kind of super drug that would insert new genetic code into the DNA of the person who took it, giving him or her superpowers. Trouble was, the lab trials were problematic at best, because it affected every test animal differently. But before he could do any more work on it, an asshole named Gordon Carson got wind of the drug. He broke into Dad's lab, killed him, and stole every dose he could find. He used the drug to become Nightwolf."

Meg's eyes widened. "My father's partner!"

"Exactly. And before that, the first villain we fought. Luckily, Carson didn't know Dad had a couple of extra vials of the drug locked in a safe in his bedroom. Adam and I took them after we found out what happened. I ended up getting the muscle and animal senses, while Adam got the speed and agility. But Nightwolf was damn near a match for us both. It took us three years to bring him down." Richard bent and turned off the taps, then switched on the jets. Straightening, he made a sweeping gesture. "Your bath awaits, milady."

"Thank you, kind sir." Stepping into the tub, Meg settled, sighing, into the frothing water. He got in, too. She dragged her eyes away from all that magnificent bare skin with difficulty. "I'm sorry about your father."

Richard met her gaze as he moved to sit behind her. "I'm sorry about yours. If I'd caught him when he was still working with Nightwolf, he'd have gone to jail instead of forcing you to become Sneak Thief." He grimaced and settled into the tub, folding his long legs around hers. "An idea he probably got from me and Adam."

"Yeah, he thought the teenaged sidekick concept was really cool." She shook her head and settled back against her lover's sculpted chest. "Asshole."

Richard gathered her against him, cupping her breasts gently. "You don't know the half of it. He came so damn close to getting you sent to jail. When we arrested him, Detective Sanders put two and two together and decided Bankbuster's daughter had to be Sneak Thief. I had to talk fast to convince him he was wrong. Said the scent was different." He shook his head. "Luckily, he believed me."

Startled, she twisted around and looked at him. "You lied for me? To a *cop?* Why?"

"I saw Gerald's police record." Angry passion ignited in Richard's eyes. "How many times was he charged with domestic violence? How many times did Social Services take you away from him when you were a kid, only to give you right back? The system failed you. Damned if I was going to let it screw you again."

She took a deep breath and revealed the guilt that had gnawed at her for years. "I did commit crimes, Richard. I helped him rob those banks."

"And we finally caught him because of a tip to Cougar's hotline from an ER payphone." Gently, he pushed the hair out of her face. "That took a lot of guts, Meg. If we'd failed to catch him, he'd have known you dropped a dime. He'd have killed you."

"I knew Cougar would get him." Meg shook her head. "Besides, he would have eventually killed somebody else on one of his jobs. He had to go down."

"And we took him down, didn't we? You and I and Adam." Richard tilted up her chin and lowered his head.

The kiss started out slow and gentle, a sweet mating of lips and tongues. In a heartbeat, it heated to a blaze as Meg determined to give him everything she had. He tasted so hot, his mouth alone was enough to make her nipples peak. With a hungry groan, she tried to twist around so she could reach him more easily. He picked her up and rearranged her to sprawl across his broad body so they were face to face at last.

Long fingers cupped her breasts, caressing the tight points to full erection as they kissed slowly, tongues sliding back and forth, teasing one another. Meg sighed, losing herself in him.

* * *

She tasted so damn good, like heat and sex. By the time she pulled away with a low groan, his cock was hard as stone against the satin skin of her muscular little belly.

Dazed, Richard looked up at her. Long red hair tumbled around her slim shoulders, freed at last from the hood that had constrained it. Her eyes were a soft pale green, witchy and wide in her heart-shaped face. Those deliciously full lips pouted at him. Seduced, he lifted his head to take them again in a hungry kiss. His hands found the soft, full weight of her breasts, cupped and cradled them. Her nipples jutted, silently begging for his fingers. He found them, rolled them. Watched her throw her head back to pant, those lovely eyes closing.

God, he loved her.

His Meg, grown from battered young girl to fierce, hot woman, intelligent and funny and sexy. When she'd told him last night she wanted to end it because she didn't trust him, it had felt as if she'd rammed a knife into his chest. He'd been willing to do anything to get her back, even tell her everything.

Even put on that kinky little act with Adam by way of revealing his secret.

And it had worked.

With a groan of mingled passion and relief, he caught her by the back of the head and dragged her down into another desperate kiss. By the time he let her up again, her lovely green eyes were dazed.

He had no doubt his were, too.

He needed to touch her. Needed to pleasure her gently just as he'd dominated her the night before.

Richard reached for the bar of soap. She watched with hot, slumberous eyes as he worked a lather between his hands. "Sit up," he said, his voice more than a little hoarse. "Astride me. I want to wash you."

A little smile curving her mouth, she obeyed, planting a knee to either side of him. Richard caught her full, soft breasts in her hands, groaning at the feel of warm, silken skin. Gently, he caressed her with his soap-slick hands, not touching her urgently peaked nipples. Not yet. He traced his hands up, easily spanning her slim torso with his long fingers, finding the deceptive fragility of her shoulders, then sliding down her long, slender arms.

She was so delicate, so fragile. Whenever he thought about Bankbuster hurting her, he wanted to explode. He hoped to God the bastard never got out of prison, because Richard wasn't sure he'd be able to resist the urge to kill him again. It had been all Lynx could do to talk him out of it the last time.

And that was before he'd fallen in love with Meg.

Now he stared up into those beautiful green eyes and watched them go vague with desire as he washed every inch of her slim body with soapy hands. Her head fell back, and her long hair brushed his wet thighs. The sweet tickle made him groan in lust.

Goaded, he reached between her pretty thighs and found the hard little nub of her clit with a forefinger. Slowly, gently, he circled it.

"God, Richard!" She arched her back convulsively as if reacting to raw, intense pleasure.

"Like that?" Wickedly, he gave her another stroke.

Meg looked down at him, a hot, wild glitter in her gaze. "Oh, yeah. In fact..."

Before he could react, she reared off him, grabbed the thick erection trapped under her backside, and angled it upward. He hissed in startled pleasure as she found her opening and impaled herself in one long plunge.

"God, Meg!" he gasped.

She grinned. "Thought you'd like that."

Then she planted those soft little hands on his chest and began to ride, jogging up and down on his cock as the water lapped and splashed around them. With every hot stroke, pleasure curled around his spine, coiling tighter and tighter over his balls.

Richard threw his head back, pressed his shoulders against the cool porcelain of the tub, and arched upward, grinding up as she ground down. He reached for her, catching her by both breasts, thumbing the peaks as she rode him at a sweet, fast bounce that drove him to madness.

"I love you, Meg!" he gasped, pleasure curling through his consciousness in ribbons of sweet flame.

Her eyes kindled with an incandescent joy. "God, I love you, Richard!"

And the fire took them both.

* * *

When they both could breathe again, they emerged weak-kneed from the tub to find the bathroom awash in bath water. Laughing, they collected towels and mopped it up, then staggered back to bed to collapse together in a damp, happy pile.

He rolled her under him, feeling her wrap long legs around him with a sigh of pleasure. "Marry me."

Her eyes widened in surprise before pained vulnerability shuttered them. "Don't make those kinds of jokes."

Stung, he rose on one elbow. "I'm not joking. I've been thinking about this for months." As she watched, he rolled over and slid open the top drawer of the nightstand to pull out a small, blue velvet box. With a thumb, he flicked up the lid, revealing an engagement ring set with diamonds and a single emerald the same pale green as her astonished eyes. He pulled the ring from its satin nest, took her left hand in his, and slid it onto her finger.

Her gaze flew to meet his, her lips parting in astonished shock. "You're serious."

"God, yes."

"But ... But I was Sneak Thief! I robbed banks!"

"When you were a kid whose only alternative was being beaten to death by an abusive bastard. You're not a kid anymore." Gently he tilted her head up and bent down to kiss her. "You're the woman I love.

By the time he let her up for air again, he could see the belief in her eyes.

So he asked her again. "Will you marry me?"

"Yes. Oh, God, yes." She threw herself against him with a shout of joy and laughter. Relief surged through him, and he pulled her tight.

* * *

They were dressed and making plans over breakfast, Meg in a pair of snug blue jeans and a T-shirt she'd left on a previous visit. Richard, shirtless and clad only in a pair of black jeans, was just about to slide an omelet onto her plate when Adam skidded into the kitchen.

Richard looked up in alarm, recognizing the grim expression on his brother's face. Adam had been on scanner duty down in the Lair; he must have heard something serious to get that look.

"Richard..." Adam broke off, his blue gaze flicking to Meg's startled face, obviously wondering how much he could say.

"Yeah, she knows all of it," Richard said. "What's going on?"

"Nightwolf's escaped. Killed a guard."

"Shit." He dumped the omelet onto Meg's plate, then strode to the sink and threw the frying pan in. "I'm going to have to go, sweetheart. We've got to catch that bastard before he kills somebody else."

Together, the two men turned toward the great room and the hidden passage to the Cougar's Lair.

* * *

Heart in her throat, Meg watched, frozen, as they started out. Nightwolf was an even bigger psychopath than Bankbuster.

And the man she loved was about to go up against him.

"Where's my suit?" she demanded, jumping up to follow them. "I'm going with you!"

Startled, Adam whirled to look back at her, blond brows lifted. "No way. That guy is a killer, Meg. And you..."

"...can fly and turn invisible. And he and my father were partners. The two of them had set up a new hideout before you caught Nightwolf the last time. I've been there. I'll bet money that's where he's going now."

Adam frowned, his *GQ* handsome face concerned. "Then you can tell us where it is and we'll..."

"Look, Richard trusted me with your secret. Trust me to take care of myself. I've been dodging assholes like Nightwolf for years."

"Nightwolf is in a league by himself, Meg."

"But she's got a point, Adam," Richard said suddenly, frowning. "Either we trust her, or we don't."

Adam turned to stare at him. "Are you nuts? We can't take her into that kind of danger!"

Meg braced her fists on her hips and glared at them both. "And I'm not going to sit on my ass while the man I love goes off to fight a lunatic! Look, I can use my invisibility, fly in and reconnoiter, pinpoint exactly where he is, and help you take him with a minimum of risk to either of you."

Slowly, Richard nodded. "Sounds good."

Adam glowered, his expression troubled. "What if she gets hurt? I know how much you love her. If something happens..."

Richard straightened his impressive shoulders in sudden determination. "Something can always happen. And I've learned the cost of not trusting Meg. It's higher than I want to pay."

Looking into Richard's wolf-pale eyes, Meg smiled slowly as a bubble of warmth rose in her heart.

* * *

Pushing her suit as hard as she could, Meg flashed down the sewer tunnel, Nightwolf roaring in pursuit. "Bitch!" he raged. "I'm going to rip your fuckin' head off and stuff that camera down your throat!"

"Only if you can catch me, Nighty!" Lowering her voice, she murmured into her new headset, "Here we come, boys."

Nightwolf bellowed another string of vicious curses, sounding like a rampaging bull as he splashed after her.

He was gaining.

The opening of the tunnel was ten feet ahead, if she could only make it. Desperately, she flexed her toes, trying to wring a little more acceleration from the suit.

And shot out of the tunnel like a bullet.

Nightwolf thundered after her—just as Cougar stepped into his path and launched a savage roundhouse that hit him square in the face. The villain's feet flew out from under him as he went flying back into the tunnel.

Cougar and Lynx lunged after him before he could roll to his feet. Heart in her throat, Meg floated in to watch as the three fought in a frenzy of punches and kicks. It seemed to her that Cougar pounded his fists into Nightwolf with even more grim fury than usual. It wasn't long until the villain went down and didn't get back up.

"Damn, I don't think we've ever taken Nighty this easily," Lynx said, snapping the cuffs around Nightwolf's thick wrists. "We'll have to use that trick again."

"Told you it would work," Meg said smugly, maintaining a careful hover well clear of the murky water.

"You did good," Cougar told her. "Despite the five minutes of stark terror after you set off that flash in his face."

Indignantly she said, "I wasn't that scared!"

He looked at her. "I was."

Lynx nodded. "Me, too." He reached into a belt pouch and brought out a small cloth patch, then slapped it against Nightwolf's thick forehead. It would keep the man out until they could get him into custody.

Cougar swung the villain into a fireman's carry, then started off down the tunnel with him, his partner splashing at his heels. Meg, visible again, floated after them. Adrenaline was still snapping and sizzling through her body, filling her with a certain wicked recklessness. "So," she purred, "after we drop off the creep—anybody in the mood for another…hero sandwich?"

Startled, Lynx looked over his shoulder at her, then at his brother, both brows lifted.

Cougar gave him a wicked grin. "Now that you mention it, I am feeling a little hungry."

Lynx cleared his throat. "I wouldn't mind a bite. But I thought you two were…" He trailed off.

"Oh, we are," Cougar said. "Deeply. But every once in a while—the three of us do make a pretty good team."

"Oooooh, yeah," Meg breathed with wicked anticipation. "A very, very good team."

~*~

Angela Knight

Angela Knight's first book was written in pencil and illustrated in crayon; she was nine years old at the time. But her mother was enthralled, and Angela was hooked.

Whatever success she has enjoyed would be hollow without the love of her husband, Michael, and her son, Anthony. Her parents, Gayle and Paul, have been unfailing in their support and encouragement. Her sister Angela, whose name she adopted, was her first and most helpful editor.

Hot Blooded, a Jove anthology featuring Angela Knight, Christine Feehan, Maggie Shayne and Emma Holly, hit #31 on the New York Times' extended bestseller list. *Bite*, another Jove anthology featuring Angela Knight, along with authors Laurell K. Hamilton, MaryJanice Davidson, Charlaine Harris and Vickie Taylor, made #23 on the New York Times' bestseller list its first week out. Other popular books by Angela Knight include *The Forever Kiss* (Red Sage), *Master of the Night* and *Jane's Warlord* (Berkley Sensation).

You can visit her on the Web at www.angelasknights.com or email her at angelanight2002@bellsouth.net.

Candy for her Soul

Sheri Gilmore

Prologue

"Happy Valentine's Day, David," Natalie said, holding her breath as the handsome quarterback of Biloxi High School turned to her. Butterflies danced in her tummy when his blue eyes crinkled while his white teeth flashed into a big grin.

He walked over to her and reached for the Valentine's card she held out to him. Her hand shook and her heart beat faster. She'd had a crush on David Scott since kindergarten, but he never seemed to notice her.

"Hey, thanks, umm…"

"Natalie. Natalie Pasqua."

"Yeah, that's it." He snapped his fingers then pointed at her.

He remembers! Her heart leapt into her throat at the brush of his fingers against her own. Then, she held her breath as he opened the envelope that contained all her pent-up teenage love.

She watched his pale fingers work under the seal. The sound of paper ripping made her stomach clench. She bit her lip. *Almost there.* He'd know of her love, then look at her and realize he felt the same.

"Whatcha got there, Dave?"

No! Not Nico Bui, high school bad-ass. Torn jeans, shaggy black hair, and an old black leather jacket covered his lean frame. This couldn't be happening. Natalie heard a distressed squeak escape her lips when he snatched the card from David's fingers.

"That's mine, Nico. Give it back."

She watched David try to take the card back, but Nico stood two inches taller and held the Valentine above his head. David was probably the only friend Nico had, but the taller boy insisted on tormenting him lately.

"Yeah, who's gonna make me? You?" His laugh echoed through the school yard.

David nodded his head. His hands clenched at his sides. "Yeah."

Tears welled up in Natalie's eyes at the sight of her *hero* standing up to her nemesis. Nico had always been a loner and kept away from everyone, except when he taunted and teased her. She knew she stuttered, and her clothes were out-of-date. She pushed her glasses up. "Give it back, Nico!" She stamped her foot. No other boy could make her angry like him. Her rage vibrated through her body in small tremors, and each breath burned through her lungs. She couldn't believe she was standing up to him. She swallowed hard when his gaze landed on her.

He's a demon!

Nona Pasqua had told her tales about demons. How they would set their eye on a girl and tempt her to do acts no "good" girl would ever think of doing if not otherwise influenced. Like the dreams she'd had of Nico Bui. Dreams she didn't dare tell anyone about. The merest thought of the sexual acts she and Nico enacted in those dark fantasies caused her cheeks to flush.

His gaze narrowed on her, like he could read her mind. His scowl turned into the evilest smile she'd ever seen. *Evil and...sexy.*

Natalie fought the urge to cross herself. Her bottom lip quivered, but she refused to back down when he stepped toward her with his eyes never leaving hers.

"Getting brave, *Braces?*"

When he stood directly in front of her, he pulled the card free. Natalie watched the envelope drop to the ground. A tear of frustration eased down her cheek.

"Let's see." His eyebrows rose. "'To my *love,* my *life.* My love is forever. Happy Valentine's Day. Natalie.'" He snorted and shoved the card against David's chest without looking at him.

"How sweet."

Around them, several of the more popular girls laughed.

"All that devotion of yours is wasted on him."

Natalie's tears flowed freely. David's face grew red, and he glanced around with a nervous twitch of his head, shoving the card into his backpack without reading it.

"Uh, thanks, um..."

"Natalie." Her whisper caught on the breeze to float away like a fallen leaf.

"Yeah, that's it." He stepped around Nico and her. "Well, gotta go to practice. See ya later." He left with the usual football groupies close on his heels.

"Give it up, *Braces.* He's never gonna fall for someone like you."

"Shut up!"

"You're a brainiac and he's…a jock." He leaned close. So close Natalie felt his breath, hot against her cheek. "He can have his pick of whichever cheerleader he wants. It'll never work."

Rage and humiliation boiled over. Natalie balled her fists and struck out, coming in contact with Nico's chest. He didn't budge. He stood like a stone wall, always blocking her way. "I hate you!" She hit him again.

He grabbed her wrists to stop her assault. "Yeah, I know, but one day you'll understand why David Scott's not the one for you."

His fingers were warm against her skin, but Natalie refused to enjoy his touch. With a sob, she wrenched her hands away and ran toward home. She rounded the last curb and tripped over an uneven patch of concrete, stumbled, and fell.

Her knee scraped hard and she landed facedown in the grass. Her glasses clattered against the sidewalk, and she heard the lens shatter. She bit her lip but couldn't stop the sobs that burst forth. She laid her head on her arms. Her shoulders shook with the force of her tears.

Why didn't he leave her alone? What had she ever done to him? She knew she looked different, but so did he. While she tried to stay hidden in the shadows, Nico Bui stood out from everyone around him like a flashing neon light. She didn't want his attention. *Or did she?* She couldn't deny her fascination with him. Her latest dream of him surfaced and she moaned.

"I'll put a hex on his butt." Her head still down, she mumbled into the dirt, watching an ant crawl by through her fuzzy vision. She didn't hear the footsteps on the sidewalk approach.

"Hmm, that's not a very nice thing to do on Valentine's Day."

She jerked her head up, conscious her skirt had ridden up over her knees. She twisted to her side and pulled the material down, wincing at the sting of her skinned knees. She squinted.

A tall man with black hair stood over her. She felt she should know him, but knew she didn't. Natalie eased onto her bottom and glanced around, but no one was in sight, except for the stranger dressed in black.

He held a hand out as if to help her up, but she flinched away from him. Her eyes settled on the gold ring he wore engraved with the initial *L.*

When she refused to take his hand, he knelt beside her, his hands hanging loosely between his knees. "Who would you put a hex on?"

She looked into black-as-night eyes. The urge to tell him her darkest secrets rose within her. When he smiled, she couldn't resist. "I-I want to hex Nico Bui. He's determined to ruin my life. I hate him."

"Tsk, tsk. *Hate* is too strong a word for such a beautiful girl like yourself."

Natalie looked down. Her lip quivered. She didn't hate Nico, but he made her feel "things"—anger, lust, frustration.

"I'm not beautiful." Her voice sounded husky with tears, which threatened to spill again. "If I were, David would love me."

A black eyebrow arched. "Love you?" He took her chin in his long fingers and lifted her face. "You're but a baby. What do you know about love between a man and a woman?"

Natalie felt her cheeks flush. "I'm seventeen." She pulled away from the man's disturbing touch. It hadn't been creepy. Just the opposite. She'd...*liked*...him touching her. She swallowed on that acknowledgement and shook her head. She frowned and studied the man from beneath her lashes.

He knelt closer, and his face came into focus. He reminded her of Nico. Something about the way he carried himself. The eyebrow rose again, and she knew he found her scrutiny humorous.

"I have to go home." She pushed up, ignoring the throb in her knees. "My grandmother will be worried."

"Ah, yes." He nodded. When he stood, he dwarfed her by a good foot and a half. Another similarity to Nico—tall, lean, and...dangerous.

She shivered.

He bent and picked up the broken glasses. "I'm afraid these are no longer any good." He handed them to her.

Natalie sighed. She and her grandmother barely made ends meet. She hated to think what a new pair of glasses would cost them.

"Contacts are a lot cheaper than glasses these days, you know."

Natalie glanced at the man, sharply.

He gave a short nod of his head and placed his hands behind his back. "Before you go, may I offer you some Valentine's candy?" He pulled one hand in front of him and held it palm up to her. In the center lay two heart-shaped candies wrapped in bright red foil.

Her mouth watered. No one ever gave her Valentine treats. Nona couldn't afford the chocolate. She reached out, tempted to take what the man offered. "Which one can I have?"

"I offer you both." He worked the candies between his fingers to hold up one. "One is light and sweet." He worked his fingers again. "The other dark and bitter." The candies circled and twirled between his fingers, then rested in his palm. He held them out to her.

Her mouth watered at the prospect of tasting two such different but decadent flavors. She reached toward temptation, but snatched her hand back at the last minute. She wasn't sure, because his lips didn't move, but she thought he said, *Such a smart girl.*

"I can't accept candy from strangers, but thank you." She glanced up to see if he might be offended. He didn't look like the type to piss off.

He smiled. "I understand." He turned and walked a few feet away, then stopped.

"Happy Valentine's Day, Natalie. Try not to put any hexes on anyone." He laughed. "And may all your heart's desires come true."

"Thank—" Her glasses slipped and she bent to rescue them. "—you." When she looked back toward the stranger, he had disappeared. She frowned. After the initial shock, she picked up her bag and started home. Ten steps later, she stopped and turned back. How had he known her name?

* * *

The lone figure moved within the shadows of the oak tree. He took a pull on a cigarette, then discarded it into the dewy grass with a flick of his fingers. He let the smoke filter through his nostrils into the crisp dark air as he watched the light in Natalie's room snap off.

Her body would shine like alabaster in the moon's light. The image of her firm muscles, rippling across her arms and legs as she danced, would be such an erotic sight with the silver beams caressing her throat and nipples like a lover.

He knew she would be perfect. He could teach her all the secrets of night magick. He sighed and looked into the darkness. Not yet. She was still too young. She needed a few more years of life's experiences to learn what a true sorceress she could really be. He'd have to wait. He turned to the narrow street, taking solace in the chill of the night.

Chapter One

"How long you back in town for, Natalie?"

"Don't know, Joe." She smiled at the man behind the bar. A dirty apron covered his round stomach and a dull white cap his head. "I'm in between jobs right now."

"You quit the fancy teaching job in New York?"

"Yeah, the *Big Apple* isn't all it's cracked up to be." *Neither are the fast city boys.* But she wasn't going to go there with the neighborhood gossip. Joe and his sons were worse than the local beauty parlor when it came to rumors. By this afternoon, the whole town would know she was back home and out of a job.

"You're just a small town girl. Stay down here on the coast with your grandmamma." Joe wiped an oyster knife on his apron and continued to shuck the day's catch to serve up fresh on the half-shell, or baked with seasonings and parmesan on top.

"Hmm." She'd heard the same advice over and over for the past two days she'd been home.

Home. She looked out the window at the sun-speckled waves of the Mississippi Sound. She had thought New York City home for the last eight years, until Rudy had ruined whatever security she had felt there with his harsh betrayal.

"Got a boyfriend, Nat?"

Natalie glanced back at Joe's youngest son. He hadn't changed much from high school. Black hair, brown eyes, and a gorgeous smile, like the majority of the boys she'd grown up with. *Except David.* The name sent a jolt of pain through her chest at the remembered unrequited love she'd carried around with her all those years ago.

With the thought of David came the even more painful thought of Nico. Over the years, she'd realized he had been the boy she had really loved. At seventeen, she hadn't known how to show him, or tell him, with his bristly nature. The image of a stray dog, snarling at anyone who tried to be nice to him after all the malice others had shown, entered her mind.

"No, not anymore."

"Ahh...left the boyfriend with the city, huh?"

Damn. That's what she got for daydreaming about Nico. Natalie smiled at Joe's all-knowing nod, hoping that little tidbit wouldn't be all over town, too.

"Probably best. You need a man who understands where you come from, my baby."

Joe Jr. nodded in agreement with his father.

Natalie sighed and resisted the urge to roll her gaze to the ceiling. She'd heard these words, too, over the last few days, like a broken record. She was only twenty-five, for Pete's sake, not forty-five. She still had several more good years before she needed to worry about settling down with one man. Rudy had taught her that.

Instead, she nodded and agreed. "That's what Nona says, too."

"She's a wise woman, is our Sophia." Joe handed Natalie the bucket of oysters, then crossed himself. "God bless she knows the *old* ways. Saved Joe Jr.'s life when he was a baby."

Natalie smiled, but cringed inside. *Not another story!*

"I remember, Joe." She cut him off before she had to stand here another hour listening to stories she'd heard a million times. "Thanks for the oysters."

She turned and headed out the door. The bells jingled and the outside glare blinded her on the way out. She missed the step and would've fallen flat on her face, except for the steely grip that saved her.

"Oh...God." She laughed. "Thanks, I forgot about that st—"

Brown eyes stared into hers and the strong fingers tightened around her biceps. Her heart did a flip-flop in her chest at the same time her clit twinged with excitement, like it always did.

"Hello, *Braces*." The exotic, brown-eyed gaze swept over her from head to toe. "All grown up, I see."

"N-Nico!" His name stuttered from her lips before she could stop herself. He was the last person she had expected to see. *Shit.* She hadn't stuttered in seven years, now listen to her.

He smiled and released her.

Natalie took a deep breath, hoping her pulse would come back down from hyperspace speed. *He scared me, that's all.* Didn't have anything to do with the way his jeans fit like a second skin, emphasizing the healthy bulge between his hips, or the smell of warm, clean man swamping her senses. It didn't have to do with any of that.

He reached down. His hand wrapped around hers and the handle of the bucket.

Natalie jumped in reaction to the feel of his hand over hers. *Electric.*

"I'll carry that for you."

"Uh…weren't you going in?" She released her grip and felt a few seconds of disappointment at the loss of his touch.

"I can come back later."

"Oh. Then, sure." She smiled, not sure at all. Nico Bui being nice had to be a new experience. "Thank you."

"Welcome. Where to? Your grandmother's?"

"Yeah, but I don't expect you to carry that all the way there. I'm quite capable."

A wicked look flashed in his eyes and a black eyebrow lifted with a twitch of his lips. "I bet you're capable of quite a few things after living in New York City for so long."

So much for nice. Natalie's cheeks grew hot, but she refused to let him intimidate her like he used to when they were younger. She was a grown woman. Sophisticated—he leaned closer—and capable of handling good-looking men. "Nico—"

"Welcome home." His mouth touched hers in a brief butterfly kiss, but the pressure inserted strong enough to make her forget what she'd been about to say.

"Umm. That's what I like."

"What?" Her voice squeaked, so she cleared her throat and tried again. "What do you like?"

"A woman with her mouth shut and her face dazed and confused from my lovemaking."

"Nico?" He was unbelievable. *An arrogant son of a bitch!* She put her hands on her hips. The door to Joe's opened and two local women stepped out and looked over at them. Immediately, their heads bobbed together in discussion. Natalie cringed.

Nico gave her a lazy grin and turned toward her grandmother's house. His look asked if she was coming, or going to stand around to become fodder for the local gossipmongers.

Natalie shook her head, but followed. "You never change, do you?"

His eyebrow cocked. "How do you mean?"

"You snap your fingers and expect women to jump."

He shrugged. "All of them but you." He stopped. The look he gave her over his shoulder held a mixture of respect and something like sadness. "You never ran to me. Always away, even though you wanted me." The frown disappeared. "Just like you do now."

"Dammit, would you listen to yourself?"

His gaze narrowed. "You never cursed before." He shook his head. "I don't like it."

Natalie laughed. "Tough." She'd stopped a couple of feet behind him. Her finger pointed at him and her foot tapped the concrete. "I don't take orders from *any* man."

"Why? Did some man hurt you?"

Yeah. You, David, and Rudy. But, she didn't say that. Instead, she shook her head.

In two steps, he stood in front of her. Natalie blinked, not sure how he'd managed to move so fast. The bucket of oysters sat on the sidewalk where he'd been seconds before. She glanced up, but only saw a blur of his face before his mouth crushed hers.

She fought against him, but a strong arm wrapped over her left arm to pin it to his body while her other arm lay trapped between them. His hands massaged the small of her back and the base of her neck. And, his mouth... *God, what a mouth.*

He devoured her with his tongue and teeth, nipping her bottom lip. She moaned and opened her mouth wider in surrender. His tongue slipped in to play havoc with the sensitive flesh inside. The twinge in her clit became a sharp pain, demanding release. Her panties grew damp. She clenched her thighs to ease the throb.

If she'd known he kissed like this, she would have begged him to fuck her years ago, instead of dreaming about it.

His teeth bit her bottom lip harder.

"Oww."

He didn't release her, but lapped the wound with his tongue. His mouth still on hers, he smiled.

"Like that, don't you?"

"Um hmm." She squirmed enough to get one arm free and pull him closer, but he stepped back.

"I bet, if we put it to the test, you'd like taking orders from a man."

He's teasing me. She pushed at his arms, embarrassed to find herself panting. Her lips tightened. He wasn't even breathing hard.

He stepped away from her and picked up the bucket. "I've waited a long time to do that."

She wanted to kick herself for enjoying his kiss, but touched her swollen lips instead. "What? Tease me again? Was it worth it?"

He grinned. "You're wet, aren't you?"

He didn't wait for her response, but turned and walked down the sidewalk like he knew she'd follow.

Natalie bit her lip to stop the scream of frustration. Some things never changed. He could still make her angrier than any man she knew. If they weren't going to her house, she'd go the other way, just to prove him wrong.

* * *

The oysters sat in the bucket, forgotten, on the counter. The sight of Natalie's hips swishing in the tight denim skirt as she washed the dishes had his cock throbbing. The kiss they'd shared earlier hadn't helped the situation, but he ignored it. Hell, he'd gotten good at ignoring his body's needs for Natalie. With a small grunt, he adjusted his fly, liking the flick of his fingers down the length of his shaft.

Her hips moved once more in a gentle swaying motion, and the image of him sliding deep into her cunt forced him out of the chair. Three steps and he stood behind her, looking down on the top of her head. Her head came just below his shoulder. He'd always liked the fact she was so much smaller than him.

His hands settled on either side of her hips. She stiffened beneath his touch, but continued to fool with the dishes. Soapy hands glided over the bowls and plates with slippery ease. Nico groaned. He had waited long enough. He had tried to hide his desire years ago through taunts. He loved that she responded all hot and bothered, stomping her foot and stuttering whenever he came near her.

"Do that to me."

Silverware clattered to the bottom of the sink. She stood still beneath his touch, except for the tiny tremor he felt go through her body.

He leaned down. The smell of her hair made his head spin like a drunk's, and he wondered what the hair between her thighs smelled like.

Ambrosia. He pushed his cock closer into the small of her back.

"I-I don't think this is such a good idea." Her voice sounded uncertain, but husky with desire.

He grinned at the sound of her little stammer. "You know you've wanted me to get into your panties since we were kids."

Nico heard the sharp intake of her breath. That turned him on almost as much as her habit of stuttering. His grip on her hips tightened and he pushed into her warmth harder, needing to get closer. "Why do you think I tormented you for all those years?"

"Because you liked to be a bully?"

He leaned further and nibbled her ear before he ran his tongue around the edge. He felt her shiver, and whispered, "Wrong. That's how long *I've* wanted to get into your panties. I didn't know how to tell you."

He heard a choking sound erupt from deep within her throat. He had to make her understand he wanted her more than any other woman he'd ever met, but the words he knew he needed to say wouldn't come. If she rejected his heart, he'd never recover. He had to use the one weapon that he knew she wouldn't reject…his lust.

"I knew the minute you became sexually aware of me." His hands moved down the short length of her skirt. He liked the fact she'd always worn skirts instead of jeans. For hours, while he worked on his bikes, he'd picture her long legs and imagined them wrapped around him.

"You'd been trying to ignore me all day, but the second I kissed Katie White, you got this odd look of *need* across your face."

His fingers touched skin, smooth as silk. "You'd never looked at me like that before." He continued his quest back up beneath the soft denim material. "That's when I knew."

"I-I did not."

"Oh, yeah. You did." He bent his knees, then stood slowly. The material of her skirt caught on his belt buckle and lifted, letting his cock ride the crease between her ass cheeks through the thin strip of her panties. He rotated his hips and heard her hiss.

"That's when I knew I'd get to fuck you…one day."

Her hands gripped the sink so tight that her knuckles turned white. He knew she fought what he made her feel. She'd *always* fought her baser need for him. He wished he knew the sweet, soft words a woman liked to hear. The words he'd heard Dave use.

"You're *so* romantic, Nico."

His fingers had reached the top band of her panties. With a quick plunge of his middle finger, he dipped beneath the scrap of material and into her hot cunt. Her head came back hard against his shoulder.

Jesus! He could come right here with just the feel of her body sucking his hand in tight. He took a deep breath and fought the urge. His heart pounded against his chest.

He worked his finger deep, then back out to circle her clit. The tiny bud knotted beneath his touch. Her quick, shallow breaths told him she would go over the edge any second. He pinched the sensitive area with his index finger and thumb. He smiled when she bucked hard, caught between his body and the counter.

God, he wanted her. She'd given David Scott everything without hesitation, but he'd had to drag and force any and all responses she'd ever given to him. Even now, she fought him.

He groaned. She might have given David adoring looks, but it was him she'd wanted with those hard, hungry stares she hadn't even been aware of throwing his way. He'd sell his soul at that moment for the chance to give her everything and anything she asked for. He wanted more from her than Valentine's cards. He just had to convince her and remind her body that she wanted to give in to him; but would she?

She will. the little voice in his head promised. Just like it had promised him years ago when he'd first seen Natalie Pasqua walk onto the school playground with her plaid skirt, pigtails, and glasses—she belonged to him.

"You want romance, sweetheart, go talk to David." He added another finger to the first. She tilted her ass up against his cock, and his fingers slid deeper. She moaned. His other hand tightened on her hip to pull her closer. "But he won't give you what I can."

"Well, I should hope not. At least not before we eat."

"Nona!" Both he and Natalie stiffened and spoke at the same time. He eased his fingers, sticky with her juices, from her body. He gave Natalie a second to pull her skirt down before he stepped away from her heat. His cock protested with a sharp pain through his groin, but he resisted the urge to adjust his fly.

Nona stood in the doorway to the kitchen with her hands on her hips and a glare in her eyes. Nico moved his hand behind his back, but knew it was too late to hide the evidence of what he had been doing to the old woman's granddaughter.

"Go get cleaned up." There was a movement on the porch. "We've got company for supper." She waved at the person behind her.

David Scott. Nico clenched his jaw. *Shit.*

Chapter Two

"So, David, what are you doing now?" Natalie smiled across the table at the man she'd worshiped from afar years before. "Handsome" still described the blond, blue-eyed ex-quarterback. At twenty-seven, he looked like he could go all night.

Natalie choked on a green bean at the sexual thoughts her mind led her to tonight. First, with Nico at the kitchen sink; now fantasizing about David at the supper table. No wonder Nona watched her like a hawk. This was not how she acted under normal conditions. *Normal?*

She almost laughed as she looked around the table at Nona, David, and…Nico. He sat at the head, opposite Nona, like he had the right. His long legs stretched out, with one hand resting on the tabletop and the other… Lord only knew where his other hand lay beneath the tablecloth.

She could imagine that other hand stroking up and down the length of his cock. He'd bring himself to the edge of orgasm, then back off enough to enjoy the pain of unattained release. His gaze had been on her all night. She'd caught movement beneath the thin cotton of the tablecloth several times throughout the meal. She bit back a silent groan at the thought of him masturbating while he watched her eat.

Normal? No way in hell was this meal normal by any means. Never in her wildest fantasies had she ever imagined she'd be sitting at supper in her kitchen with the two men she'd always loved and lusted after.

"...been working with my uncle at the used car auction over on Pass Road."

David's voice broke into her thoughts. Natalie sat straighter in her chair and focused on him, sitting across from her. "I'm sorry. You said you're working with your uncle?"

"Yeah, but just until I get on my feet. The divorce cost a lot more than I thought it would. You're lucky you and that guy you lived with in New York weren't married."

Natalie took a quick glance at Nico, not liking the way his eyes narrowed at the mention of Rudy. He was a little too possessive after a couple of kisses and caresses. Couple? Hell, if there had been anymore like the ones he'd been giving her, Nona would've found them on the floor, rutting like deer in the fields. Her body felt branded from the heat of his fingers deep in her vagina.

Her neck and cheeks grew warm, and she reached for her water. Taking a few sips to ease the heat at the remembered events earlier in the evening, she missed what Nona was saying. Luckily, her grandmother addressed Nico.

"How is your mother?"

"Fine."

"Is she still looking for a roommate?"

Nico nodded.

A man of few words. He'd never been much on conversation. His eyes had always done most of the talking. She looked up, and her breath caught at the sensation that he could see into her soul and knew every thought circling through her mind. She took another sip of water.

He sat up. His other hand came from under the table. Natalie couldn't take her gaze off those fingers, wondering what they'd been up to undercover with that long, hard— She closed her eyes and bit back another groan.

"Natalie, are you okay?"

Her eyes opened to find everyone staring at her—Nona in concern, David in confusion, and Nico...in satisfaction.

"What?"

"You groaned, dear. Are you in pain?"

You could say that! "Um, no, no, I'm fine."

Nico's mouth turned up at one corner. Natalie wanted to crawl under the table. He knew what she'd been thinking. *Fuck him!* And that's exactly what she wanted, no, *needed* to do—she smiled at Nona—but couldn't at the moment. She tapped her finger against her plate.

"I forgot to ask you what you're doing now, Nico?" Her fingers stilled, but clenched the edge of the porcelain. "Where are you working?"

His fingers played over the pattern of the tablecloth, but he didn't hesitate to answer her. "I have a refurbishing shop down on Caillavet for old motorcycles."

"Sounds interesting." Natalie wasn't surprised that he worked with motorcycles. He'd always been tinkering with the things in high school and had ridden a big, black machine at the time. She heard the pride and satisfaction he had for his work in his voice.

"I like it." He shrugged and the movement drew her gaze to the broad shoulders that had surrounded her and made her feel dominated. She shivered and tried to get control over her wayward thoughts, but couldn't resist looking at those shoulders again.

So wide—not like most Vietnamese men she'd met. Nico wasn't only wide in the shoulders; he was tall and big. He must take after his unknown father.

"Yeah, you ought to go check it out, Nat. He's got some awesome bikes." David leaned forward with a genuine look of admiration on his face.

She knew they were friends, but she'd always wondered what it was that brought them together. From all outward appearances, they didn't have anything in common—David, super-jock, and Nico, super bad-ass. And here they were sitting down to dinner with her, super-nerd. She pushed a bean around her plate with her fork.

The sound of silverware clattering on a plate brought her back to focus. Nona stood with the dishes in her hand. "Natalie, would you help me with the plates? Then I'll start the coffee."

"Sure, Nona." No meal went without coffee to round off the mouth-watering morsels her grandmother cooked. The coffee, thick and rich, came from the neighborhood's old Cajun influence. Over the years, the number of true Cajuns had dwindled as more and more different peoples settled in the community of Pointe Cadet, but that just added to the unique atmosphere of Biloxi.

That's how it worked. One ethnic group moved in, then moved out, and another group moved in. First, the Cajuns, then the Croatian immigrants, now the Vietnamese. Pointe Cadet could be classified a veritable melting pot of various cultures, especially with the rise of casinos only blocks away, lining Highway 90. Even though small in size, the coast reminded Natalie a lot of New York with the mixture of peoples, religions, and cultures.

She stood and reached for David's plate, having to bend slightly to retrieve it. Catching his gaze on her cleavage, she felt her cheeks grow warm. She threw a glance at Nico to see if he noticed.

Of course. Old eagle-eyes wouldn't miss a thing. A little irritated at the disapproving look on his face, she couldn't help feeling a surge of pleasure that both men were paying attention to her. She smiled first at David, then raised an eyebrow at Nico before turning away from them.

Her panties were so wet she wanted to strip them away from her skin and ease the tight throb between her legs. Yep, this situation was downright...stimulating. She almost giggled on the way to the kitchen.

* * *

"What the fuck do you think you're doing, Dave?"

Natalie had barely disappeared through the swinging doors before Nico attacked the other man. David had had his chance at her in high school. It was *his* turn now.

"What are you talking about?"

"You know what I'm saying. Natalie." Nico nodded toward the kitchen.

David shrugged. "She looks damned good. New York must've taught her a few things."

Nico held back the urge to lunge across the table and grab him by the throat.

"Back off."

"Are you kidding?" David leaned forward. "She's hot, and I don't plan on throwing away what's offered this go-around."

"If you didn't notice earlier, we kinda have a *thing* going on."

David raised his eyebrows up and down. "How could I not notice, bro? My cock went to full attention when I looked through the back door and saw you two." He groaned. "Wish Nona hadn't been with me; I would've liked to watch."

He should have been annoyed, but the thought of David watching him and Natalie fuck made him hard. Nico shook his head. "I've decided not to waste opportunities, either." He sat back. "She's mine. I've waited a long time for her to grow up." He looked at David and frowned. "I thought you liked men, anyway." Nico watched a dull red tinge creep over David's cheekbones.

"You know I like both. Anyway, I think that's for the lady to decide. She's always shown more favor towards me."

"Not anymore."

David grinned. "We'll see."

"Wanna bet?"

"Hey, man, the casino is a block down the road, but I'll take you on."

Nico nodded. "Then, it's a bet. The one who has her in his bed on—" He looked at the calendar Nona kept on the wall. "—

Valentine's Day gets to keep her without further interference from the other."

"Ooo, a whole two weeks of fun and games. You're on."

The two shook hands. Nico refused to acknowledge the little *frisson* of electricity he felt at David's touch. Nico planned on winning, whether he had to use "outside influences," or not. He'd heard all the rumors that were whispered in the Vietnamese community about his father. He didn't know who, or what, his father might be, but if all the rumors were true, the old witch over on Pass Road would know how to contact a demon. The old man had never done anything for him. Now would be a good time to call in all that back "child support" he'd never received. Natalie belonged to him.

* * *

"What do you think you are doing?"

Natalie pulled up short as she walked through the swinging doors into the kitchen. Nona stood facing her with her hands on her hips and a frown across her face. Natalie looked behind her to see if one of the men had followed her, not sure who her grandmother spoke to. When she didn't see anyone, she had her answer.

"I'm not sure I understand."

"No, you don't." Nona sighed and took the dishes out of Natalie's hands. "You're playing with fire if you intend to lead those two on."

"Lead them on? They're the ones coming on to me!" Natalie bit her lip and glanced over her shoulder, not wanting either Nico or David to hear this conversation.

"But you're letting them." Nona shook her head. "Nico Bui has a short fuse, granddaughter. Don't push him too far."

"His 'fuse' didn't feel too short to me." Natalie clamped a hand over her mouth at the unexpected words.

"Natalie Marie Pasqua!" Nona admonished her, but Natalie saw the gleam of humor in her eyes. After a second, Nona even smiled. "He is a good-looking devil, isn't he?"

"Nona!" Natalie laughed. She'd never heard her grandmother utter anything sexual in her entire life. "Listen to you."

They giggled, and Nona took her hands. A serious expression replaced the happier, carefree one. "Promise me, you will decide wisely."

Natalie sighed. "I'm not choosing a husband, Nona. I'm just—" She waved her hand. "—having a little fun."

"That's how people get hurt."

"We're all adults. I think we all know how to handle a 'no strings attached' kind of relationship." Natalie tried to laugh, but the effort sounded weak. "David just got divorced less than a year ago, and I just broke up with Rudy. We don't want anything serious right now."

"What about Nico? He looked serious to me when he had his hands all over you today." Nona sniffed and scooped coffee into the old percolator. "He's always…liked you."

"You mean he's always liked to torment me." Natalie sat cups on the tray. "I know how to handle Nico."

"That's what I'm afraid of."

Natalie leaned against the counter and listened to the old coffee pot perk. The smell of rich coffee filled the room. "Does he have a girlfriend?"

"Nico?" Nona waved a hand. "Women are all over him like they were in school."

"Oh."

"But they are not like you."

"Oh? How's that?"

"They are cheap; you are not."

Natalie snorted. "Meaning, I'm dull and boring." She could hear Rudy's last cutting remarks, as he walked out of their apartment with a bleached-blond bimbo bitch on his arm. "Story of my life."

"You are not."

"It's okay. Even Nico called me a 'brainiac.'"

"That was years ago and he was jealous."

"Jealous? He was being his usual obnoxious self."

"You had given another boy a Valentine. What did you give him?"

"Nothing." Natalie watched Nona finish arranging the coffee tray with dessert cakes. She frowned and thought about his confession in the kitchen. Guilt pulled at her heart for not realizing earlier how she felt about Nico. "I never gave him anything. Ever."

"Well, maybe this Valentine's you will be a little nicer to him." Nona picked up the tray and headed for the dining room.

Yeah, but with any luck, it won't be some silly card he gets from me. Natalie smiled and followed. The image of a dark hand offering two pieces of candy came to mind. The image intensified when she went through the swinging doors to find the two men sitting smug in their chairs, looking at her. *One, light and sweet; the other, dark and bitter.*

"Hey, guys, ready for something sweet?"

David grinned and his blue eyes sparkled. Nico raised that imperious black eyebrow over narrowed eyes. The sight of both men, so opposite, but so right, made her heart flip-flop. Maybe she'd give them both something on Valentine's Day.

Chapter Three

Natalie tiptoed into the living room. Flashlight ready, she angled the beam toward the bookcase. One step and she stubbed her toe on the side chair. It took all her willpower not to scream *Shit!* at the same time she fumbled to keep a grip on the flashlight. She swallowed hard against the shooting pain from her big toe and managed to hobble the rest of the way across the room.

James Bond, I'm not. She leaned one hand against the wall and let out a sigh of relief. So far, so good if Nona hadn't been awakened by her midnight meanderings. Carefully, she scanned the bookcase for Nona's old journal full of gypsy spells. Nona would tan her butt if she ever learned she'd been using this family gem for years. Coming from a long line of gypsies had its advantages.

Ah, there. Covered with dust and sitting back from the rest of the books on the shelf, she found the little journal she'd been hunting. She pulled it free and blew a thick layer of dust from its jacket. Nona must not use it anymore.

Natalie limped over to the sofa. Curling her legs beneath her, she turned the pages, using the dim light from the flashlight to find the spell she wanted— *If you are undecided between two admirers, magick can help...*

Well, she hoped so, because she had a dilemma. She had enjoyed the attentions of both men, but she needed to know which one she really wanted. Natalie bit her lip. She'd always pursued David, but deep down she'd always wanted Nico. She flipped the pages. Maybe a spell existed that would help her keep them both. Now, that would be an interesting scenario. She stopped her perusing and stared into the darkness. Her eyebrow rose, and she covered her mouth on the giggle that threatened to give her away.

* * *

Easing into Natalie's bedroom was easier than she'd expected. With Natalie busy searching the spell book in the living room, it would only take a second to do what she had to do. Nona smiled in the darkness. Her granddaughter thought she didn't know of her dabblings in gypsy magick, but she'd always known. Although they went to Mass every week, the Pasqua women had always followed the "old" traditions.

A floorboard creaked and Nona froze, listening for Natalie's footstep. After a second, she realized the old house had settled. Walking to Natalie's bed, she pulled the pillow up and placed a bay leaf between the pillowcase and the pillow, then laid the pillow back against the bed. She gave the goose down a pat. Tonight, her baby's dreams would tell her which man she needed to focus her attentions on.

* * *

Take two tulip bulbs. With a new pin, scratch the name of one suitor on each bulb. Remembering which bulb represents which lover, plant the bulbs beside each other in a pot. Whichever one blooms first will be the one most deserving of you.

"Bullshit." Natalie cringed at her whispered outburst. She'd been going through the journal for thirty minutes and still hadn't found a spell to do what she wanted—fast.

She wanted to know how to make both men hers before Valentine's Day. She yawned and flung the book across the cushion to land in a patch of moonlight shining through the window. It had been a long day, and she really needed to go to sleep. The pale beams called to her, and she knew what she had to do before she went to bed.

She got up to stand in front of the window. For years she'd gone to the moon whenever she needed something. In New York, her nighttime rituals were impossible to perform with limited outside spaces and privacy. But, here—she pulled the sheers back and looked into the backyard—she could practice her magick without interruption.

Remembering the chair, she eased through the living and dining areas into the kitchen. At the door, she rummaged through the counter drawer for the needed items then removed her nightgown and panties. The slide of the door chain sounded louder than she remembered. After slipping it free, she waited for any reaction from Nona. When none came, she stepped through into the chilly January air.

Her nipples peaked and her pussy clenched at the cold that nipped her body. She breathed deeply of the crisp night air. She loved winter nights. With a quick dash, she ran across the frost-covered ground to hide beneath the live oak tree. Here in the shadows of the old gnarly limbs and leaves, she could perform her ritual without anyone seeing her.

A concrete bench sat beneath the tree. Sweeping leaves and twigs from the surface, she used the flat area for an altar. With gentle care, she placed the single candle and box of matches she'd retrieved from the kitchen drawer then crossed herself.

Lifting her hands to the moonlit night, she whispered the incantation she'd designed years before. "Moonlight that shines on me, hear my wish and grant my needs."

She held her stance for a few minutes, but couldn't stop the yawn that claimed her. A faint breeze lifted the hair around her shoulders and she closed her eyes to let her meditative trance take her. In the distance, she heard the sounds of the night—cars on the Biloxi bridge, the train crossing two streets over, dogs barking into the night air, and someone breathing.

Her eyes opened with a snap and she whirled around. A hand covered her mouth when she would have screamed. Her heart pounded against her chest and she kicked out with her bare foot.

He laughed. "Nice try, sweets." The raspy voice whispering in her ear sounded familiar. He pulled her closer and she realized he was as naked as she. "That's right, don't fight. You'll only get hurt trying to resist me."

A warm, wet tongue trailed down her cheek. When he reached her neck, his lips joined his tongue in a soft sucking motion against the vein that throbbed in fear and...something else. While her mind screamed "run," her body screamed "give in." Desire wound its way down her neck, across her breasts, and settled in her groin. She pressed her thighs together to fight the need that swamped her senses.

He released her neck to trail back to her ear. "Hmm, you taste as good as I imagined." The arm around her waist loosened. "Sweeter than that candy I offered you when you were seventeen."

His hand wandered over her body. First he slid his fingers up to pinch her nipple between his forefinger and thumb, then he feathered down to twirl a finger around the curve of her navel. "You've grown up quite nicely. No wonder he wants you."

Natalie moaned and shifted her hips. Whether in pleasure or an attempt to break free, she didn't know. The more he touched her, the more her cunt grew wet and throbbed.

He laughed, the warmth of his breath puffing small clouds of mist into the cold air. His hand slipped further south and hesitated above her pubis.

The anticipation became a physical pain. Through the pressure of his fingers, she muttered, "Come on."

He did. Long, hot fingers combed through her pussy hair to reach their destination. When he entered her cunt, he released the hand over her mouth and she heard their moans of pleasure blend together. The familiar ache grew so acute she thought she would fall, but his arms held her tight against his body. The outline of his cock pressed into her back, and she thought of Nico.

"Don't think of him." He plunged his fingers deeper. "Not yet. Think of me and the pleasure I'm giving you."

Fantasy and reality blurred together, and Natalie couldn't be sure if she were dreaming or actually letting a complete stranger take control of her body. But…he wasn't a stranger. She'd seen him before. The haze of desire swamped her senses.

She didn't care. Between the cold of the night and the heat of his fingers and lips, she lost all touch with reality. One minute they were standing with him behind her, his fingers deep within her body; the next moment he stood before her in the cold night air.

He reached past her head and produced a long-stemmed rose with petals so red they looked black in the moonlight.

"It's beautiful." Her voice sounded like she spoke inside a tunnel.

"Like you, my dear." He trailed the bud across her shoulders and between her breasts.

"I'm not beautiful."

"Oh, but you are." He smiled. His teeth flashed white in the pale light. "I know at least three males who think so." The bud circled her breast. "Myself, Nico, and David."

Natalie sucked her breath in at the throb between her legs. Why had he stopped what he'd been doing to her earlier? She wanted—

He continued the assault of her senses and teased her nipple to a point.

She bit her lip to keep a cry of utter need from escaping.

"Nona—"

"Can't see or hear us."

"Who are you?"

"I'm the answer to yours and another's prayers."

She shook her head. "An angel?"

He laughed and the black eyebrow rose. "Not the last time I looked in the mirror."

"You're...the devil?"

The smile disappeared. He bowed. "I'm but a lowly servant."

"Why are you here?"

"With your body..." He stepped closer and sniffed her neck. "With your cunt, you have the ability to tempt the soul of one who needs what you can offer."

"You have more power than I to do that."

He shrugged. "But I'm not what he wants."

He walked behind her and stood so close, she felt his cock against the small of her back. Again, the image of Nico surfaced, but quickly dissipated when the *man's* hand circled her waist, sending tiny, threadlike shivers across her abdomen and down to her clit. Moisture eased between the folds of her pussy. If he didn't fuck her soon, she'd go insane.

"Do you want me?" He kissed her temple.

She nodded.

"If you let me take you, then we have a pact. Do you understand?"

"Yes." Her whisper filtered into the night air.

"I can give you pleasure." The soft petals of the rosebud caressed her clit, and she sighed. "Or I can give you pain."

His hand covered her mouth and muffled her scream as the rose's thorn pierced her labia above her clit. A warm trickle of blood mingled with the juices of her pussy to run down the inside of her leg.

"Whichever sensation you wish, my sweet." He kept the thorn in place as he eased a few steps back to sit on the bench. Once situated, he pulled her onto his lap. The head of his cock pushed at the wet folds of her vagina, and she spread her legs without hesitation to take him into her body.

His ankles captured her calves, spreading her wide and more open to his control. Slowly, he worked the thorn above her clit while he speared his hips up against her body.

Her hips moved against his rhythm, forcing her cunt to widen and accept his thick mass. *She'd never had a cock so large. So thick.*

"That's right...give me what I need." He sank deeper. "I'll make all your desires come true."

The thorn pulled her labia tight at the same instant his dick shoved into her. He used nature's beauty like a clit ring, and the sensation had her squirming to get closer to the *man* beneath her.

"I'll promise your lover's cock will feel better than mine."

She wanted to deny the pleasure she experienced at what he did to her, but couldn't. She craved more. She wanted more. A whimper escaped between the press of his fingers.

"Shh. Don't fight what I know you want." He bent his head to circle her nipple with his mouth and sucked hard.

Natalie bucked with the force of her orgasm, but he held her tight with his arms, legs, mouth, and cock. Her body rocked hard against his with the contraction of her pleasure, on and on. Finally, spent, her body went limp, and he released his punishing hold, but his cock stayed buried inside her body, hard and long. She lay dazed and panting within the circle of his arms.

"My turn." His voice growled against her ear. He swiveled, but kept his hands firmly around her waist, and pushed her, chest down, over the cold concrete bench.

She tried to struggle up, but his weight held her down. "You accepted me into your body, Natalie. You have to complete the pact." He rammed into her hard. The feeling of fullness increased with the swell of his cock.

"Oh, God, yesss…"

"He's not part of this bargain, sweet." He pulled out, then surged back into her again and again. His fingers tangled into her hair, and he pulled her head back. "It's you and me."

One last thrust had her going over the edge for a second orgasm. This time he followed, and her scream blended with his, loud and animalistic through the cold, night air. The steam of their breaths panted fast in a white mist. Hot, scalding semen bathed her womb.

What have I done? She wanted to escape this…*thing* that held her, but she didn't have the energy.

He pulled out. The sensation of fullness evaporated, leaving her feeling…empty. Her eyelids grew heavy. *Have to get away…* But all she could do was curl up and close her eyes.

A large, calloused hand smoothed the hair from her forehead. Firm, sensuous lips kissed her cheek. Muffled words filled her mind, and she frowned, but couldn't wake.

Sweet, Natalie. Sleep now, and I'll make sure your wish becomes reality tomorrow.

Chapter Four

Music reverberated around the crowded room. The table vibrated beneath David's arms with the bass as he leaned on the scarred wooden top. Cradling his beer, he watched the moisture trickle down the sides into a pool at the base. A cheer rose from the crowd when the band completed the first set to take a break. Loud conversation took the place of the rock music.

He glanced around, but didn't see anyone who would recognize him. That was the beauty about sneaking over to New Orleans. No one knew him or his family. He could do whatever he wanted, pick up anyone he wanted.

"Whatcha havin', hon?"

David jumped at the waitress's question. His gaze traveled from her high-heeled sandals over long bare legs topped with a miniscule black skirt. His eyebrow rose with his smile. "Whatever you can give me."

She hesitated over her gum-chewing and studied him closer with narrowed eyes. "Uh huh. How 'bout another beer, then?"

David felt his smile falter to be replaced by a frown. That line usually worked. The waitress walked away toward the bar. He angled his head and took a swallow of his beer. She had a nice ass with those legs, too. He could imagine them wrapped around his waist and back. "Umm."

"You can say that again."

David turned toward the voice. A tall man in black stood beside his table. His face lay hidden in the shadows of the dim room. Cigarette smoke curled in lazy swirls around the outline of his body. The noise level droned into a distant rumble as the man pulled out a chair and sat opposite him. The smoke followed in a cloud to hover above the stranger's head.

David swallowed. A chill raced down his spine and settled in the base of his abdomen. "W-Who are you?" He fought to control the catch in his voice. Unexplainable fear took hold in his mind. He shook his head and looked at the number of beer bottles on the table.

"Oh, you're not drunk...yet." The stranger's mouth quirked at one corner, his eyes still shrouded by the dark. A lean, dark hand, tattooed with a greenish-black pentagram, reached out and took the bottle from David's hand. With slow precision, the bottle lifted to the cruel slash of the man's mouth. Firm lips covered the rim of the bottle.

David watched in fascination, not able to look away. When the man's tongue circled inside the neck, his balls clenched. A slow throb spread to his cock and his anus quivered. He resisted the urge to adjust his jeans and settled on pulling the neck of his T-shirt away from his collarbone. The heat in the room rocketed ten more degrees.

David cleared his throat. "I asked who you were, mister."

The bottle came down, and the stranger leaned forward. The overhead light cast jagged shadows across high cheekbones, giving the guy a haunted appearance. Black hair fell past wide shoulders and feathered above black eyebrows and eyes.

David sucked in a breath. *Nico!* But—he looked closer—not. This guy looked like an older version of his friend. A black T-shirt stretched over a muscled chest and firm abdomen. Intricate tattoos in some sort of Celtic design circled each bicep. Dark and dangerous, just like his friend, but more...menacing.

"Like what you see?"

David sat straighter, anger and excitement coursing through every vein. "Look, you son-of-a—"

"The name's Luke." A long finger reached out and traced a small pattern over David's knuckle, cutting off his words.

His cock, rock hard, strained against the restraint of his jeans. His breath came in short, quick gasps through clenched teeth. David fought the reaction without success.

"What...do...you...want?"

"The same thing you want."

David tried to pull his hand away from the questing finger. Every caress sent tingles through his balls.

The man placed his palm flush to the back of David's hand and prevented further movement.

Spirals of electricity raced over David's skin and up his arm. He gasped. "Don't."

"Why not? You like it; I like it." Luke shrugged. "Why not?"

David swallowed hard, closing his eyes against the glittering stare that reached into his soul and found his darkest desires. Sweat peppered his upper lip and forehead. Taking a deep, shuddering breath, he snatched his hand away from the temptation Luke offered. He'd wanted to get laid, but with someone he could control. From the look of the man in front of him, David knew who would be calling the shots.

"Get the fuck away from me, you pervert."

Instead of anger, the man threw his head back and laughed, long and hard.

David glanced around, catching the curious stares of several patrons. He pushed his chair back and stood. Taking a few bills from his pocket, he threw them on the table. His hand shook, but he didn't care. He had to get the hell out of here. He shouldn't have come here tonight, but after spending the entire evening looking at Natalie's legs and Nico's ass, he'd needed some relief. But—he looked at the stranger watching him—this wasn't it.

"You sure?"

David hesitated at the question, not sure he hadn't spoken out loud. He watched the man stand with a lithe animal grace, slow and smooth. Again, he thought of a younger man he'd been lusting after since high school. "You're not related to Nico Bui, by chance?"

A black eyebrow rose and the quirk returned. "I'm related to a lot of people."

David shrugged. "Never mind. I'm outta here."

Steely fingers wrapped around his wrist next to his thigh. "Not yet." Luke stepped closer, dwarfing him by half a foot, and whispered in David's ear.

"Imagine your wildest, darkest desire."

A finger flicked across his crotch. David groaned. The thought of Luke's larger frame wrapped around him surfaced.

A burst of hot air tickled his neck. "That's only the beginning."

He opened his eyes to find Luke's face close to his. Black eyes stared straight into his, commanding him to relent. A knot formed in his throat at what he knew he'd do. David nodded. The guy wasn't Nico, but the similarity was too strong. He couldn't resist.

Luke smiled.

* * *

Strong hands pushed him against the wall. David grunted with the impact. *Shit!* What had he been thinking when he'd invited this guy home? *Nico.* That's what. The need to have the one he most desired touch him, suck him...fuck him made him sweat and pant with lust to the point he picked up a stranger.

Muscled arms wrapped around him. The hands moved down his sides to grasp the snap to his jeans. The large body pressed into his and hot breath fanned his neck and cheek.

"Relax, lover boy. I'm not going to do anything you haven't been dreaming about."

"What do you know about my dreams, asshole?"

Luke's laugh held humor and a dash of aggression. His thumbs hooked on either side of David's briefs. With one vicious tug, the cotton lay at his feet. The cold air on his ass made his cock tighten.

"Hmm, I know you want me to be Nico."

David stiffened, but Luke pressed into him harder. "And that's okay with me, except the price for release might be a little steep."

A hand snaked around his waist and hip to grasp his dick. David turned his forehead to the wall and closed his eyes against the sensation. In his mind he pictured Nico behind him, massaging him, giving him what he needed.

He swallowed. "W-What do you want?"

The calloused hand tightened in reward. "Natalie, you, and Nico. Together."

"Why?"

"Let's just say Nico's had a hard life, and I'd like to see him happy."

David snorted. "Not asking for much, are you?"

The hand moved up, then back to feather a caress across his balls.

"Goddammit, who the fuck are you?" He couldn't take much more. His balls ached with the need to release their load. Sweat covered his arms, chest, and back. The back of his throat burned with the effort of breathing through clenched teeth to hold his orgasm in check.

"I'm the one who can give you that ultimate Freudian high you've always wanted." The other arm and hand worked around his middle. The fingers holding his cock disappeared, only to reappear, wet, against his rectum. "You just have to relax, enjoy the moment, and give me what I want."

His anal muscles tightened in defense, but the questing hand burrowed deeper with a thumb and middle finger, forcing his ass cheeks apart. Luke's forefinger teased around the opening to David's anus.

Hands flattened against the wall curled and fisted in frustration. He groaned in surrender. "Okay, okay, I'll do it. I'll get the three of us together."

* * *

His foot on the last step, Nico came to a halt at the rhythmic thud that sounded familiar, coming from David's apartment. He frowned.

"Oh, God...don't...stop! Don't...stop."

The *thud* grew stronger, harder; the cries louder.

Nico's eyebrow rose. He'd known Dave liked his sex both ways, but he'd never had proof of others. David's voice begged for more. The thumps increased in rhythm, indicating that whoever had him didn't mind giving him what he asked for. Nico shrugged, trying not to imagine what that scenario would entail.

He turned to leave, but hesitated when David's pleas became moans of deep and utter pleasure. His own cock tingled, and his teeth clenched. He *wouldn't* be turned on by the fact David and some other guy were "sucking and fucking." He took another step.

Yesss!" David's release tore through the night air.

Nico closed his eyes at the same time his cock hardened. His hand gripped the rail and he pulled his body away from the unwanted desires that called to him. He'd given in once, long ago. Reaching the pavement in the parking lot, he glanced up to David's darkened apartment. He couldn't give in again. He didn't understand that side of himself. How could he crave Natalie and at the same time want David?

* * *

He lay facedown against the mattress. Sweat covered his body from head to toe. He shivered when the air conditioning kicked on, but didn't move. He couldn't.

Fuck! He'd never had it that good. Dragging what energy he could find, he turned his head and scanned the darkened room for him...Luke.

The tip of a cigarette glowed red. A second later, a trail of smoke curled up and around Luke's head as he sat in the corner, cloaked by shadows.

David could see his silhouette against the cream-colored drapes. He moaned and let his head fall back to the wet sheets and watched his newest lover. There had been nothing gentle in what the other man had done to him. His ass throbbed and burned, but it had been worth the pain...so good.

"You liked that?"

"Um hmm." He couldn't speak; it took too much energy.

"Enough to let me fuck you again—" Smoke circled down to the floor. "—and again?"

"Yes." The word hissed from David's dry lips. His heart rate increased with the fear Luke wouldn't return after tonight. He lifted his head, feeling weak and lethargic. "I-I've got to have it."

A quiet laugh emerged from the dark. "I know you do, Davey." The silhouette stubbed the butt into the nearby planter, then leaned forward. "But here's what you've got to do for me."

* * *

Natalie sat straight up in bed with a gasp. She looked around at the familiar knickknacks of her bedroom, smelling Nona's coffee brewing in the kitchen. She frowned. The last thing she remembered had been saying her incantation under the light of the moon, then…everything afterward seemed fuzzy and distorted. She'd been naked.

She looked down at her nightgown beneath the covers she clutched in her hand. Lifting the covers back, she pulled her gown up to reveal her panties. The frown on her forehead deepened. She eased her forefinger beneath the scrap of silk and touched her clit. *Humph.* The little nub quivered, but didn't ache with the pain she remembered from the rose's thorn.

Murky images ebbed back and forth beyond her reach. A flash of David—she angled her head and closed her eyes—a flash of Nico. The picture blurred, then sharpened. She almost had it—

"Natalie, breakfast!"

"Damnation." She punched the pillow as the vision disappeared. She looked around the room once more, not sure how she'd gotten back here, or if she'd ever really been outside at all. With another groan, she eased out of bed and grabbed her robe. One thing you didn't do at Nona's was walk around in your nightgown without a robe. Heaven forbid if the cat saw the outline of your nipples, or something. She bit back a laugh.

Nona would pass out if she'd seen her all those times she'd strutted around in the backyard, performing her midnight rituals. She'd heard rumors of Nona's gift, but had never seen her grandmother dance with the moon. She shook her head and shrugged. Maybe the rumors weren't real. Maybe she was the only one here who believed in magick. Stretching her arms above her head, she walked into the kitchen and yawned.

"Sleep well, my baby?"

A loud *whack* accompanied the question and sent Natalie stumbling two or three steps to the kitchen table. Her eyes fully open, she watched her grandmother beat the can of frozen orange juice against the counter's edge.

Shaking her head, she stepped to the end of the counter and took the can from the old woman's arthritic fingers. "Here, Nona, let me. If you keep on, you're going to break your fin—"

Her words trailed off as her gaze focused on the concrete bench under the old oak tree in the backyard. The sun shone bright in the morning air. Birds whistled from their perches in the tall tree. And, sitting where she'd left them, were the candle and box of matches from the night before.

Dizziness hit; she gripped the edge of the counter. *A hot, wicked voice whispered in her ear while long, lean fingers explored her pussy.* Natalie heard a small moan escape her throat. *Oh, God…it couldn't have really happened!*

Chapter Five

"What do you mean, you put a bay leaf under my pillow?" Natalie looked up from the mug of steaming tea and gazed into her grandmother's concerned face. The little woman held her hands together in front of her chest, wringing them over and over.

"It's an old gypsy fortune-telling trick."

Well, she had her answer. Nona really *did* practice the "old" ways of her ancestors, but...a bay leaf? "What does a bay leaf do?"

"If you'd just ask me to let you study the book, you'd know. It's one of the first 'tricks' you learn when you become a seer."

"A seer?" Natalie put the cup down. "I'm not a seer, Nona. I've just borrowed a few of the spells I've found in there."

"I thought you liked David."

Natalie sighed in frustration. Her fingernail worried a chip in the cup.

"I do." She didn't know how, but she had to ensure that both men ended up in her bed. "Is there a spell you know besides *bay leaves* that I can use?"

Nona poured water into the pitcher of juice. "Well, there is one…" She stirred the frozen pulp. "…where you take a piece of the person's hair, tie a knot in it, and place it between the tarot cards for their birth sign and yours." She stopped stirring and looked at Natalie.

"You paperclip the cards and place them somewhere you will have frequent contact, like in your purse. This is supposed to help 'bring your true lover to you.'"

"Do I say any type of incantation?"

"You need to study, granddaughter, if you're going to use magick." Nona shook the wooden spoon at her. "You need to know the 'why' and not just the 'how to' of the spells you're trying to cast."

"Okay, okay." Natalie stood. "First, let's find a hair from each of them." She grinned at Nona's frown and headed for the dining room where they had all eaten the night before.

The darkened room sat quiet in the morning hours. With the drapes pulled, the atmosphere clung in thick, depressing waves. Natalie loosened the tie of her robe. "Turn the light on. I can hardly see my hand, it's so gloomy in here."

Nona snorted, but flipped the switch for the overhead light. Natalie blinked against the sudden glare. After a second, her vision adjusted and she bent to search the cloth-covered seats where David and Nico had sat.

Nona lifted a blond hair. They grinned at each other, but when Nona turned, Natalie slipped a black strand into her pocket.

* * *

Her left hand clutched her purse while she smoothed her right hand over her jeans. The cards were tucked securely in the side pocket of the purse. Everything in place, Natalie walked through the door of Bui Motorcycles.

The smell of oil and tires mingled to tickle her nose. Several customers were present but didn't glance up when she walked across the concrete floor to the service counter. She thrummed her fingers against the countertop. She didn't see any sales personnel, or Nico. She decided to wait.

To the right side of the entrance, Nico had arranged a sitting area with an old black sofa and several metal-framed chairs covered in the same dark material. A low coffee table rested between the furniture and a small color television. Natalie sat on the sofa and looked around. Not the most beautiful design, but comfortable. She picked up a magazine and flipped through the pages, eyeing the hallway to the back of the shop.

She heard him before she saw him. Angling in her seat, she watched him come out of the warehouse carrying a box. His biceps strained with the effort of supporting the parcel's weight. Her mouth watered at the sight of the muscles as they rippled back and forth. The black T-shirt and faded jeans he wore fit him like a second skin.

My, my, my. Her hand searched out the cards in her purse. She hoped they picked the right man, because both subjects were in prime physical condition. At that second, he looked up and spotted her. His gaze narrowed, but he didn't acknowledge her any other way. He continued to speak to his customer, ringing up the sale, writing a receipt.

Natalie hated the nervous flutter in her stomach. She wiped her palms down her jeans. One more customer, then they'd be alone. She wondered if he would continue where they'd left off yesterday, or if he'd be upset with her for flirting with David last night. She couldn't help it. That contagious smile of his did it to her all the time.

The drawer of the cash register *pinged* and slid closed. Natalie looked up in time to watch the last customer walk out the door with Nico close behind. Her mouth opened to protest, but closed when she saw him flip the "open" sign to "closed." She stood, not sure if he wanted her here, or not. The frown on his face grew darker with each step he took her way.

What in hell was she doing here? He'd barely gotten an hour's worth of sleep last night between thinking of her pinioned between him and Nona's sink, then listening to David getting fucked. He sighed, raked a hand through his hair, and turned to her.

His frown deepened. She wore jeans. He'd never seen her in pants. He walked within a foot of her and looked her up and down. The movement of her throat as she swallowed caught his attention. He liked the idea she might be nervous.

"You're wearing pants."

She blinked, and her hands skimmed her thighs. "Uh, yeah."

"I like you in skirts." He stepped closer. Her breath came in a little *huff* to brush across his chin. The minty smell of her toothpaste passed across the fringes of his awareness. It was the sight of her lips pressing into a tight line that caught his curiosity.

"What, don't care for me telling you what I like?" He reached up a finger and stroked across her bottom lip. The tremor he felt could have come from either of them. He leaned forward and touched his lips to hers.

She jerked in reaction, but his hands caught her upper arms. A small protest escaped her mouth but was muffled when he brought her to him, hard. She struggled for a second, then relented. Nico smiled against her lips. His hands eased down her arms to settle on the curve of her ass.

Hmm, might be benefits to jeans, after all. His fingers trailed up over her hips and caught her belt loops. With a quick, hard tug, he pulled her against him; his pelvis snuggled into her stomach. Air whooshed from her mouth along with a low moan. Their lips searched for each other; tongues mated and swirled; sucking sounds echoed through the showroom.

Nico pulled back, realizing where they were. He nipped her lips, glistening with their combined saliva, with his. "Upstairs."

Fused together again, he tugged and pushed her up the side stairs to his apartment. Head buzzing, he got them through the door, barely. When he had her within a foot of the entrance's path, he pushed her back against the door. It closed with a loud *bang.* Neither of them noticed.

Hands bumped hands, trying to push clothes out of the way. Her fingernails grazed his skin and he shuddered. The snap of her jeans loosened and he eased both hands into the warmth. The musky smell of her body rose to push his need over the edge.

Releasing her lips again, he tugged the denim to her ankles; on the way back up her body, he caught her behind her knees and lifted. She kicked one leg free from her pants and wrapped both around his waist. Nico anchored her against the door with his weight.

"Put your arms around my neck." When she did, he undid his jeans and pushed the denim down far enough to free his cock. That done, he angled his hips in preparation of entry.

"Wait." She reached between their bodies and wrapped a hand around his dick. "Wait." Her breath came in short pants.

"*What?*" Nick clenched his teeth against the interruption and the feel of her hand around him.

"C-Condom." She bumped her head back against the door in apparent frustration.

He leaned his forehead against hers and closed his eyes. Thank God one of them still had enough wits to remember precaution. Nico breathed in deep, then swallowed. "Right."

Not releasing his hold on her, he shifted her legs higher on his waist then reached down into the back pocket of his jeans. After several fumbles, he tore the wrapper from the condom and freed the rubber, then eased the lubricated latex over the head of his cock.

"Shit!" His hands shook so hard he couldn't get the prophylactic in place.

"Here, dammit." Natalie leaned closer. "I thought you did this sort of thing all the time."

He had to laugh. "I don't know about 'all the time,' but I do have some experience." Nico let her take the condom and pulled her up with his hands around her thighs.

"I've never forgotten to use a rubber before, though." Their eyes met, and he saw the surprise in her gaze at his admission. The touch of her cool fingers easing the condom over his skin forced his hips to twitch toward her cunt.

"Hurry up, Nat. I'm dying here." The husky note in his voice didn't come from lust alone. He needed her to understand how much this moment meant to him. If he could just tell her—

"Okay, okay, it's on." She shimmied back, then pushed her hips down.

Nico's body had a mind of its own as he rammed forward. All the loving, sweet words he'd thought of saying disappeared with the sound of her scream. The feel of her body around his consumed him like a forest fire. He'd waited so long to do this. He pushed harder, harder, working his hips deeper into her heat. His lungs burned with the need for oxygen, but that didn't stop him from digging, grinding...fucking...his way into her cunt.

"God...so tight. So fucking...tight."

Natalie strained to take him deeper within. She'd wanted him for so long. She hadn't realized how badly. Sweat pooled beneath her breasts. She arched her back, hoping to get closer to him. She didn't want to just fuck. She wanted their bodies to meld into one—one body, one mind, one being.

Her hands locked behind his neck, and she brought his head down. Their gazes locked mere centimeters apart. His hair clung to his face in sweat-soaked clumps. With his pupils dilated, he looked like some wild beast. Her pussy clenched, and he groaned.

"Fuck me."

His eyes narrowed, his lips pulled away from his teeth, and he ground his cock into her, pumping. Faster...faster. Harder.

Natalie threw her head back to release another scream that ripped through the room, followed by his. Tremors wracked them both as they came down from their lust-filled high. One leg, then the other, she dropped her feet to the floor, but when her muscles spasmed, she clutched his shoulders for support.

Nico's hand went to her waist. "I got you." An arm wrapped around her. Letting him pull her forward into the room, they ended up on the sofa, panting and exhausted.

She lay back against the cushions and turned her head to him. His eyes were closed, and his cheeks stained with a dull red flush. A bead of sweat worked its way down the angle of his jaw. She leaned over and swiped the salty trickle with her tongue.

"Umm, you taste good."

His eyes, glazed with satiation, opened. He lifted her hand to his lips and kissed her fingers, then let their joined fingers drop.

"You do, too." His smile took her breath. Here was one beautiful man.

She smiled back at him; then they were both grinning.

"That's been overdue."

She nodded. "If I had only known."

God, she's so beautiful. Nico wanted to open the window and yell out into the neighborhood that he'd finally gotten the woman he wanted. He took a deep breath and let his fingers trail over her face. The little burst of hot air across his chin told him she liked his touch.

His dick tingled to life. He placed his fingers and thumb around the contour of her jaw, trying to memorize the feel of her face. When he leaned forward to kiss her, she met him halfway.

Slowly this time, he savored the taste of her lips and tongue. There was no reason to rush. He shifted his weight and pushed her down into the cushions, never letting his mouth leave hers. His knees straddled her hips, and he reached between them to undo the tiny buttons on her blouse.

That done, he pushed the material aside to work on the front closure of her bra. With a twist the clasp opened and her breasts fell free. The breath died in his throat at the sight of the soft mounds in front of him. He looked up.

Her face held an expression of anticipation. Her eyes were closed and her lips were parted with the tip of her tongue held between the edges of her teeth.

He lowered his mouth to first one nipple, then the other, marveling at how the dusky peaks hardened with the flick of his tongue.

Natalie's breath hissed, and he looked up again to find her lips compressed at the same time her thighs clamped together beneath him. He smiled and a rush of triumph forced his cock to harden further.

He moved away enough to remove the condom and drag the jeans the rest of the way off her body. The musky scent of their earlier encounter rose from the warmth of her skin to tease his nose. With a moan, he pushed her legs apart and aimed for the dampened curls laid out like a feast.

Her hands fisted in his hair as he lapped her juices. The tangy taste of her cunt coated his tongue. With one hand he caught her pussy hair and pulled the slick folds aside so he could latch onto her clit with his teeth.

He pushed his mouth closer to devour all of her. His nose snuggled against her bush and he breathed deeply—his eyes closed, but he didn't stop until she lay panting beneath him. Three more laps and one bite, he had her bucking like a wild horse while her orgasm peaked, then ebbed. He propped his weight on his elbows and watched her chest heave up, then down with her ragged breaths.

She opened her eyes and stared at him. Her pupils were dilated and her nostrils were extended in exhilaration. Strands of her hair lay tousled across her face and neck to give her that "just fucked" look. She smiled at him.

His heart thudded hard twice, then settled into an uneven pattern. Without a word, he eased up onto his knees and pulled another condom from his jeans. His hands still shook, but he got the rubber in place with the first try.

Her giggle at his success turned into a deep, hungry groan when he slid his length into her heat. Sharp fingernails bit into his back as he thrust slow, but deep, into her body.

When her legs wrapped around his waist and she tilted her hips at a different angle to allow the entire length of his cock to be swallowed by her cunt, he couldn't hold back any longer. His thrusts intensified to the point the sofa moved several inches across the floor. The eruption of his orgasm caught him by surprise and had him gasping for breath.

Their hearts beat together for several seconds, then settled into two separate, distinct patterns. He leaned his forehead against hers and kissed her gently.

"T-That was good." His voice sounded husky and unsteady.

"Y-Yeah."

He smiled when he heard her stutter, knowing that meant he'd affected her on some deep level. He pulled her close. She was his.

"Stay with me tonight." The words were an order, not a request. The smile had disappeared and his eyes gleamed with an emotion she couldn't define.

A knot formed in her belly. Making love with Nico confirmed how much she had always loved him. She shuddered at the strength of the emotions she felt at that moment. Her chest tightened with the realization that he could ask her to do anything while under his influence and she wouldn't be able to resist him. Fear surfaced from the turmoil inside her.

Nico's persona could easily take over her own newfound freedom. She'd left Rudy. Did she want another man who would dominate her? For a second, the thought of another man forcing her to bend to his will scared her more than anything. She had her freedom and wanted to be in control of what she did and when she did it. "I-I can't."

She felt Nico's withdrawal even though his expression never changed except for a tiny flicker in his eyes. "I made dinner plans with David."

He stood and the loss of his body heat forced her to reach out, but he took a step back and adjusted his jeans.

"He's my friend." She watched his eyebrow rise at the word "friend." Sometimes Nico could say more with his body language than someone who knew the entire dictionary. She sighed. "I didn't mean it like that, and you know it."

"Do I?" He grabbed his boots off the floor and scooped his keys off the coffee table. "You've been chasing him for years." He turned.

"Nico!" She kneeled up over the back of the sofa. "It's not about David, or you."

He halted in the doorway, but didn't look at her.

"Let me explain."

"No need." He walked through the opening and down the stairs. "I understand completely." His words faded with his footsteps.

A few seconds later, she heard his bike rev, then fade into the distance.

"Arrrgh... He drives me crazy!" Natalie sat back and punched the sofa cushion hard, wishing it were Nico's head.

Chapter Six

"How's the shrimp?"

"Great! How's the crab?"

"Pretty—"

Natalie looked at David; David looked back, then they laughed. She put her napkin down on the table. "Sorry, but we sound like we've just met, or something."

"I know." He glanced around the restaurant.

She frowned. He'd done that at least five times since they'd sat down.

"What's wrong?"

"Nothing. It's just—" He turned his head toward the front door. "—I keep expecting Nico to sneak up on me like he used to do in school whenever I got anywhere near you."

"Oh, yeah, I *do* remember those days." She wiggled her eyebrows up and down. Reaching for her water, she looked up through her lashes toward the door. She didn't want to admit to

David that she'd been expecting the same thing. It was too weird not having their "buddy" interrupting their conversation.

"He actually let me speak to you in whole sentences last night."

Natalie choked on her water. Coughing and laughing, she placed the glass on the table. "Nona wouldn't have let him get away with the stuff he used to do in high school."

"High school, hell, he's acted like that since the day he met you."

Natalie felt a blush spread up her neck. She shook her head. She didn't want to think about Nico while she had an opportunity for once to have quiet time with David.

"He loves you."

Natalie's smile froze, then faltered. She shook her head. "No, you're wrong there. He's never indicated *that* to me." She speared a shrimp with her fork. "Lust, maybe…possessiveness, probably."

"'Possessive' is a good word. He did always act like he owned you, telling me and any other boy who came within three feet of you to stay away."

"He wasn't that bad."

David didn't smile as he looked at her. "Yes, he was. He broke Tim Robichaux's nose when he threatened to ask you to the prom."

"What?" She couldn't believe what she was hearing. Nico had physically harmed someone out of jealousy, but hadn't had the courage to ask her out himself. She'd sat at home, crying all weekend, because no one had asked her to the prom.

A worried expression passed over David's features. "Look, don't say anything to him, okay?"

Her eyebrow shot up. "Are you scared of him?"

Now David looked uncomfortable. "Yes, I am."

"David!" Her mouth fell open. At one time, she'd been scared, too, but after she'd stood up to him on Valentine's Day, she'd given as good as she'd received from him. He had deserved every bit of the animosity she'd given, too. Well, maybe not all of it. "He's all hot air. He's always acted tough to hide the pain of his mother's people not acknowledging him."

A twinge of guilt surfaced in the back of her mind. She could have been nicer to him over the years, then maybe he wouldn't have felt compelled to be so aggressive toward her and, apparently, other guys. She took another bite of food. He *still* deserved her wrath for making her sit alone on prom night in the dark, waiting for someone to give her her first kiss.

"He's an intimidating guy."

"Let's talk about something else." She smiled, not wanting to ruin the time she spent with David. Nico had a way of making her lose her control with just a thought.

"You love him?"

"What?"

"You heard me." He took a bite of his crab, then smiled.

Nico had been in her head too much today. He'd walked out on her after they'd had such good sex, without letting her explain how confused she felt about him and David. The more she thought of it, the more she realized she did love him. She just didn't know if she was ready to admit that to him, or anyone else. "I-I don't know."

"Okay, let's talk about us having sex."

"Us?" She didn't know what to say. She'd fantasized about him for years, but never thought she'd hear him say that. "Like how?"

"How do most adults have sex?" He leaned closer and motioned with his forefinger for her to lean toward him. "I don't know about you, but I think we should go somewhere private." He winked.

Natalie sat back. She'd been waiting for this forever, but... "I don't think that's a good idea. I have to tell you that Nico and I..." She sighed. "...we..."

David raised his hand to stop her. "Don't say any more. You just answered my question whether you loved him or not." He resumed his meal. "Lucky girl."

"David, just because I slept with him doesn't mean—" *What did he say?* "What do you mean 'lucky girl'?"

A pink tinge shadowed his cheekbones. He glanced everywhere except at her.

Hell. He'd done it now. David looked her in the eye. "I'm in love with...Nico." The last part of the sentence crumbled as the waiter walked past.

The look on Natalie's face said it all. His lips pressed together and he let out a sigh. He shouldn't have told her. She wouldn't understand.

"How long?"

David blinked. She hadn't jumped up in horror and run. "I can't even remember when I realized. I've always admired him for his toughness and 'take charge' attitude. I guess it happened sometime in high school."

"Oh, my God." The words were soft; the tone incredulous. She stared at him like she didn't know him, but she stayed seated. It had to be the shock. Any second she'd bolt, like his ex-wife had when he'd told her about his bisexuality.

"But, you were married."

David shrugged. "Yeah, well, I think you can see why the relationship didn't work."

"She knew?"

"Not about Nico in particular, but I told her I needed men to be...complete."

"You didn't know this before you married her?"

David signaled the waiter for the check. "I think that's called *denial.*"

"Didn't you want kids?"

He shook his head. "I can't father a child. I'm sterile." His fingers played with his silverware. "Nancy knew that fact before we got married. We had discussed adoption, so infertility hadn't been a problem." He sighed.

The lost look on his face forced Natalie to reach across the small distance that separated them and hold his hand. She knew how it felt to lose someone.

"I didn't have the courage to tell her my other 'secret.' I'd never been attracted to men, except for Nico. Then, a couple of years ago, it just...happened. I met someone who reminded me of him. After that, I couldn't keep lying to her. She deserved to know."

He knew Natalie's next question by the look on her face. "He knows."

Her mouth opened, then closed. She sat silently while he paid the bill. He could tell by the way her eyes darted back and forth across the contents on their table that her mind overflowed with questions. As soon as the waiter left, she leaned forward. He stopped her.

"In the car."

She nodded.

He put his hand on the small of her back, hoping Nico was *somewhere* watching. It was a game they'd played, quietly, for years without Natalie knowing. He wanted Nico; Nico wanted Natalie; Natalie wanted… David narrowed his gaze on the pretty brunette. "I believe you and I are in competition."

"I don't know what you mean."

"You're not stupid. We both want Nico, but he'll never admit he wants me unless *you* say it's okay."

"What?" She stopped in the center of the parking lot. Several customers looked their way at her exclamation.

David took her arm and urged her forward. No sense in causing a scene. They could have this conversation in the car. Or, better yet, at his apartment, where Nico could only wonder at what decadent overtures David would offer Natalie. He'd lost their Valentine's bet, but he could still make his friend sweat a little. Besides, he had to get Natalie to agree to this threesome, not only to pay Luke back, but to finally show the two people in the world that he cared the most for what they meant to him.

He shivered. He didn't know for sure who Luke was, but he had a good idea, and it scared the hell out of him. The man oozed sex appeal and danger. The kind of danger that would find you burning for all eternity.

"Let's get in the car before I explain." He opened the door; she slid in, but not before he kissed her lightly on the lips. Straightening, he glanced around the darkened parking lot, but there was no sign of the man they both wanted. But he was there, somewhere.

* * *

Nico didn't move. He watched David search the pier area. *I'm here. Right fucking here.* David cranked the car, then reversed. Gravel crunched beneath the tires before the car pulled away. He knew where they were going. He also knew David expected him to follow.

He shoved his hands into his pockets. He would, of course, but not yet. He'd make David sweat a little. He leaned back against the side of the boathouse with his knee bent and foot resting on the faded wood of the wall. The echo of seagulls, looking for scraps left by late-night customers, screeched in the darkness. Distant bells clanged far out on the Gulf of Mexico as the channel markers sounded their lonely desolate positions.

The north wind picked up; Nico hunched his shoulders. Making love with Natalie had not turned out the way he had anticipated. She hadn't declared her love and stayed in his bed. He pulled a toothpick out of his pocket and chewed the tip.

The thin strip of wood snapped in two with the pressure of his clenched jaw. *Shit.* Nico threw the jagged sliver into the nearby trash can.

"Sweet game you three got going."

Nico turned to the voice. A man stood fifty yards behind him, hidden in the shadows. The voice sounded gravelly, like the owner smoked too much. Nico glanced around, but there was no one else near. The man was speaking to him. "Not sure what you mean, mister."

The stranger laughed. "Sure you are." His hand gestured in the direction David had driven. "The good-looking jock and that sweet piece of ass with him."

Nico shifted his neck to ease the sudden tension that shot from his back into his shoulder. He fought the need to put his fist down the guy's throat at calling Natalie a sweet piece of ass. "I think you need to mind your own business."

"Sure, son, didn't mean to pry." The man threw his cigarette over the side of the rail. Hot ash against cool saltwater hissed with impact and the stale smell of smoke rose into the clean air.

Nico pursed his lips, refusing to waste energy chastising someone who didn't give a rip for protecting nature. Walking to his bike, he realized what the guy had insinuated. He kicked one leg over the seat and settled his crotch into the cradle. *David, Natalie, and...him.* Whether the idea appealed to his mind or not, his cock and balls tightened at the idea of the three of them together—fucking.

His jaw tightened. He'd thought about the idea a lot, years ago, but had pushed the fantasy deep within the recesses of his mind. With an utterance of a few words, the stranger had released Nico's private demon. "No way, no how would Natalie go for that." He turned the ignition and the bike revved to life.

* * *

"What are you talking about?" Natalie sat with her back against the car door, looking across at David in the dim light from the dash. "You know he knows that you were the one I always wanted in school."

"Right. I never saw you react to me the way you reacted to him." David shrugged. "And you just admitted you two had sex today."

"I wanted both of you, but in different ways."

"Like now?"

She breathed deep and released the tension slowly. This date had not turned out like she expected. She'd expected to have a nice, quiet supper, reminiscing over old times, then going back home for a pot of Nona's coffee. Now... "When did you tell him you loved him?"

"When we were on a camping trip in school. We were eighteen." He laid his head against the back of the seat and stared at the night sky through the moon roof.

Natalie heard the regret in his voice. She reached out and touched his arm with her hand. "What happened?"

She didn't think he'd answer her. The interior of the car grew so quiet she could hear the ticking of her wristwatch. Just when she felt compelled to tell him not to worry about it, he shifted in his seat and looked at her.

"We filled my uncle's old skiff full of booze and snacks and went over to Deer Island. You know, the inlet on the south side, where no one can see you."

Natalie nodded but didn't say anything, scared he would stop talking. In her heart, she knew she didn't really want to hear what he was telling her, but she needed to understand. The two men had been friends since they were five years old; then one summer that friendship had disappeared, as if it had never happened. She'd never known what had caused the two to separate.

"We drank and talked about girls, you in particular." He reached over and feathered his fingers through her hair, tucking a strand behind her ear. "We ended up drunk, lying out on the sand, staring up at a full moon." He laughed.

"How romantic can you get, huh?" His hand dropped and he turned to face the front. He wrapped his fingers around the steering wheel. His knuckles showed white in the darkness. "I looked at him and I just couldn't stop from kissing him."

Natalie heard her indrawn breath. She closed her eyes. David's pain at the renewed memories made her heart ache. "What did Nico do?"

"He was shocked at first and didn't do anything. When I pulled him closer and told him to pretend I was you, he responded."

David turned his face to her. In the dark, she saw his drawn features. His eyes glittered with regret. "I knew then the only way to have him would be through you. I gave him everything I could, but in the end it wasn't enough."

Natalie cried out when David grabbed her upper arms and pulled her close. His lips were hot and hungry against hers. She turned her head left...then right. "D–David!"

"I want to know what you have that I don't. Your lips aren't any softer than mine." He sighed. "God, I sucked his cock that night. When he came, he called out *your* name."

Silence tore through the car. Natalie didn't struggle against the hands that bit into her flesh. David hurt, and she wanted to help him.

"The next morning when I woke, he'd swum back to shore. We've not been friends since."

His grip eased and she sat quietly in his arms while he held her, rocking back and forth in the dark, taking what little comfort she could offer. She lifted a hand and petted his head. "I'm sorry."

"I don't want to be alone tonight, Natalie." He raised his head. "Stay with me?"

She shook her head. A part of her still wanted David, but the other part knew she belonged to Nico. "I can't."

"You can have the bed. I'll take the couch."

He looked so earnest in his offer. His mouth turned up in that devious smile of his and his eyes begged like a lost puppy. "Please?"

"Don't be silly; we can share the bed."

The eyes twinkled in delight. "But strictly platonic, huh?"

"Yes." She watched his smile fade into a sadness she could relate to, as he got out and walked to her side of the car. He opened her door and held out his hand. She didn't hesitate placing her hand into his. This man she could trust.

"I lived with a man for three years while I was in New York." She slipped her arm through David's. "I thought I loved him."

"You didn't?"

"No." They walked up the stairs to his apartment with slow, relaxed steps. At the door, she turned to him. "Turns out he just reminded me of someone I thought I couldn't have."

"Nico?"

David's key scraped into the keyhole and clicked. He swung the door wide for her to walk through.

Natalie stood on her tiptoes and kissed his cheek. "He reminded me of you."

She stepped past him and entered the darkened apartment. The stale aroma of cigarettes permeated the air. She reached back and took David's hand. "Let's go to bed."

He squeezed her fingers before he closed the door. Tonight they accepted their relationship—friends, not lovers, like she'd dreamed in the past. But tomorrow brought another day with a hope for something new and exciting. He'd offered her a way to have both the men she cared for, if she only had the nerve to reach out and take what could be hers.

Neither saw the lone figure sitting quietly in the shadows of the building, watching their every move.

Chapter Seven

The music had an eerie quality, but she didn't mind. Today was her wedding day. She clutched the bouquet in her hand tight and stepped forward. She looked down the aisle and found the two men she'd always loved. They must have made up, because they stood side by side in their tuxedoes. Natalie smiled up at the man who led her down the aisle.

The smile turned into a frown. She tried to pull her arm away, but the man held her tight.

"You're not running away again, Natalie. This time, you will accept the candy that is offered you." He nodded his head toward the altar. "One dark, one light."

"Noooo..."

Natalie sat up with a jerk, clutching the bed covers to her chest and gasping. Sweat clung to her skin and she could feel the heat from the morning sun, streaming through the bedroom window. She took a deep breath to steady her pulse. *Where the hell had that come from?* She'd never been known to have nightmares. Now in the space of a couple days, she'd had two.

"Nona's damn bay leaves."

"What's that?"

She looked up to see David coming through the bedroom door with a tray. He kicked the door shut with his foot, then headed for her. She shook her head in response to his question and waved her hand. "What's all this?"

"*This* is to thank you for last night."

Last night? Natalie glanced around, hoping she hadn't forgotten something very important. She didn't remember drinking anything stronger than Irish coffee after supper, but—

"For lending me a shoulder to cry on, so to speak."

"Oh. Yeah. Right."

"Had you worried there for a second?"

She shook her head, but when she saw the laughter in his eyes, she smiled. "Well, for a second."

"Don't worry. When we sleep together, you won't forget it."

"*When?*"

David placed the tray across her lap, then picked up the red rose. The image of another rose drifted across her memory. He feathered it under her nose. The fragrance, strong and sweet, tickled her nostrils. "I think we should give Nico what he wants."

Natalie reached for the orange juice on the tray. "And that is…what?"

"Both of us."

She choked. Her juice spluttered over her plate. "We had this discussion last night. It sounded...intriguing, but I don't know."

David grabbed the napkin and dabbed her face and mouth. Natalie tried to take the paper from him, but he continued his task and his proposition.

"Think about it, Nat. He wants you. I want you—"

"Wait a minute. Since when do you want me?"

"I've always wanted you, but I just wanted him more. I didn't say I don't like women." He snorted. "I love women. I just prefer men."

Natalie waved her hand in the air. *Makes perfect sense to me.* She picked up her fork and stabbed her sausage. "I'm confused. Last night you were crying in your cup over Nico. Now, you want me to believe you want to have sex with me."

"I do, but with the three of us together." He leaned over her and took a bite of the sausage before she could get the meat into her mouth. "He'd love watching me fuck you."

"Aha! That's why you want to have sex with me." The sight of his white teeth clamping into the sausage flashed an image she'd tried to repress. The image of him and Nico, having oral sex while she watched. Her clit throbbed, and she squeezed her thighs together.

"Yeah, but I think you're attractive, too." He lifted the covers and scooted into bed beside her. "You've always wanted me, so how 'bout it?"

Natalie opened her mouth to respond, but there was a loud *bang bang bang* on the front door. She looked at David. He shrugged and got up, letting a bout of cool air swish in over her legs. She shivered and pulled the blankets closer around her before she resumed her breakfast.

Two bites later, the bedroom door crashed open and she spilled her juice a second time. "Dammit, David—"

She looked up into dark eyes beneath fierce black eyebrows drawn together into a scowl. David inched into the room behind Nico, trying to explain.

"Look, it's not what you think."

Nico glanced at David, and his eyes narrowed further. "Yeah? What *is* it then?"

David looked at her; she looked at him. "Okay, you caught us."

"David!" Natalie couldn't believe what she was hearing. He had decided to put his "plan" into motion without her agreement.

"We slept together last night." He turned and pointed a finger at Natalie. "And don't you try to deny that you were in *my* bed all night."

She opened her mouth, then stopped. She couldn't deny being in David's bed all night, because she had been. She just hadn't been having sex in said bed. She opened her mouth again.

"I think actions speak louder than words. Don't bother trying to explain."

Nico's words were spoken in a soft voice, but she heard the venom beneath. She closed her mouth again. There would be no use in trying to defend herself when he was in this kind of mood. He hadn't listened yesterday; why would he today?

She shrugged. "If you've made up your mind, there's nothing I can do to change it, is there?"

"No." He turned and left the room with David following close behind.

Natalie flinched when he slammed the door. The eggs and sausage lay on her plate, but she couldn't have eaten if she'd tried. A movement caught her eye. She glanced up to see David leaning against the door frame, rubbing his chin. A red mark spread beneath his fingers.

"He hit you?"

"Yeah."

"You deserved it."

David grinned. "I got his attention though."

* * *

Sisters of Mercy blared through the garage, loud enough that David had to cover his ears when he walked past the speakers. He'd never understood Nico's taste for Goth rock. Granted, he always wore black and his hair always looked as if it could use a trim, or two, or three, but he didn't fit your stereotypical Goth.

Climbing over a row of boxes containing motorcycle engine parts, he spotted Nico's long frame stretched out on the cement floor with one leg bent at the knee and leaning to the side. The view of his crotch caught David's attention.

Nice package. His cock hardened at a sight he hadn't seen in a while. David clenched his jaw. This wasn't the time to be drooling over the man's gorgeous bod. Natalie had sent him on a mission. *Explain, or else.*

It was the "or else" part that had him scared. For such a tiny thing, she sure could dish out the orders. The image of her standing over him and Nico with a whip flashed through his mind. He bit back a groan and shifted his hips to relieve the sudden pressure against his fly.

"You gonna stare at me all day, or is there a reason you're here?"

Nico had caught him. "Never could sneak up on you. With that crap blowing a hole through the stratosphere, I'm surprised you can hear any—"

The song ended.

"—thing." David's voice ricocheted off the metal walls of the building. Before another one could start, he walked to the stereo system set up against the far wall and turned the volume to a dull roar. "Jesus, man, where do you find this stuff?"

Nico rolled his large frame, bent his knees, and stood, wiping his greasy fingers on a stained rag. He shook his head, examining his hands. "Here and there."

A man of many words. That was the problem. Nico never told anyone anything, and trying to probe the layers of his mind was like pulling teeth—damned big, long molars that wouldn't let go. David sighed. "Nico—"

"Don't bother, Dave. You won the bet. She's always wanted you." He threw the rag into a box filled with other dirty rags in the corner. "Now, she's got you. I hope you don't decide you can't stand pussy anymore and go for a big, fat dick." Nico pointed a finger at him. "Because if you hurt her, I swear I'll kick your ass."

"Wait a minute." David's voice rose. He looked around to make sure no one was within hearing distance. He took a step closer to Nico. His lips compressed against what he really wanted to say. "I came here because Natalie made me."

"Never figured you'd end up pussy-whupped, bro."

"Fuck you!"

Nico had him by the collar so fast David hadn't been able to blink. He felt his feet leave the floor, his back shoved against the cold metal of the wall. Tools scattered and clanged to the floor. Nico leaned close, so close that his breath came in hot spurts across his cheek. David swallowed the fear that rose in his throat. The sheer power of the other man's body rippled beneath a thin layer of cotton. Nico could make mincemeat of him if he wanted, without working up a sweat.

"You already did that, *friend*. Or have you forgotten?"

The words were soft, but David heard the lethal note in the seductive voice. A shiver of excitement mixed with the fear; his cock twitched. He placed his hand around Nico's wrist and squeezed, hoping the contact would ease Nico's grip.

It didn't. His collar tightened to the point of asphyxiation; he coughed. "I remember." His voice sounded husky and strained. "I also remember how you enjoyed what I did to you...*ack*—" David's hands clutched and pulled at the pressure around his throat.

Nico growled, but David ignored the unspoken threat. With one hand, he reached down and did the only thing he could think of that would force Nico to release him. He smoothed his palm up Nico's crotch, letting his fingers caress the bulge. The cock had looked massive before he touched the outline, but now, the pulsing flesh hardened and quivered, growing longer and thicker beneath the rough denim fabric.

Nico stiffened.

David's fingers tightened, then withdrew. He angled back across one of the work tables with Nico's shove. He swallowed, wincing against the searing pain in his throat as saliva coated his esophagus. He sucked the much-needed oxygen in through his mouth and gagged. The cough sounded like a bark, raspy and deep.

He watched Nico pace back and forth like a caged animal. He raked his hands through long strands of black hair. The resemblance to Luke struck; David's gaze narrowed. The build, the loose-limbed gait, the coloring... They had to be related.

"You ever meet your father?" The question escaped before he had a chance to think over the reaction he'd receive. Dread pitted in the base of his gut.

Nico's agitation came to a halt. He turned to face David with a frown on his face that resembled a murderous black mask. "What...in...hell...does my no-good, bastard *father* have to do with any of this?"

"N-Nothin'." David shook his head, held out a hand in denial, and stumbled forward, still needing more oxygen to clear the dizziness that had overwhelmed him a few minutes before. Any longer, and he'd have passed out from the pressure of Nico's fingers around his windpipe. "I'm not thinking...clear."

"Get out of here." Nico pointed to the door. "Don't come back."

"Natalie—"

"*What* does Natalie want?"

David stood straighter, trying to get the words out, but the pain in his throat had him doubled over in a fit of coughing. Through the tears that pooled in his eyes, he heard a soft, feminine voice.

"*She* wants the three of us to become lovers."

Natalie! David spotted her through the bout of coughing and moisture. *A sight for sore eyes.* If anyone could tame the beast before him, it'd be her.

Chapter Eight

Everything happened in slow motion. One minute she'd been standing by the car, waiting for David. Then she glanced across the street and saw him; he was dressed in black like he'd been years before. He held up two pieces of candy wrapped in a shiny red cover. His words and actions from long ago echoed through her mind.

"I offer you both." He worked the candies between his fingers to hold up one. *"One is light and sweet."* He worked his fingers again. *"The other dark and bitter."* The candies circled and twirled between his fingers, then rested in his palm. He held them out to her.

She blinked, then he disappeared. "Dammit, not again." She stepped closer to the street; she looked left, then right. Nothing. Not a soul in sight. A loud *crash* from Nico's garage caught her attention. With one last look across the street where she could have sworn the guy from her dream had stood, she turned toward the commotion that continued to grow louder.

The transition from the bright sunlight to the dimness of the garage blinded her. She could hear Nico threaten David, but couldn't see anything. Then the two men came into focus. Nico had David pinned against the wall and a work table.

She took a step forward, but stopped when David touched Nico's crotch. Her breath caught and her abdomen muscles tightened in anticipation of how Nico would react.

His big body quivered; moisture pooled in her panties. He took a deep breath; she held hers. He took several steps back away from temptation; she moved forward.

When he ordered David to leave, she wanted to scream. She had them both together, alone. *Now,* she needed to tell them what she wanted. What she needed. Before Nico withdrew from the situation.

"*What* does Natalie want?"

"*She* wants the three of us to become lovers." The words came out. She frowned. The voice sounded like hers, but she looked behind her to see if someone else had spoken. She saw him again, closer this time. He leaned against the hood of David's car with a smile on his face. He winked.

"Say that again."

She turned back to Nico. He watched her like she'd gone crazy. Maybe she had. A quick glance over her shoulder showed the man was gone. The palms of her hands grew moist, and she wiped them against the wool fabric of her skirt.

"I-I want to have sex with both of you." She looked from Nico to David and back. "Together."

Neither man moved. Nico's eyes were narrowed on her while David's were narrowed on Nico. No one said a word.

Sisters of Mercy wailed in the background. Natalie fought the urge to cover her ears and scream, *Turn that shit off!*

She shook with disbelief at what she'd asked of both men, but knew the moment of truth had to be now, or never. She'd waited too many years. After the fiasco with Rudy, she refused to put her desires and needs in the background any longer.

Nico stepped toward her. She released the breath she hadn't been aware of holding. When he drew level with her, her body quivered with his anticipated touch. Her nipples hardened with every tortured breath she took. The puckered skin scrubbed against the thin material of her bra. She knew he could see the points through the rough fabric of her sweater. The idea caused a flood of moisture between her legs.

He stepped around and behind her. Close enough for the heat of his body to warm her back and buttocks, but he didn't touch her. He leaned forward, then stopped when his mouth lay next to her ear. She shivered and closed her eyes.

"Sure you want that, *Braces?*"

The whispered sound of his old nickname for her caused her to shake in violent reaction. *Hell,* yes, *she was sure.* She nodded, not trusting her voice not to stutter, like she'd always done. She didn't want to give any hint of indecision on her part. The time for uncertainty had died when he walked out of David's apartment that morning, leaving her with the feeling her entire world had crumbled at her feet. She loved him.

She looked into a security mirror in the corner above her head and spotted David. She loved them both.

"Don't move." Nico stepped away.

She bit back a groan of protest, but did as he had instructed. Her back to him, she heard him pull the garage doors into place with a snap of the lock, loud and final. She'd made her decision. Whatever happened this afternoon would seal their fate. She glanced again at David's reflection.

He, like her, stood still as a statue. By some unspoken agreement, they took their lead from Nico. That's what they'd always done. He oozed dominance and authority. Rare were the occasions she'd stood up to him. When she had, he'd looked surprised, but pleased at her bravado. Today, all her courage had been spent in voicing her need. Her energy had waned, and she could only stand where he'd left her and wait.

Suddenly, her body angled backward. She screamed until Nico's shoulder and arm caught her upper body while his other arm hooked beneath her knees. He hefted her weight up and closer to his chest. Natalie clutched his shoulders with her hands.

He felt strong. Muscles rippled beneath the palms of her hands. The smell of his aftershave tickled her nose. She breathed in deeply and closed her eyes against the warm male scent of his skin.

"Let's give the lady what she wants."

Her eyes opened and she looked over Nico's shoulder to see David following close behind. Their eyes met, but they didn't speak. She could see anticipation and desire on David's face. The same desire she felt spiraling out of control through her body.

Nico's knee pushed against her bottom at the same time his other shoulder butted the door, leading into his apartment. The shades were drawn and the lights were off. The small space lay in darkness, but he didn't stop. His stride steady and determined, he headed for the bedroom.

Natalie's mouth watered. She swallowed and wondered at what they would actually do to and with each other. She buried her face against his shoulder.

"Don't go getting shy, *Braces,* after you've promised me the moon, the stars...hell, the whole fucking universe."

He let her go. With a *whoosh,* she fell into the softness of the mattress. Pillows scattered across the bed and floor as he followed her down. Before she could respond, his mouth covered hers, and she drowned in the heat that consumed her. She thought she heard David moan from the corner by the door.

At the sound of David's moan, Nico's cock throbbed harder. He knew what to do. The night he'd let David suck him off, he'd pretended his friend had been Natalie. But not today. He would take Natalie every way he'd ever imagined; then he'd take David like he'd always wanted, but had denied.

He was tired of fighting the truth. He wanted...no...*needed*...both of these people. He pushed his tongue deeper into Natalie's mouth. The sweet mewling escaping her shimmied up his spine. His hands tore at the hem of her skirt. If he didn't get inside her quick, he'd come. He heard David move up behind him.

Nico tore his mouth away from the woman he held pinned to the mattress. His gaze met David's. The desire he saw mirrored his own. David moved forward.

"Let me undress her."

Nico nodded, then moved back where he could remove his own clothes. Within seconds his jeans and T-shirt lay in a jumbled mass on the floor. He watched David and Natalie together on his bed. While David pulled her sweater loose and over her head, her nimble fingers unsnapped and unzipped his jeans. Long fingers from each caressed and teased in the process while hungry lips searched for relief.

David reached for the front clasp of her bra but hesitated to pinch a hardened nipple. Natalie arched into his hand with a hiss from between clenched teeth. In retaliation, she slipped her hand beneath the denim of David's pants and cupped his balls. David groaned.

Nico smiled. The sense of urgency faded. With one foot he hooked an old ladder-back chair from beside the door, twirling it around where he could straddle the back of the chair and sit down to watch the festivities playing out in front of him. No way in hell would he miss these two fucking each other in *his* bed—every fantasy he'd ever had, acted out live and in color.

When they were naked and panting, they turned to him, waiting for instructions. A sense of power vibrated through him, and his cock twitched. Without taking his eyes off his companions, he wrapped his hand around his arousal. With one long stroke, he clenched his teeth and looked David in the eye. "Eat her pussy while..." He shifted his gaze to Natalie. "...you suck his dick."

Not once did they blink in refusal. David shifted his hips and body around where he could delve into Natalie's wet cunt. His cock dangled, long and thick, in front of her face before she licked the shaft from base to tip, then sucked the head deep into her mouth and throat. All three moaned together.

David grasped her thighs with both hands and forced them farther apart. The coolness of the room fanned the moisture coating her skin. Natalie shivered at the sight she must be offering Nico. From his vantage point, he could see everything. The thought that she and David could drive him over the edge with what they did to each other urged her to take David's cock deeper into her throat.

She heard him moan at the same time his tongue plunged deep into her pussy. The sensation of his hot tongue licking her clit had her rotating her hips harder against his mouth. She released his cock to suck in a much-needed gulp of air. "Oh, yeah...oh, yeah...just like that, please."

David could only oblige her demand. He would never have imagined Natalie could taste so sweet. The slightly acidic flavor of her pussy just added to her own unique spirit. He felt her tremble with the beginnings of her orgasm, so he eased the pressure of his tongue. He wanted to see how Nico would react to the sight of Natalie's juice on *his* lips and face. He raised his head.

Nico's gaze zeroed in like David knew it would. The black eyes narrowed and his nostrils flared, like he tried to smell what David could smell. David closed his eyes and breathed in deeply. "Ah, she's heaven." He opened his eyes to find Nico a half-inch from his face. He tried to move his head back, but Nico fastened a hand around his neck to pull him close.

David watched in fascination as Nico breathed in the musky scent; then his tongue traced the outside of David's mouth to obtain the liquid essence he sought. David's eyes closed at the touch of Nico's mouth against his. His body shuddered at the combined ecstasy of Natalie's hot mouth wrapped around his cock, sucking him while her hands kneaded his sac.

His body jerked once, then Nico pulled him off Natalie. His balls ached for release. He looked down at Natalie's surprised and dazed expression. They turned to Nico.

"Not yet."

* * *

Nona mumbled and turned another card face-up. She looked at the Celtic spread in front of her and frowned. *Queen of Pentacles, Ten of Swords, Knight of Cups.* She tapped her chin with her forefinger. Beside the cards, her tea steamed into the chill of the night air. The cards represented Natalie, Nico, and David, but didn't tell her what she needed to know. Something didn't feel right about their liaison. There was an outside influence somewhere. She shook her head and flipped another card. She gasped.

"Ah, my favorite." A low, raspy voice emitted from the corner of the room that lay in darkness. "The Devil."

Nona's heart beat faster. She reached for the cordless phone, but her hand shook so hard, she knocked her tea over onto the tablecloth. Hot liquid scalded the skin of her right hand. "Ahh…"

"Who were you planning on calling?" His head angled. "Ghostbusters?"

The figure moved forward into the light, and she stared in horror. He looked the same as he had years ago, when he'd visited her at the age of eighteen—black hair, long and curling past the nape of his neck, long legs, and lean body. His eyes fringed by those black eyelashes, he could tempt a nun into his bed, much less a naïve, lonely girl.

"You're as beautiful as ever, Sophia."

Nona made a tsking noise with her tongue. "And you're as smooth-talking as ever, Luke."

He smiled; she didn't. She nodded toward the cards.

"What are you doing with my granddaughter?"

His smile widened to show white, even teeth. "Nothing she doesn't want *done* to her."

Chapter Nine

Natalie straddled David's hips. They'd been working each other for at least an hour, and now it was time for a position change. She hadn't asked Nico for permission, but didn't care. She needed to feel a thick, hot cock deep inside her. As turned on as she was, she didn't care which one she had, either. She leaned down and kissed David's abdomen, liking the play of muscles beneath his skin. She felt his dick tighten beneath her and moved to take him into her cunt.

Strong fingers worked into her hair and pulled her head back, hard. Nico's mouth rested against her cheek. "What do you think you're doing?"

Her gaze found his, narrowed. A dull red tinge highlighted his cheekbones and his nostrils were flared in either excitement or anger; she couldn't be sure which. She'd made a decision without him, and he didn't sound too happy. Anger flared within her.

"You weren't participating, so I decided to heat things up a little."

The grip on her hair tightened. "Ouch!" She refused to let him know that little move had made her wetter than anything so far tonight. Her nostrils widened. She wanted him to get rough.

"You're going to climb off him and do what I tell you to do."

"Oh, yeah?" Maybe if she defied him. She shivered in anticipation of the reaction she'd receive. She'd never tell him she liked him to dominate the situation. The more he ordered, the more she defied, and that usually led to some very combustible reactions, with him getting more aggressive.

"Yeah." His tongue sneaked out to lick up the side of her face to the outer edge of her earlobe. He worked it like a snake and circled her ear, then plunged deep within.

Natalie whimpered and rotated her hips against David. David moaned.

"Damnation, let her finish. You've dragged this torture session on for an hour." He shifted his hips beneath her. The rustle of the sheets blocked most of his tirade. "...bringing us up to the point of no return, then backing off. I'm about to explode."

"You complaining?"

"If he's not, I am." Natalie grabbed Nico's wrist to force him to ease up on her hair. "Let's get this show on the road. I need one of you inside me, like yesterday."

Uh oh. That black eyebrow rose and his mouth quirked at the corner. She knew that look. Exhilaration and fear coursed through her at the same time. She tried to scramble away and off the bed, but Nico caught her hips and drove her down onto David's cock.

David arched up at the same time she arched back into Nico's body. His thighs encased hers and his weight drove her further onto the thick pole between her legs. A searing pain spread from her vagina into her thighs. She bit her tongue to keep from screaming. She refused to give him that satisfaction. She knew this would be her punishment for defying him. *What a way to go.*

"You're enjoying this, aren't you?" His question held a mixture of excitement and frustration.

"Aren't you?" Her teeth clenched against the spasms of her muscles as her body tried to adjust to David's size. She'd never expected him to be this big. The crown of his cock had to measure at least three inches across. Where his cock had thickness, Nico's had both width and length. Moisture flooded her vagina with the thought and she slipped further down David's length.

"You wanted to fuck, so go ahead and fuck him hard, baby." Nico had her arms captured at the wrists to prevent her from scratching him. He pushed his weight into her again, and she gasped as her body stretched to accept David, little by little.

"I should...hate...you." Sweat covered her body in a light sheen. Her breathing grew ragged, but she couldn't fight what she craved. Her hips worked her cunt further onto the man beneath her.

"Probably." He kissed her neck. "But you know you love me, too." He released her wrists long enough to push her forward where she lay, chest to chest with David.

"Hold her tight."

Natalie tried to struggle up, but David's hands held her biceps in a grip that denied freedom. She grinned at him. He looked like the cat that had lapped up all the cream. "You bastard, we're supposed to be on the same side."

David laughed, his face flushed from their exertions. "Baby, if he's gonna do what I think, I'm with him. This is what fantasies are made of."

"What are you doing?" She twisted to see Nico. At the sight of him spreading a thick, clear gel over his cock, she stilled. His gaze caught hers, and in that second, she knew what he intended.

She bucked her hips, but David caught her calves with his and held her arms tighter, locking her to him with his cock. The pressure of him inside her made her relax a nanosecond before she felt Nico come up behind her.

"Nothing you won't like." He pushed her forward.

David's mouth caught hers with his tongue plunging deep at the same time Nico's fingers, coated with lubricant, played around the entrance into her rectum. The combined pressure—David's cock and Nico's fingers—worked her to the very point of orgasm.

With the tip of his finger, he pressed inward.

She moaned her pleasure into David's mouth, and her body squeezed around Nico's finger. He pushed farther, then held still. Her muscles contracted and expanded again to accommodate the deeper invasion. The fullness made her clit throb. She rotated her hips to grind her pubis against David's, the need to orgasm strong.

"Not yet." Nico eased his finger out.

Natalie pulled her lips free from David's mouth. "Damn you, Nico, what are you waiting for?"

* * *

"What do you mean by that?" Nona didn't like the way Luke had phrased his answer. "What is being *done* to Natalie?"

"Now, Sophia, do I really have to spell it out to you? Use your imagination."

Nona's heart flip-flopped. There could only be one scenario that Luke knew about, playing out somewhere in this city with Natalie, and it involved two men.

"You bastard!"

"I believe that's what she called my son, too."

His son! "Nico Bui is your son." Nona fell back into her chair and closed her eyes. How had she been so blind? The resemblance between the two couldn't be denied.

"You said it yourself, Sophia. 'He's a good-looking devil, isn't he?'"

"Damn your demon hide." The words she'd spoken to Natalie nights before came back to haunt her. In her own way, she'd blessed any union between the two that might arise. She sat up and reached for the cards, hoping there could be a way to stop what Luke tried to accomplish.

"Too late...on both counts." His hand covered hers. Black fingernails tipped the strong fingers as he laced their hands together. "I'm only granting the young lovers what all three desire." He leaned closer. "I believe you promised me, when I granted your request, that I could have anything I wanted."

"That was fifty years ago!"

"And you thought I'd forget?"

"I thought that you got what you wanted with Nico's mother."

"Oh, she gave me a son for the favor I granted, but I didn't take into account how her people would ostracize a child born out of wedlock." He raised her fingers to his lips. "I've had to sit back and watch him being tormented and ridiculed his entire life."

"Why didn't you step in and help him?"

"I'm not allowed to do certain things, like tamper with the natural outcome of everyday life."

Nona snorted.

"There's a time and a place for everything. In his torment, he's learned to appreciate life...and love...more."

"So, now that he's grown, he'll get his revenge against all those who wronged him?"

"Payback's hell, but I'll get my reward, too." He kissed her hand. "Just be thankful you don't have to relinquish her to another. There are much worse demons than I."

* * *

Her words bit into his soul. *What are you waiting for?*

"I don't want to hurt you." He couldn't fight the need for her much longer. Both hands on her waist, he eased his cock up against her anus. He pushed gently. The head of his cock slipped through her relaxed sphincter. All three gasped, moaned, and groaned with the impact.

After several seconds, she pushed back against him. He could feel her muscles grip and tighten to pull him in deeper at the same time he felt the outline of David's cock thrust deep into her pussy. The heat from her body sucked him in, and he threw back his head in complete surrender to the sensations.

David recovered first. He spread his legs wider with his feet planted flat on the mattress. With his teeth clenched and eyes closed, he rocked his hips into Natalie's cunt.

Natalie's gasps for breath were short and fast. She rocked down into David's thrust.

When she tilted her hips back, Nico thrust deeper, allowing the tight grasp of her sweet ass to overpower his senses. He'd wanted to do this for so long, and now he could. He wouldn't deny himself anymore.

"That's it, babe." He rubbed his hands over her back and hips. "You like this, don't you?"

"Y-Yes." Her words were broken, her creamy skin was flushed, and her hair hung in damp tendrils down her gorgeous back.

With her admission, they set up a rhythm. When she pulled up, he pushed down to meet David's upward thrust. It didn't take long for them to work themselves into a sexual frenzy. The orgasm caught him in the balls first, with a burning sensation that spread into his abdomen and down his legs to his toes. Without thought to any rhythm, he rocked deep and hard into Natalie's body, while his cries of completion mingled with David's.

Natalie lasted longer, but when her orgasm came, he felt the ripples through her entire body. Wave after wave rocked them until she cried out in exhaustion.

She fell flush against David, and Nico fell on top of her, sandwiching her between the two of them. She belonged to them both, and they both belonged to him. He sighed.

The feel of David's cock rubbing his through the thin membrane between her rectum and vagina almost made him hard again. He kissed Natalie's temple where damp strands of her hair lay plastered to her skin. He nibbled his way to her ear and felt her shudder beneath him. "Tell me you love me."

"Umm." She smiled with her eyes closed, but didn't make any further response.

"What's that mean?" He finally had the two people he wanted in his bed, and all she had to say was *Umm?*

He looked at David and frowned. He had a smile on his face, but shrugged muscular shoulders covered with the sweat of his exertions.

"Don't look at me. I told you how I felt a long time ago."

"Do you still feel the same way?" Nico knew he'd treated David badly. He wouldn't blame him if he answered no. David's smile disappeared, and Nico's stomach twisted in fear.

"I've never felt differently, but I'd like to know how you feel."

Nico's jaw clenched. He didn't know if he could say what David and Natalie wanted to hear from him. He took a deep breath. "I've got the two people that mean the most to me in life right here in this bed."

Natalie raised her head. "And?"

Nico frowned, not sure what else she wanted. "And I don't intend to let them go."

David's eyebrows rose. "And?"

"What the fuck do you two want to hear?"

Natalie's eyes opened and she looked at David, then him. "The same words you want us to say."

David nodded; Nico sighed.

"Fine." He pulled his body up and out of the warmth of Natalie's. Sitting on the edge of the bed, he felt their gazes on him but couldn't turn around. He reached for his jeans, not bothering with socks or shoes. He needed to explain but didn't know how. He raked a hand through his hair.

"My mother never told me she loved me. Her family and community never accepted me, because of my being illegitimate." He stood and zipped the jeans, leaving the snap undone. He turned to his lovers. "You two are the only people I've ever...loved." He heard the husky note in his voice and coughed to clear his throat.

The softness glistening in Natalie's eyes caught him off guard. Her approval almost caused his undoing. He headed for the bathroom. He wanted her to be happy, but this sentimental stuff got to him. He hoped he didn't have to say "I love you" too often. Surely they could tell that he cared for them by his actions.

"Where are you going?" David jumped off the bed, but Nico kept his back to his friend.

"I need to shower."

"Want me to scrub your back?"

Nico turned and saw the expression on David's face. He knew David needed him to *show* him, now, that he cared and wanted him as his lover. Nico glanced at Natalie. Her eyes were closed and a smile rested on her beautiful face.

"If you're worried about me, don't." She yawned and rolled onto her stomach. "I'll be here when you two get through."

Nico lifted his eyebrow. *Women!* She'd be no help at all in navigating him through this scenario. He looked at David. "I guess we're on our own."

"Luckily for us, I know just what to do." David winked and took his hand.

Natalie watched Nico lay his head back while the hot water massaged his neck and shoulders. His hands fisted at his sides as David knelt in front of him, working Nico's cock with his lips and tongue, up and down the long shaft.

First the engorged head, a ripe plum color, then the shaft disappeared into David's mouth and throat. A low moan escaped Nico and shivered up her spine. She stood at least three feet away, but swore she could feel every lick of David's tongue and every nibble of his teeth. David wrapped his fingers around the base. With every downward swallow of his mouth, his hand worked lower, then up when his mouth and lips released their suction.

The longer the encounter, the faster their momentum became with Nico's hips thrusting forward to crash into David's eager mouth—over and over. Nico's sighs and moans became hers. She eased her back down the side of the bathroom wall at the same time she slid her fingers into her cunt, brushing her sensitive clit along the way.

She worked her fingers in and out, then around her clit in sync with David's motions. When Nico arched his back against the shower wall, she arched hers into the bathroom wall, letting her orgasm crest with his. Their cries of release mingled in the hot, misty air of the room. David swallowed Nico's cum as her juices slid down the cheeks of her buttocks.

She watched David give Nico one last stroke and lick the end of his penis. Still the men were unaware of her presence, so caught up in their pleasure of each other. Their ecstasy was her ecstasy, and when Nico pulled David up and shoved him against the wall, her breath caught in anticipation.

His strong hands grasped a bar of soap, working the suds into a lather before he drew the bar down David's back and between the firm buttocks exposed to her view. His hands followed the trail of the soap, and Natalie imagined them on her breasts and hips.

The bar slid to the shower floor, and long fingers disappeared into the crevice. She moaned, rocking herself against the wall with a small thudding motion. Her skin tingled with every caress of Nico's fingers over David's willing flesh. She knew what he intended, and a fresh flood of cream oozed from her pussy. She realized she had been chanting "Put it in" when her breath caught at the moment of entry.

David's head came back against Nico's shoulder, and Nico's hips surged forward. Nico stood still for a second, and both men grunted in pleasure. Then, with a growl, Nico wrapped one arm around David's waist and another around his thigh before he drove home, riding David with everything he had.

The shower might be on, but Natalie swore the rivulets of moisture cascading down their bodies had to be a mixture of water and sweat. Her skin burned all over, but she refused to interrupt the scene in front of her.

She'd let them get situated in the shower before she'd slipped into the bathroom, so she could watch her two lovers together. She knew they needed time alone to get accustomed to each other without her influence.

Nico groaned, and she came out of her daze to watch David reach back and work the base of Nico's cock hard while he massaged the tight sac between Nico's long legs.

Water sprayed and trickled down David's jaws and neck. The memory of his tongue swirling against her clit made her bite her tongue in an effort not to give her voyeur's perch away. She discovered she liked to watch, especially these two. They meant everything to her, always had.

The two male bodies moved in unison—Nico's hips, driving against David's ass. The sight so beautiful that when his orgasm came, and Nico latched onto David's hair and pulled him closer, Natalie moaned with the joy of watching Nico's mouth open wide in release.

David cried out his release at the same time, then leaned against the wall before he fell. Easing from him, Nico kissed the throbbing flesh around his jugular before turning him in his arms. Their gazes met, Nico's still intense and fearsome from their encounter. The dark eyes closed and Nico laid his forehead against his.

David's heart flip-flopped in his chest at the gesture. He worked his hands over Nico's abdomen and chest. He paused a second over a darkened nipple, leaned forward to suckle and nip, liking the surprised gasp he heard escape his reluctant lover. He smiled. Nico wouldn't be reluctant too much longer after he taught him a few things.

He'd reached his full height, which might be two inches shorter than Nico, but tall enough to reach his lips. David angled his mouth over Nico's. The expected stiffening came, but lasted only a second before Nico gave in and let his tongue mate with David's.

Heat lanced through his abdomen to settle in his groin. His cock thickened and throbbed. He needed to feel Nico's heat around him, but knew it would be too soon for his friend to accept anal penetration. But, soon...

The shower doors slid open. Steam escaped into the cooler recesses of the room as Natalie stepped into the small confines. David looked at her, and she smiled before she took each of their cocks in her hands. Sliding to her knees, she took the bar of soap and lathered their cocks, cleaning every inch with her skillful fingers. His cock hardened, then jumped when she licked one, then the other. Both men groaned at the pleasure of her hot mouth.

"You...know?" David closed his eyes with a gasp.

"What?" Nico's voice wasn't much stronger.

"She's got us right...where...she wants us."

"Don't I know it." Nico leaned to him, and David met him halfway.

Natalie lifted her head in the steamy atmosphere. "You two love me?"

"Umm." That was the only response they could give as their lips searched for what the other could provide.

* * *

Ah, another Valentine's Day. His favorite time of year, next to Halloween. The sun shone bright, and a brisk, chill breeze scurried down the neck of his shirt to cool his ever-hot skin. He had the family he'd always wanted. Something his *boss* didn't seem too happy about, but...what the hell.

After seven years, Nico and Natalie were pregnant with his second grandchild and living with Sophia. Without cutting down the old oak tree, they'd renovated the old house to include rooms for David and several babies. There, the three could share the unique love they all held for each other.

With a growing family to protect, what more could he ask for? Luke adjusted his sunglasses on his nose, then turned and walked down the sidewalk. He didn't answer that question and ignored the stab of loneliness that encased his cold heart. Technically, he still had the same job. No woman in her right mind would accept what he was. But—he shrugged his shoulders—he'd met all his obligations, as he'd promised. Well, maybe not all...

A little boy with black, curly hair and big brown eyes lay sprawled across the concrete, crying, while his glasses lay broken beside him. A gang of bigger boys walked away, shouting taunts over their shoulders.

Luke frowned and drew nearer. He heard the boy mumbling into the dirt.

"I hope they rot in—"

"That's not a very nice sentiment on Valentine's Day."

The boy looked up. Luke smiled at the smudge of dirt on the boy's upturned nose. He had his mother's pretty face...

"Well, I'm gonna tell my mom and she'll put a hex on their butts."

...and colorful imagination. Luke's eyebrows rose. Without a word, he removed a piece of candy, wrapped in red foil, from his pants pocket. He offered the sweet to the boy, who had his father's and grandfather's eyes.

The boy accepted the candy with a smile.

"I'm sure she will." Luke threw his head back and laughed.

~*~

Sheri Gilmore

When Sheri Gilmore isn't creating erotic romantic fantasies for her readers, she's a registered nurse, wife, and a mother of three. Her most favorite cities are New Orleans, San Francisco, and New York City. The one place in the world she would like to visit is Machu Picchu.

Her hobbies include reading, photography, cooking, and studying other cultures and religions. Her goal in life is to know and learn everything she possibly can and be the best 'Sheri' she can be.

You can learn more about Sheri and her writing at http://www.sherisecrets.com

Fortune's Star

Morgan Hawke

~ 0 ~

Armored Media Corporation
Estrella City, Temperance Prime

Luxi smiled as the data from the feed jacked into the base of her skull flowed smoothly through her internal computational array. The upgrade had been well worth the credits. The department's incoming and outgoing communications data was barely touching her conscious thoughts, with not one trace of lag-time.

She turned her face to the tall windows right by her desk and peered out over the city's vista. Sunlight gleamed on the towers and spires of Uppercity's business district. Below her, two-man gliders and private sedan cruisers wove around massive freight hovers as they zipped along the traffic-filled airways.

Musing on the different levels of speeding air traffic, she ran her fingers lightly over her hair, making sure that the silver clip was still securely fastened. She didn't need her rolled and coiled waist-length hair unraveling and getting caught on the data-jack. As curly as her hair was, the bright red strands had a nasty habit of wrapping tightly around the feed wire. She utterly refused to cut it, not when it was her best feature, so keeping it tightly bound was her only option.

The entry door chimed gently, then slid to the side, opening with a soft hiss. A tall businessman stalked in from the outer hallway.

Luxi stared at the tall man filling her tiny receptionist alcove and felt every hair on her body rise. Her throat tightened for no good reason whatsoever. "Welcome to Armored Media Corp." Her voice came out breathless.

There was something terribly wrong with him.

He didn't *look* odd; in fact, he might have been considered handsome. He had strong, clean-shaven features and his shoulder-length sable hair was neatly trimmed. Broad shoulders filled out his simple but sedately expensive fawn overcoat with no sign of the paunch that most Uppercity businessmen carried. The single-button chocolate dress suit he wore under his long coat was also understated, but the superfine material and the tailored cut reeked of money.

She'd seen lots of businessmen dressed like this, and quite a few from off-world that were dressed far more exotically. None of them had ever given her a case of the chills.

He turned to Luxi and smiled. "I'm here to see Gentle-fem Symposia?" He held out his data card.

And every instinct in Luxi's body screamed that she was in danger.

Luxi took the card very carefully so as not to make actual physical contact with his fingers. She swallowed. "One moment please." She swiped it through the desktop scanner, then routed his data to Gentle-fem Symposia's office. His information consisted of a single name, and that was it.

Vincent

Luxi frowned. *He must be some kind of private consultant.* She handed the card back.

He turned away and stared at one of the tasteful but boring prints on the cream wall by the inner door. Luxi was clearly beneath his notice, and that suited her just fine.

Mercy Symposia, director of the Executables department of Armored Media, strode briskly into the reception alcove from the inner door. As usual, she appeared conservatively professional with her dark blond hair in an elegant upsweep, yet sleek in her tailored black suit-dress. Chin up and smiling, she took Vincent's outstretched hand. "I'm so glad you could see me on such short notice."

Vincent bowed over Gentle-fem Symposia's hand then released it. "I found an opening in my schedule that permitted."

Luxi transferred data while keeping half an eye on the pair. What was it that set her off? Very casually, she stood up to get a better look. She swept her hands down her sleek and less-than-expensive, but nicely tailored, dove-gray business dress. She fiddled with a few folders on the upper ledge of her desk while trying not to look directly at either of them.

Mercy's smile faded as she spoke with the gentleman. The conversation sounded like any other business discussion, and yet she seemed nervous.

Vincent stood with casual deference and nodded in complete understanding. He spoke in mild and polite tones, but his smile seemed a tad sharp and his eyes...his black eyes...

Luxi awakened her quiescent mental talent from the depths of her mind and focused it on what she was feeling. Synchronicities, the lines of coincidence and possibility ruled by the decisions made in the here and now, clarified and stretched outward into bright skeins that created the warp and weft of potential futures. Her attention slid down the threads of prospect, decision, and chance that the unnerving man shared with her boss, seeking the future they would create.

She cringed. This man was a con-artist that preyed on fear. If Gentle-fem Symposia did business with him even once, her boss would never be rid of him.

Luxi turned away. If she said anything to her boss, she would have to tell Gentle-fem Symposia how she knew. She had no doubts that she would be believed. Psi-talents were not unknown. Most people showed some trace of telepathy or telekinetic ability, but strong talents were rare. And her talent was very reliable.

That was the problem.

Exposing the existence of her particular talent would cost her her job. The ability to track potential futures was just too much for any company to deal with. No one wanted to know that someone else was privy to their business decisions before they even made them. It didn't matter to them that she wouldn't know if she didn't actually look. They were all so busy angling for an advantage over the next company it wouldn't occur to them that *she* simply did not care.

But if she didn't say anything, Luxi would lose her job anyway. The company would not take kindly to Gentle-fem Symposia's embezzlement to feed this man's need for cash. The office would be closed for months during the investigation.

Mercy would be indentured to the company for life and her staff disbanded, including the receptionist.

Luxi's possible futures burned in the back of her mind. No matter what she chose, her future was no longer here in this office. There was nothing she could do to stem the tide. The real decisions were not in her hands. Once that man had entered Mercy's life, Luxi's future had been doomed. Keeping silent would not save her.

But Gentle-fem Symposia's gratitude might.

There was one slim chance that Luxi would not end up living in the under-city slums—but it was slim indeed.

Luxi shut down her holographic display, pulled out her data jack, and set the communications switchboard on auto. *Damn it, I really liked this job!* She took a steadying breath and lifted her chin. "Ms. Symposia, that man cannot be trusted."

Mercy turned a sharp look Luxi's way. "Luxi, you have no idea what you're talking about. He's a monk."

A monk? Luxi swallowed but held her supervisor's gaze steadily. "Gentle-fem Symposia, with all due respect, he's a blackmailing con-artist."

Her supervisor frowned. "What?"

The man suddenly focused on Luxi. His black eyes narrowed. "Miss, do you know what you are saying?"

Luxi stared coldly into his eyes. "Yes, as a matter of fact, I do." Abruptly, her small secondary talent stirred within her. She had no grasp on it or control over it; the talent came and went as it pleased. It wasn't particularly useful. All her little talent saw were the threads of the past—and ghosts.

As she stared into Vincent's black eyes, her second talent suddenly opened wide and showed her why her skin was crawling.

Vincent was possessed by a second soul. It was staring straight at her from within his eyes with malignant intent. It was very dead, and very hungry.

Vincent suddenly smiled. It wasn't pretty.

Luxi literally felt the ground move under her feet as her future abruptly reshaped itself.

* * *

Mercy Symposia's office was not particularly large, but it boasted a full wall of solid windows that overlooked the heart of Estrella City's corporate district. Her broad desk was an understated work of art made of real imported blackwood. Mercy tapped at her keyboard and frowned thoughtfully at her holographic display.

Luxi sat in the elegant back-curved chair before the desk with her hands folded quietly in her lap. She had been right. Mercy had not had any difficulty believing, once she understood Luxi's odd talent. Fortune-tellers were a dime a dozen, but none of them in Estrella, upper-city or below, had the accuracy that Luxi possessed. It was not something she talked about.

The silence lay thick in the office.

Luxi swallowed hard. "I'm...I'm sorry, Gentle-fem Symposia."

Mercy sighed and folded her hands on her desktop. "I have been having strange dreams and odd...occurrences in my condo.

I was led to believe that this man was an expert on such things." She gazed at her hands rather than at Luxi.

Luxi turned to get her purse, which was hanging on her chair's slender arm. She pulled out a slim data card and set it on the desk. "This is a friend of mine. She'll take care of that for you, and she won't ask for more than she's worth. If you have any other problems, she'll tell you who you can trust."

Mercy took the card. She glanced briefly at it then tapped the edge on her desk. "When you told me what you told me...I was under the impression that there was a lot more that you...didn't say."

Luxi closed her purse and nodded. With the entire company hard-wired for surveillance, "embezzlement" was the one word that never came out of your mouth.

Mercy's hands clenched into fists. "You just saved my career, didn't you?"

Luxi clutched her purse. "None of that will happen now. You're safe. He's not after you anymore." *He's after me.*

Mercy pressed her fingers to her brow and released a breath. "Damn it, Luxi, you just saved my ass and I have to fire you!"

Luxi nodded miserably. She had done the right thing. She knew she'd done the right thing, but it still hurt like hell. "The company cannot afford to have me work in their offices." She closed her eyes. "I'm a...an information leak."

Mercy leaned back in her chair and glared at her closed office door. "It's also company policy to report strong talents. Once it's recorded on your personal essay, it goes on your resume. Not one company will hire you."

Luxi stared at her purse. "I know."

Mercy scowled at her hands. "You could have kept your mouth shut."

I would have lost my job anyway. Luxi lifted her shoulder in a half-hearted shrug. "I'm a nice girl. It's what nice girls do."

Mercy blinked, then smiled bitterly. "Nice girls, huh?" She stared at her holographic display and tapped her desktop with a manicured nail. "Loyalty should be rewarded—not punished!" Abruptly, she leaned forward. "Luxi, can you look for yourself? Can you see if there is any way I can help you? Any way at all?"

Luxi's fingers tightened on her purse. Within her mind, her talent hummed and possibilities dropped into place. This was it. She had reached the juxtaposition moment she'd been waiting for, the turning point in her personal future where everything came together and hinged on a single decision. She glanced up at her former supervisor. "As a matter of fact, there is."

Chapter One

Port Destiny Station
Imperial Space - Outbound Corridor

"We are approaching dock to Port Destiny spaceport," the shuttle's gentle voice announced. "Please secure all personal belonging in preparation for return to gravity."

Luxi woke from her nap and stretched in her padded chair. The shuttle had taken nearly an hour to cross the distance from the starliner to the spaceport. A zero-gravity nap had filled the time nicely.

She peered up over the heads of the other shuttle passengers. The yawning mouth of Port Destiny's sixty-five-meter-wide docking bay door filled the forward view-screen. The cylindrical station slowly took on truly gigantic proportions. All of a sudden, Luxi had no trouble at all believing that the station employed over sixty-five hundred people.

From the starliner's stateroom view-screens, the station had appeared small. Measured against the spaceport station she had transferred from, Port Destiny station *was* small. It was only a little over eight kilometers long and archaic in design. Rather than a modern docking ring around a habitat globe, Port Destiny was an old Terran-built station that was tubular in shape. The entire barrel-like body of the station turned, generating nearly normal gravity the old-fashioned way, by centrifugal rotation.

Luxi pursed her lips. Port Destiny was practical rather than aesthetically pleasing, but practicality had its advantages. Since the entire station turned, pocket regions of the station were less likely to lose gravity through unexpected power outages.

"Please remain in your seats until the shuttle has come to a complete stop," the shuttle's voice continued. "Please have your data cards ready for swift assessment through customs. Thank you for traveling with Imperial Princess Starlines."

Luxi reached into the zip-sealed breast pocket of her deep-violet jumpsuit and pulled out her holographic data card. The card marked her identity, such as it was, the last of her personal credits, and her passage through the corridors of space on her way to a new planet, a new job, and a new life. A reward from Ms. Symposia for her loyalty and the price she had paid for it.

The first moment she had touched the card, Luxi's talent for reading the future betrayed that her arrival at the card's final destination would mark the beginning of a long, stable career marked by utter misery.

She was going to loathe her new life.

However, a crossing thread marked a single moment in time heavily weighted by chance, hinting that an opportunity for a better future could cross her path before she ever arrived. It was only a whisper among the tangled threads of synchronicity. A possible knot of juxtaposition whose threads were not yet in place. Others had yet to make decisions that would bring this moment of opportunity forth.

That slim possibility had been enough to make Luxi sell every trace of her entire life. One hand-carry bag and the card were all she had left.

Luxi's hands tightened on the arms of the chair as the view-screen filled with the interior lights of the station's dock. She had traveled for sixteen days and eight jumps from star system to star system, on two different starliners, to reach that moment. It was here, on Port Destiny station, that the tangled threads of opportunity, chance, and decision would cross. It was here that her last chance for happiness would occur. Her talent hummed actively within her. Possibility was coming closer to being opportunity with every breath she took.

Luxi hoped with everything in her that the opportunity presented itself soon, because yet another moment of synchronicity was actively chasing her with malevolent determination.

The ghost-possessed monk, Vincent, was trailing her across the stars.

She could feel his vile intent crawling across the threads of possibility into her future. Her talent warned that no matter what course she charted, sooner or later he would catch up with her. From that meeting, all her lines into the future ended in a single moment marked by a single decision, a decision that was entirely in her own hands.

With not one hint of what that decision would bring—or cost.

* * *

Customs was a huge, well-lit, and crowded hallway that curved to the right. Three lines of passengers moved at a crawl past plain and featureless cream walls painted with a broad band of bronze. The long lines ended in a wide doorway blocked by full-body scanners and armed guards in dark uniforms. Their snug, half-armored doublet coats were emblazoned with *Sojourn Corp.* across the breast, and swords graced their hips. In the sealed environment of a space station, where a pinhole could mean the deaths of thousands, energy weapons were tightly controlled. Even the state-of-the-art live-steel blades worn by Imperial officers could not cut through armored plating.

Luxi tucked an errant wave of her red mane behind her ear. The shuttle's zero-g had really done a job on her hair. She was going to have to dig out her brush and re-braid the whole mess.

Boredom weighed heavily. It had been a long, dull flight, then a long, dull wait, and then this long, dull walk.

She arrived at the gate to enter the station proper, and had to force herself not to yawn in the guard's face.

He winced. "Please don't yawn," he said softly. "I'll start doing it, then the rest of the guys will do it, and it looks really bad on surveillance."

Luxi smiled to cover the almost-yawn. "You? Yawn, when you have such an exciting job?" She turned over her data card for assessment.

"Oh, yeah..." He rolled his eyes and grinned. "I'm so fulfilled." He slid her card through his hand-held reader. The light over the doorway scanner went green. He returned her card and handed her a folded flyer emblazoned with the station's logo. "Welcome to Port Destiny Station." He leaned closer and added in a stage-whisper, "…where nothing ever happens."

"Thank you." She glanced at the station flyer. "Personally, I've had enough adventure already."

The guard snorted. "Then you are going to love Port Destiny."

"I certainly hope so!" Luxi grinned and stepped through the scanner, towing her overstuffed hand-carry bag on its small wheels. No alarms went off. She released a small breath and continued on, grinning foolishly as she strode past another set of guards and out of the customs ring. It was time to find her future.

The good news was that she didn't have to worry about getting on the next flight for a whole thirty hours, so she had thirty hours to figure out where she needed to be—and be there.

The bad news was that she didn't have the credits to get even a cheap room to rest in for any of those thirty hours. Her berths and meals were included on the starliners, but the spaceport stopovers had proved very expensive. According to her personal account, she had just enough credits left to get a cup of kaffa and a snack. If she wanted a decent meal before her next flight, she was going to have to do something to make the credits to buy it. Luckily, there wasn't a spaceport that didn't have a kafé, or a kafé that didn't appreciate a good fortune-teller.

Letting the corporate office know that she could read the future could get her fired, but here in the middle of nowhere, it was a way to make a little cash.

Luxi held up the paper flyer the customs officer had handed her, reading as she walked. According to the flyer, there were seventeen kafés in the station's Garden District concourse. And according to her talent, she definitely had an appointment with one of them.

Luxi approached the row of lifts that would drop her on the Garden District concourse. Her talent shifted within her.

Something didn't feel right.

She stopped, letting the other shuttle passengers brush by her. *Now what?* She frowned in concentration, trying to get a better grasp of what she was feeling.

Synchronicity was out of place. Taking the lift wouldn't put her in the right place, in the right moment in time, for the future she was chasing.

Luxi rolled her eyes in disgust. *Great, a complication...* Following the lines toward the future was proving to be a real pain in the ass. She glanced around. *Okay, so if I'm not supposed to go down the lift, where* am *I supposed to go?* There was a small hallway off to her right. Something clicked into place. *Ah...*

Following the thread of synchronicity, Luxi slipped through the line of passengers and into the small hallway.

The hall ended at a single lift access. According to the sign by the call button, this lift led to the cable-car tramway that traveled from one end of the station to the other, right through the station's center. No one was waiting for the lift.

Luxi's brow rose. Apparently, it was not a popular mode of transportation. But this was where she was supposed to be, so... She pushed the call button.

Chapter Two

Luxi stepped out on the tramway deck, trailing her bag, and grabbed onto the rail that ran all the way around the tram station. Gravity was very minimal this close to the station's center.

Not one person was waiting on the tram.

On the other side of the deep track where the cable-tram would pull in was a huge window, and beyond it, the floor of the world turned upward very slowly, meters and meters, and meters, away—all the way overhead. *Oh, glory...*

She suddenly felt as though she were falling, and falling, and falling...

Luxi had to consciously make an effort not to fall over. According to her sense of perspective, the entire world was rotating sideways at a dizzying distance. She tore her gaze away and turned her back to the window. *Okay, let's not look at that anymore.* She swallowed, suddenly understanding why the tramway had few passengers.

According to the chrono on the wall between the two lifts, she had about five minutes to wait for the next tram. Once she was on it, the tram would reach a stop just short of every five minutes, and she had seven stops before she would reach the stop she wanted. *That should be long enough to do something about my hair.* Brushing her hair would also give her something to concentrate on, rather than the dizzying view. She knelt and dug into her bag to retrieve her brush.

Brush in hand, she stood to tug the elastic free from the end of her braid, then dug her fingers into her thick curls to get them out of the braid. It took more effort than she thought it would to untangle the long coils enough to pull a brush through them. The bright copper of her waist-length mane blazed in a cloud of sunset waves against her deep-violet suit. She winced. Her hair was beyond frizzy. The shipboard sonic projection vibro-showers and antibacterial lighting had not been good for it. Brushing it in low gravity did not help any. She shook her head and kept brushing. Well, at least her hair wasn't dry and crispy...

The lift door on her far left opened and three laughing people came leaping out of the lift, floating on the light gravity. The tallest was a pale young male with sleek creamy-blond hair that swept well past his shoulders. His charcoal-gray silk formal frock coat flared open to his knees, showing off the expanse of his gently defined bare chest. His trousers were skintight black velvet.

His two companions were slender, black-haired fems dressed in snug and aggressive-looking black leather trousers and tall boots. They were nearly masculine in build, with only the gentle flare of hips and the slight curve of breasts under their cropped halter tops defining their gender. They were also armed with long and short blades, where the male was not.

Their bare arms and bellies proudly displayed sword-cut scars across the light golden skin. Their mouths were wide and their up-tilted black eyes flashed with humor as they towed their beautiful companion toward the tram-track.

Luxi watched them avidly as she pulled her brush through her springy curls. From the looks of the sword scars, the fems were a lot older than their youthful forms suggested. It was entirely possible that the male was also far older than he appeared. Clearly, she was looking at an Imperial lord and his two bodyguards.

The young male turned to look at Luxi with violet eyes set in an exquisitely perfect face. His glossed pink lips opened on a spectacular smile.

Luxi froze. *Wow...pretty.*

Another man came out of the lift. His strongly masculine face was pale as marble, without a trace of blush. His metallic-silver hair was drawn back and fastened in a smooth, straight tail that fell just past his shoulders. His full-body, high-collared jumpsuit was of deepest black, yet it shimmered with rainbows. Absolutely comfortable in the light gravity, he moved with the inhumanly effortless grace of the mechanically enhanced. He was simply gorgeous in motion. He stalked around the incredible trio with the careful inattention of a predator trying not to startle his prey.

Luxi blinked. There was something odd about him... His hair was true metallic silver, a color no living hair could possibly emulate. Her mouth fell open. He was a cyborg—the most perfectly crafted, utterly human-looking cyborg she had ever seen.

He lifted his chin as though scenting something interesting and turned to look at Luxi with eyes the color of steel—and shadow.

Luxi's talent jolted hard. *Good glory...*

The cyborg was animate and conscious, but he wasn't alive. The spirit of the living man he had once been burned in the depths of his gaze, a spirit that had not fled with the loss of his living body; a ghost perfectly contained in fully robotic flesh.

Within her, synchronicity suddenly dropped into place.

The cyborg was a key to the future she was looking for.

Luxi jerked her gaze away from the stunning ghost. *A haunted cyborg?* Life was getting stranger by the second. She lifted the brush to her hair to do something rather than turn back to stare at him. Her talent shimmered within her. Apparently she was supposed to see him, and he was supposed to see her, so he had something to do with her new future, but what?

She scowled, trying to read the lines, but just could not see what was supposed to happen next. The future was still too vague. Apparently the decision to set things in motion was not hers.

Someone spoke at her elbow.

"Huh?" Luxi turned.

The beautiful young lord and his two dark-eyed companions stood only inches away. Luxi's eyes opened wide. This close, the young lord was breathtaking. His face had only the slightest touches of cosmetics outlining his impossibly violet eyes. Even his perfume was gorgeous.

He asked her a question.

She had no clue what he said. Luxi lifted her shoulder in a small shrug. "I'm sorry, but I don't understand." She really, really needed to get an upgrade for her internal translator.

"He says that you have hair like living flame. He'd like to know if you would care to join him for sex."

Luxi started and turned her head to find the cyborg standing by her left elbow. She hadn't even seen him approach. She was forced to look up. He was head and shoulders taller than she was. And this close, he was absolutely stunning. The lord was lovely, but the cyborg's arresting face was utterly, powerfully masculine. Something in her stilled, as though holding its breath.

His dark silver brows rose. "Are you all right?"

Luxi released her breath and felt her cheeks heat. She'd been staring. "Sorry... I..." What had she been thinking? She didn't have a clue. Her mind had utterly blanked. "I don't know your name."

"I'm Leto." He smiled.

"I'm Luxi." Her voice came out breathless. Glory above, his smile! She felt the listening stillness wash through her again.

Leto tilted his head toward the lord and his two fems. "He's waiting to know if you want to have sex."

Luxi blinked. "He wants...what?"

Leto lifted a pale hand to cover his chuckle. "Sex. He wants to know if you want to have sex with him and his fems."

Luxi glanced over at the beautiful lord then bit her lip. "Could you tell him, I'm flattered, but I don't normally have..." She winced. "...relations, with people I don't know?"

Leto tilted his head and replied to the lord.

The lord rolled his eyes in obvious amusement. His two companions dissolved into giggles. The lord glanced at the cyborg and asked a question.

Leto raised his chin and turned away.

The lord watched Luxi expectantly and smiled.

Luxi peered up at the cyborg. "Leto, what did he say?"

Leto folded his arms across his chest and glanced down at the deck. "Tell you what—I'll translate what he said for the price of..." He turned to Luxi and lifted a silver brow. "A kiss."

"A kiss?" Luxi's breath caught. This spectacular man wanted to kiss *her?*

His shadow-filled eyes focused on her. "Will you kiss me?"

Glory, yes! Luxi licked her lips. "Okay."

Leto's eyes widened just a hair. He leaned downward, very slowly.

Luxi tilted her chin up to meet him. His lips brushed hers. Warmth, breath... He was warm; he breathed. Her eyes drifted closed and her lips parted under his. Their tongues met, explored, parried. He tasted like fresh, clean water. He smelled of rich leather.

He cupped her shoulders in his strong hands.

She reached for him and her hands settled on his hips. His shimmering suit was warm under her palms and felt like exotic leather. Vibrancy and darkness pulsed in a delicious yet shivery combination under her fingertips. She spread her fingers and pressed her palms against him to feel more of it.

His hands skimmed up her neck, drawing tiny shivers, and his fingers slid under her hair. He cupped her head and angled her mouth to deepen the kiss, stroking her tongue, tasting her, encouraging her to kiss him back.

Heat, hunger, urgency... A small moan escaped her throat. Her hands slid around his waist, pulling him closer.

His arm closed around her waist, pulling her tight against his body.

He was warm, and excited. She could feel the hard length of his erection against her belly. Moisture dampened her panties. The simmering dark within him brushed against her heart with unexpected fire. Her talent awoke in a searing rush and suddenly she could feel his bare skin under her palms—and along her entire body where they touched.

Leto abruptly pulled away, blinking, clearly startled.

Luxi grabbed onto his belt, refusing to let him go. "Did I do something wrong?"

He frowned down at her. "I 'felt' you." He licked his lips. "You're vitae sensitive? You can feel life-forces?"

"Not exactly." She blushed. There was just no way to say this gracefully. "I feel...ghosts. I'm necro-sensitive."

"I see." Leto's brows lowered and his eyes narrowed. "Did you know that I was..." He took a breath and his jaw tightened. "...*dead,* before you kissed me?"

She nibbled on her bottom lip. "I knew that you were a cyborg with a...ghost."

He stilled then his eyes narrowed. "And you kissed me anyway?"

She frowned up at him. "Is there a reason I shouldn't?"

He blinked and gave her a sour smile. "About a million of them; all religious and having to do with necrophilia."

She raised a sarcastic brow. "Funny, you don't kiss like a corpse. You're warm; you breathe."

He barked out a laugh and stared downward. "I don't think so, either, but some people seem to have a problem with it." He shook his head and folded his hands behind him. "I was originally a nano-based cyborg. Biological machines replaced my body cell by cell. I'm not living tissue anymore, but I'm still me and perfectly functional; just not biological, so to speak."

Luxi snorted and glanced down at the heavy line of his erection straining against the seam of his suit. "You felt awfully biological to me." Her fingers tightened on his belt. She had the most incredible urge to pull him close and "touch" him again.

Trilling laughter reminded Luxi sharply that they were not alone. She turned to face the grinning lord and his dark-eyed, aggressive companions.

The lord gestured, shot out a rapid-fire list of incomprehensible statements at Leto, and glanced at Luxi briefly. He watched the cyborg expectantly.

A windy roar announced the sudden arrival of the tram.

Leto nodded at the lord

The lord grinned, then turned to his two fems, and they all moved toward the tram through the tram station's low gravity like swimmers through water.

Leto tilted his head at Luxi. "Is that your bag?"

Luxi frowned at the tram. It was going in the wrong direction. "Yes, but that's not my tram."

Leto snatched for the handle of her bag and caught her around the waist. "It is now." He jumped.

Chapter Three

Luxi grabbed onto Leto's arm as their feet left the deck in a spectacular leap boosted by the weak gravity. She gasped as Leto carried her clear across to the tram's open door.

"In you go!" He shoved her onto the tram, right behind the youthful trio.

Just outside the tram's outward-facing windows, the floor of the world turned upward very slowly, meters and meters, and meters, away.

Luxi gasped and turned away from the rolling view. Her sense of perspective and balance simply could not deal with it. The tram was windowed on both sides, with long, cushioned benches running lengthwise under the windows. Once the tram left the small station, the world would rotate all the way around, with the tram moving through the very center. It was going to be impossible to avoid the stomach-churning view.

Leto was the only thing to look at besides the floor. He was also the only thing to hold on to. She grabbed his belt. "Leto, what are you doing?"

Leto grinned at her and turned her to face the tram's interior. "We are going to provide them with some entertainment." He pushed her deeper into the tram, aiming for the cushioned bench along the left.

On the opposite side, the pale lord stretched his arms out across the back of the bench, relaxing as his fems stripped off their weapons with astonishing speed. He smiled and licked his lips, staring hard at Luxi and the cyborg pushing her down the aisle.

The two fems climbed up on the bench and knelt on either side of the pale lord, framing him. They glanced at each other and licked their lips, then leaned close to pull his coat open, baring his pale chest. They pressed and rubbed their lithe golden bodies against his creamy skin, spreading their slender fingers wide to caress his gently defined chest and smooth belly.

He groaned and shifted under them, rubbing up against them.

They pushed his creamy mane back from his neck, and pink tongues flashed as they licked his throat.

He raised his chin and tipped his head back with an open-mouthed sigh, but kept his violet gaze locked on Luxi and the cyborg.

Leto's lips brushed her ear. "Just so you know, the blond is Bel, the fem on his right is Orah, and the fem on his left is Faro."

Luxi tried to stop, but Leto was impossible to halt. The light gravity gave her feet no purchase whatsoever on the floor. "Leto, I am *not* going to have sex with them!"

"No, *they* are going to have sex." He shoved her bag under the bench "But they want to do it while watching us kiss." He caught her around the waist and dropped onto the broad seat, tugging her down across his lap.

Luxi's butt landed on the seat between Leto's thighs. She grabbed for his shoulders. "Wait a minute; they're having sex on the tramway?"

Leto shook his head and cradled her in his arms. "Haven't you ever had sex on a tramway before?"

Luxi shifted on his lap. "No! And I'm not having it now!"

Leto tightened his hold, settling her across his thighs. "Relax. *They* are having sex; *we* are just kissing."

Orah caught a fistful of her lord's silky hair at the base of his neck, opened her mouth wide on his throat, and bit down on the long muscle.

He gasped and smiled.

Faro licked her way down Bel's throat to his pale pink nipple and stroked it with an outstretched tongue. She locked her lips around the pale flesh and sucked, her mouth making wet sounds as she moaned her delight.

Bel writhed and a soft moan escaped. He wrapped his arm around Faro and pulled her tighter against his chest. He reached out and wrapped his other arm around Orah as she bit down on his neck. He whispered to them, but his gaze remained on Luxi and Leto.

Orah released her lord's throat from her teeth and leaned back to pull her top off, revealing the gentle curves of her breasts and her tightly pointed caramel nipples.

Bel pulled her tight against him and turned his head to capture her proud nipple in his mouth, but his eyes never left Luxi and Leto. His tongue flicked as he licked first one nipple, then the other. His teeth flashed as he bit down.

Orah arched, throwing her head back and moaning, tugging his hair to encourage him.

Bel reached up to catch Faro's cropped black hair in his fist and pushed her head from his nipple down toward his lap.

Faro spilled across Bel's lap and stretched out on the bench, kicking her feet up. She tugged Bel's belt open and unfastened his pants. Her hand slipped within. Her fingers were plainly defined by the elastic velvet of his trousers as she wrapped her hand around his cock and then pushed deeper to cup his balls.

Bel gasped and arched, bringing his hips up from the bench.

Luxi swallowed as wet heat pulsed in her core from the inciting view. "Just kissing?"

Leto's breath caressed her ear. "I swear I will not go any further than you want to go."

Luxi shivered. *That's what I'm afraid of.* She was already more excited than she had ever been with anyone else. Her talent hummed within her. She was still in the right place, occupying the right moment in time. She was supposed to be here, doing this. "Okay..."

Leto gave her a heart-stopping, if sly, smile. "Good." He leaned closer and took her mouth, pressing her back against his arm as the tram began to move through the heart of the turning station.

Leto's taste, clean and fresh, his scent, tinged with leather, and the determined pursuit of his tongue against hers combined into a drugging euphoria that cleared Luxi's mind of thought while crowding her body with restless yearning.

His mouth encouraged her to arch further back. "Look," he whispered. "Look at them."

Luxi turned to look at the pale lord and his fems across the aisle.

Faro, sprawled across Bel's lap, grinned as she pulled his cock free of his trousers. The pale column of his hardening length curved upward from the black velvet, fully two of her hand-widths in length. She tightened her fingers around him and stroked upward, then down. The deep-rose cockhead darkened to plum. She stretched out her tongue and licked the column of pale flesh in her hand. Her tongue lashed the flared edge of his darkening cockhead.

Bel's eyes closed briefly and he released Orah's nipple to gasp out a short phrase.

Orah pulled back from Bel's arm to stand up on the bench, her nipples wet from his mouth. She grabbed the overhead safety bar with one hand and jerked her leather pants down with her other. Her pants slid past her hips, baring the muscular curve of her ass and the neatly trimmed black hair of her mons.

Leto's fingers tugged at the throat fastenings of Luxi's suit. Slowly, carefully, he opened her suit to her heart. His hot, wet mouth closed on her throat and he licked. His teeth raked the long muscle and over her pulse.

Luxi shivered and her mouth opened on a gasp, but she kept her eyes on the pale young lord and his two fems.

Bel wrapped his arm around Orah's hips and pulled her toward his mouth. He stretched out his tongue and licked the plump lips of her exposed pussy. He tightened his hold and thrust his tongue deeper, licking with audible wet enthusiasm.

Orah whimpered, her hips rolling against his mouth, and lifted her booted foot to step over his lap.

Bel released Faro's hair and shoved the nearly naked Orah back to his side. He clearly did not want his view of Luxi and Leto blocked.

Faro, in his lap, opened her mouth and took the plum head within. Her lips tightened around Bel's cock and her head plunged, taking him deep in her mouth and into her throat. Her head rose and fell, her cheeks hollowing as she sucked with interest.

Leto slid his hand down Luxi's suited hip. He cupped, then caressed, her butt cheek.

Shivers trailed across her skin, followed by sudden heat. Luxi shifted against him, releasing a small moan. She could feel his palm as though he stroked her bare skin. It was his ghost. She was feeling the phantom within his cybernetic hand touching her, right through her clothes.

"Blood and fate, I can feel you," Leto whispered against Luxi's throat. "I've never felt anyone with my..." He hesitated for a breath. "That part of me, before."

"Your spirit?" Luxi flashed him a quick smile.

He bit his lip. "Yeah, my spirit, sure."

"Can you feel me?" She leaned back to press her palm to his heart.

"Here." He moved her hand over to the right and a little lower on his chest. He closed his eyes and drew in a breath. "Oh, yeah, right on the nipple."

Luxi shifted her fingers. She could actually feel the hard nub right through his suit. She could feel his leather suit, too, but the suit didn't seem to feel quite as real as the tight nipple under her fingers. She rubbed her thumb across it.

He pressed her palm tight, stilling her hand. "It feels as though you're touching my bare nipple, but deeper."

Luxi peered up at him. "That's what it feels like to me."

His brows shot up. "Really? How about this?" His fingers slid across her hip and over her belly, tracing very lightly over her suit.

She shivered. It was the most incredibly exciting thing she'd ever felt. "It's like...I'm naked."

His eyes narrowed and his lips curved up in a sly smile. "Is that so?"

Her pulse suddenly beat in her throat. Perhaps that had not been a good thing to say. "Wait..."

"Oh, no, you can't take it back now!" He pressed her back onto the bench, pinning her shoulders with his hands. Her long red mane spilled over the seat and onto the floor.

"Leto!" She shoved her hands up against his chest. "What are you doing?"

He licked his lips and chuckled softly. "What do you think?" He came up on one knee and threw his leg over her hips, dropping a booted foot to the floor to straddle her. "I want to see just how naked you feel!"

"Leto, please!" She could barely speak past the pulse in her throat. She desperately wanted to feel his skin against hers. The thought of it was seriously soaking her panties. She didn't think she'd ever wanted to feel anyone more. But if he actually did it, she didn't think he would stop there. Worse, she didn't think she would want him to stop there.

"Luxi..." He lowered his mouth and his lips brushed hers.

She moaned and opened to receive his kiss.

He turned his head to take her mouth more fully, his tongue making deep, slow sweeps as he slowly dropped to his elbows. His chest brushed her breasts. His warm skin swept across her hardened nipples as though nothing lay between them.

She couldn't stop her moan any more than she could stop herself from arching to press her breasts more fully against him.

His hand slid between the seat's back and her hip to cup her thigh. He pulled and her knee rose. He set his knee on the seat between her thighs and shifted his weight onto the seat. His other hand pushed her leg from the seat to get both his knees up on the seat.

And between her thighs.

Alarm washed through Luxi. *Glory and mercy!* Fully dressed, this was a perfectly harmless position, but for some reason, their clothes weren't any kind of a barrier between them.

She jerked her mouth from his, but he pursued her, capturing her lips and then her hands, pulling them up over her head. Stretched out and spread, she moaned into his mouth.

He lowered his hips against hers, groaned and arched.

Luxi sucked in a sharp breath. She could feel him. Feel his skin sliding against her skin, and his rigid cock rubbing with intimate warmth against her belly.

He released her hands and slid his arms under and around her shoulders, pulling her tight against him. "Blood and hell, you feel damned good!"

She groaned in reply. He felt damned good, too. The urge to feel more of him brought her arms up to press her hands against his back. She could feel the ridges of his muscular form under her palms. He was fully dressed, but he felt utterly and excitingly naked.

Chapter Four

Bel grinned at Luxi and Leto as he lapped at Orah's pussy while his hips bucked against Faro's mouth. He turned to look down at the sucking fem and snapped out a phrase before returning his mouth to Orah, trembling in his hold.

Her mouth full of Bel's cock, Faro unfastened her pants.

Bel slid his palm down Faro's spine and shoved his hand into the back of her loosened leather trousers. Her snug pants defined his fingers as he cupped and fondled her ass. He groaned and shoved his hand deeper, his fingers curving under and between her cheeks.

Faro whimpered as she sucked, lifting her hips and pumping her ass against his hand.

"Are you watching them?" Leto whispered in Luxi's ear. His hands slid down to cup her ass, pressing her more firmly against his cock.

"Yes." Luxi had been unable to tear her eyes off of them, even with the heat of Leto's body rubbing against her belly and breasts.

"Bel has his fingers shoved in Faro's ass."

Luxi's eyes widened. "He does not!"

Leto chuckled and his hands tightened on her ass-cheeks. "Trust me, I know what I'm looking at, and he is finger-fucking her ass, hard."

Luxi frowned and shifted under him. "And she likes it?"

"Are you joking?" He tilted his head toward the lascivious view. "She's about to come." He lifted his head and hissed a soft phrase at the sucking fem.

Faro turned her gaze toward Leto, releasing the hard cock in her mouth. Her eyes widened. She gasped and trembled, pumping hard against Bel's hand with her eyes locked on Leto. A soft moan escaped and she froze. Her eyes dilated wide and she shuddered hard. Her eyes drifted closed and she writhed with a smile on her lips.

Leto sighed. "There. She came."

Orah, locked to Bel's mouth, whimpered desperately and grabbed onto his head with both hands, grinding against his mouth.

Leto nodded. "The other one is about to come."

Bel pulled his mouth away, drawing moans of disappointment from Orah.

Leto chuckled. "Oh, that was mean. He didn't let her come."

Bel grinned and tugged on Orah's knees.

Orah fell back onto the bench with a soft gasp.

Bel snapped out a phrase.

Orah flipped over onto her belly, coming up on her elbows and knees. She put one booted foot down on the tram's floor, spreading herself wide.

Leto sighed. "Ah, that's why. They're going to fuck."

Bel turned to face Orah and came up on his knee. He grabbed her by the hips and pulled her toward his jutting cock. He jerked her pants lower and turned to look over his shoulder.

Faro grabbed her top and yanked it over her head, showing the even slighter curves of her breasts and her stiff caramel nipples. She tossed the top on the seat behind her and came up on her knees behind Bel. She tugged at the waistband of her open pants, tugging them lower. A small but not inconsiderable cock emerged as she pulled her pants down past her hips.

Luxi stiffened in surprise. "She's a boy?"

Leto snorted. "No, the little he-fem is both. Faro is fully equipped with both sexes, but her body looks female, so she's still considered a fem."

"Then she has a…" Luxi swallowed. "She has a pussy, too?"

"Oh, yes."

Luxi frowned up at him. "How do you know all this?"

Leto smiled. "Who do you think Bel invited for sex first? He was quite vocal about his little he-fem's talents."

"You were going to have sex with them?"

"Ah, no." Leto gave her a tight smile. "That young man has a dominant streak a mile wide. I wasn't interested in playing his games, but I was more than interested in watching, so I followed them up." He brushed his lips against Luxi's ear. "Bel likes to be watched almost as much as he likes fucking people he doesn't know."

Luxi whispered back. "That's really perverted."

"No, it's boredom." Leto grinned. "And you seem to be finding it rather entertaining."

Luxi ground her teeth. "Fine, rub it in."

Leto licked his lips. "Don't mind if I do."

Bel positioned himself behind Orah and gripped his cock. He grabbed her thigh and pulled her back onto him. His head came up and he groaned as his shaft slowly disappeared into the trembling fem's dripping cunt. He stopped, caught both her thighs and pulled back to suddenly thrust deep into her.

Orah shoved back against him, meeting his strong thrust.

Behind them, Faro stroked her small cock to hardness and tugged Bel's velvet trousers down past his hips.

"Oh, yeah, all three are going to fuck. Good genetic designing; the he-fem rearmed fast, though I don't envy the mess in her trousers."

Luxi blinked. "What?"

"Faro already came, remember? There's a load of cum in her pants." He made a sour face. "Not something you want to walk around in."

Luxi winced. Wet panties weren't exactly comfortable either. "Why did he let Faro come, but not Orah?"

Leto grinned. "To keep the little he-fem from coming too fast once she got her dick up his tight ass."

Faro locked one arm around Bel's hips and positioned her cock between his cheeks.

Bel stilled, waiting.

Faro arched her hips, pushing her cock into Bel's ass. She sighed and grinned, then locked both arms around his hips.

Bel groaned and licked his pale pink lips. A grin appeared. He gripped Orah's thighs and ground his cock deep into her, then pulled back, pressing himself back onto Faro's cock. He thrust, and pulled back, then thrust, fucking and being fucked, with slow, deep plunges and retreats.

Both fems gasped and moaned in obvious enjoyment.

"Speaking of coming..." Leto reached for the fastening at Luxi's heart and tugged her jumpsuit further open.

Luxi sucked in a breath as cool air caressed her flushed skin. The suit was designed to be opened for necessities, without having to take it off. It unfastened all the way down and up over her butt.

Leto's mouth captured hers as his fingers worked, unfastening her suit lower and lower...

She didn't try to stop him. She didn't have the will to stop him. She moaned into his mouth. The absolute truth was she didn't want him to stop.

He released her suit fastening all the way down and then under, as far as it would go. He grabbed the edges and pulled her suit apart, exposing her flushed nipples, her belly, and her panties. His brows shot up. "Panties?"

Luxi flushed. "Well, of course."

Leto grinned. "How sweet!"

Across from them, Bel rolled his eyes and chuckled as he continued to slow-fuck his two writhing and anxious fems. He reached under to cup Orah's breasts and tugged on her hard little nipples.

Leto leaned down and captured Luxi's nipple with his lips and his teeth.

Fire scorched from her nipple straight down to her clit, drawing an echoing throb. Luxi gasped and arched. A spat of cream released into her panties.

His hand slid into her panties, his long fingers delving past the plump outer lips of her sex to explore her intimate folds. "You're wet." He stroked her clit lightly, and insistently.

Luxi threw back her head and moaned, jolted by the bolts of erotic fire caused by his deft touch on her clit. He was really, really good. She had to fight to keep a coherent thought in her head. "I thought we weren't going to do sex?"

"Do you want me to stop?" He stroked her hard nipple with his pointed tongue while strumming her swollen clit with devastating skill.

Luxi writhed and gasped. She could barely think past the fire boiling and building in her core, but she knew for a fact she was well past the stopping point.

"Luxi," he whispered and swept his tongue across her painfully swollen nipples. He slid a finger into her core, and stroked. "Do you want me to stop?"

Luxi shivered and arched her hips up against him, deliberately rubbing against his cock. "No."

"Good." Leaving his hand in her panties, he leaned over against the backrest and grabbed the fastenings to his suit with his other hand. He jerked the clips open from his throat all the way down to where the rigid line of his cock began, then dropped back over her. He focused on her with eyes filled with heat and shadow. "Touch me."

Luxi reached up and swept her palms across the smooth skin of his chest, then ran her fingers down his belly. She could feel his other body, his phantom, his ghost, pulsing right under the smoothness of his cybernetic skin. "Oh…"

"Blood and fate, that feels good." He moaned. "Lower. Touch my cock."

His cock? Luxi hesitated.

Leto groaned and his steel eyes burned with shadows. "If I can't fuck you, at least give me your hand."

Luxi bit her lip. He had a point. His hand was already in her pants. It was only fair. And she wanted to. She really, really wanted to feel his cock. She slid her hand down his muscular belly and into his suit. Her fingers brushed against the thick root of his cock. She opened her hand and reached deeper, wrapping her fingers around him. His skin was hot and smooth. She explored his length. He was long, and very thick.

Leto threw his head back and gasped. "Bloody, fucking fate! That is fucking intense! It's like I have two and you're holding them both."

Curious, Luxi pulled him free of his suit. His cock was bone white, hot and marble-hard in her fingers. Leto was a big man. She stroked him, pulling upward toward the flared edge, then slid her thumb across the broad head.

"Oh, shit!" He shuddered and arched back with a gasp, pulling away from her hand. "I can't take it. It's too much." He winced as he tucked himself back onto his suit. "I'm going to have to settle for rubbing against you." He flashed a broad grin then dropped down on top of her. "You don't mind, do you?"

Luxi grinned. "I don't know; I kind of liked the idea of having you go to pieces in my hand."

Leo snorted. "You would." He slid his hands down her body, caught her thighs, and lifted. "Let's see if I can return the favor." His mouth took her nipple and bit down.

Luxi shivered under his teeth then felt his cock nudge and rub against the intimate folds of her body's entrance. She stiffened. "Leto?"

He licked her nipple. "Relax, my dick is still in my pants." He leaned over to take the other nipple into his teeth.

Fate and glory, he was good with his mouth! Luxi moaned. "Then what am I feeling?"

Leto lifted his head and grinned. "My…ah…spirit."

Luxi's mouth opened. His *spirit?*

"I can actually feel how wet you are. I wonder…" He thrust, entering her in one strong lunge, and gasped.

Luxi gasped with him. Regardless of the fact that his *spirit* was in her, rather than the hard cock she'd held, her body was quite convinced that a very hard cock was stretching her, and she hadn't had sex in quite a while. She shifted under him and felt the cock trapped in his suit riding right on her clit. She groaned and her body abruptly moistened, easing the tightness within her.

"That is so strange. I can feel my dick in you but I can also feel my dick in my pants."

Luxi swallowed. "You're telling *me* it's strange?"

He shifted his hips and hissed. "Blood and damnation, you feel good." He pulled back and thrust.

Luxi rolled under him, feeling his hard stroke and yet feeling his rigid cock against her clit, too. Heat coiled tight and hard. She wrapped her legs around his hips purely out of carnal greed. It didn't matter that it wasn't his cock; whatever was in her felt damned good there.

"Damn…" Leto curled his arms under hers and grabbed her shoulders. "I can't tell the difference." He pulled and thrust, and thrust…"It's feels like I'm fucking you."

"Great," Luxi panted and writhed under him. "Because I sure feel like I'm being fucked!" His strokes were hitting something inside and his cock was pressing hard on her clit, jolting her hard and fast toward a powerful climax. Her body shuddered and trembled around him.

Leto panted against her throat. "It feels like you're close to coming, too."

Luxi gasped. "Fastest one I've ever had."

"Good." He slowed down to long delicious strokes and withdrew. "But I don't want you to come yet."

Luxi moaned and ground up against him. "Leto, please?"

"Oh, I like the sound of you begging, but no."

"No?" She twisted her hips.

"No." Leto grabbed her hips to still her. He turned to look at the three writhing on the opposite bench and his mouth set in a hard line.

Bel stared hard at Leto and Luxi, moving exquisitely slow. His fems were panting and writhing in erotic agony, right on the edge of a climax he wouldn't let them have.

Leto nodded at him.

Bel grabbed Orah by the hips and began thrusting ruthlessly hard into her with merciless speed.

Faro, behind him, matched him stroke for stroke, gasping with her thrusts.

All three turned to watch Leto.

Leto held Luxi still under him, thrusting just slowly enough to keep her on the edge and drive her insane. His gaze held, locked on the three moaning across the aisle.

Orah abruptly held her breath and shuddered. Her eyes widened as she stared at Leto and her breath exploded with a mewling cry.

Abruptly, Faro threw back her head and cried out.

Bel grinned and gasped, grabbing tight onto Orah as he thrust and held. His body trembled and he thrust again, releasing a small shout followed by groaning gasps.

Luxi was suddenly aware of power sliding across her skin. It was centered on Leto. Her lesser talent stirred, the part of her that saw phantoms. A cloud of swirling, colorless energy, like heat rising from hot metal, was surrounding him.

Something dark and hungry opened and bloomed within Leto's heart. He drew in a deep breath. The swirling energy dove into him, drawn into his body, and he drank it down, absorbing, and feeding the core of his shadowy heart.

Luxi's mouth fell open. Leto was feeding his ghost on the energy given off by their orgasm.

Leto sighed with deep appreciation. "Yes..." He smiled down at Luxi with the echo of his feeding burning in the heart of his eyes. "Now it's your turn to come."

Chapter Five

Leto pulled Luxi up and sat back against the bench with her straddling his lap. He grinned. "Ready to fuck?"

Luxi grabbed onto his shoulders and moaned as the phantom cock within her shifted. She wasn't sure she wanted to feed his ghost with her orgasm, but her body didn't seem to care. It was tight with erotic tension and it wanted release. She glanced over at the exhausted trio.

Bel and his fems were cuddled in half-naked, sweaty splendor, gently kissing and cuddling in his lap.

Luxi nibbled on her lip. They didn't look at all like they had been harmed.

"Luxi…"

She turned to Leto, only to have her mouth captured in a searing and aggressive kiss. His arms closed tight around her and he pulled her hard against him, bare chest to bare breast.

She shivered and kissed him back. *Fuck it. They weren't hurt; I'll be fine.* She moaned softly and grabbed the shoulders of his suit. Damn it, she wanted to come!

He thrust up into her and moaned into her mouth. He thrust again, then again...

Luxi closed her eyes tight and whimpered in reply. Sitting this way, his cock went deep, and he was big, and hard, and delicious... Heat pooled, rose, and boiled in her core.

Leto groaned and slid his hand down to cup her ass, lifting her, then pushing her down onto his strokes.

She moaned and rocked against him. His cock, phantom or not, struck something electric within her that jolted her toward orgasm with every hard thrust.

Abruptly, he locked his arm around her to hold her still. He tipped her back and his mouth took her nipple. He bit down on the tender peak, then licked away the sting. His hand moved between them, jerking at his suit.

Luxi arched and gasped as his mouth tenderly tortured her nipple.

Leto suddenly lifted her off of his cock and reached between them to bunch the crotch of her panties to one side.

He was moving her panties? The hair on Luxi's neck lifted. "Leto?"

"Not now." He repositioned, and let her fall onto him, shoving back into her wet core. He threw his head back and shuddered. "Fuck!"

Luxi's breath exploded from her lungs. "Leto!" His physical cock was in her. She could feel them both simultaneously filling her.

He groaned and thrust, and thrust..."I'm already...fucking you." His panting breaths cut into his speech. "I'd rather...come...in a nice warm...body...instead of...my pants."

He ground up into her. "God, you feel good." He lifted her against his chest and began to power-thrust hard.

Luxi writhed on the incredible sensation of fullness as he hammered up into her more-than-willing body. "You said...you...wouldn't!"

He bared his teeth, his jaw tight as he thrust. "Sometimes...I lie." He gasped. "You obviously like it. You're dripping...down my balls."

Luxi could only hold on as she was thoroughly and mercilessly fucked. "You're...a beast!"

"Sometimes." He leaned closer to nibble on her throat. "Shouldn't you be...screaming and trying to...escape?"

She shivered under his lips and tilted her head back to give his mouth better access. "Do you want me to?"

His hands closed tight on her ass. "I'd prefer if you didn't."

Luxi groaned and twisted. "Would you stop?"

"Nope." He shuddered, and thrust faster. "Too close...to coming...to stop."

Luxi bit back her building shriek. "Me, too."

"That's my girl!" Leto grinned. "You're about to come."

"Yes," she whimpered. "Glory, *yes!*"

Leto covered her mouth with his, stealing her breath in a ruthless kiss.

Tension broke within her and pleasure exploded in waves of lightning that rampaged through her, leaving violent tremors in their wake. Luxi gasped her frantic cries into Leto's mouth and bucked hard.

His gaze caught hers—and pulled.

Within her heart, something broke free and found a place in his hungry soul. And she didn't care.

She collapsed against his shoulder, panting with repletion. She had never come harder in her life.

Leto held her, his hand sweeping down her spine. "That was phenomenal."

She smiled into his shoulder. "I bet you say that to everybody."

"No, I don't."

"Good." Luxi moaned and lifted to pull away. "Time to get up."

"Not just yet." Leto locked his arms around her hips, holding her tight onto him. "I'm still ejaculating."

Luxi leaned back to look at his face. "What? But, you're a cyborg!"

Leto smiled tiredly. "I was once completely biological. The nanotech just replaced what was already there." He rolled his hips under her and groaned. "So I still come. Thank fate!"

Luxi sucked in a breath. She could feel him pulsing within her. "But you're not biological, so what are you putting in me?"

Leto pursed his lips. "Not quite sure."

Luxi raised her brow. "You don't know?"

He rolled his eyes at her. "The composition of my ejaculate is not something I bothered to have examined." He groaned and lowered his arms, releasing her. "Okay, now my balls are empty."

"Gee, thanks." Luxi rose up and lifted her leg over him, dismounting to stand on trembling legs in the aisle. A clear, viscous liquid slithered down her thighs.

Grinning broadly, Faro held out a moist towelette.

Luxi shot Leto a sour look as she used the towelette to clean up the mess.

He grinned. "We definitely have to do this again sometime soon."

Luxi started fastening her suit, her eyes tight on her fingers rather than the view out the window or the smug cyborg. "We weren't supposed to do it in the first place, remember?"

Leto rose from the bench to fasten his suit. "Oh come on, you enjoyed the hell out of it!"

Luxi winced in guilt. He was right. She hadn't done a whole lot to put a stop to it. In fact, she had been very willing at the end. She sighed. "Look, it doesn't matter, I can't see you again." A stab of regret shot through her.

His mouth tightened. "Why not?"

Luxi shook her head. "I'm only here on layover. I leave in less than thirty hours." To go to a job she was going to loathe.

Leto folded his arms stiffly across his chest. "Don't you want to see me again?" His jaw tightened.

Luxi bit back a smile. He seemed so disappointed. "What? So you can trick me into sex again?"

He gave her a tight smile. "Well, yeah."

She shook her head. "One-track mind, and it's all in the commode."

He raised a brow and gave her a feral grin. "I'm male. Sue me."

The tram suddenly pulled into a station and halted.

Bel and his fems rose from the bench, once again fully dressed, and fully armed. They strode up the aisle toward the exit.

Luxi lifted her head. The tram was supposed to stop every five minutes, but it hadn't. Now that they had…finished, it stopped. She frowned. "Why didn't the tram stop before?"

Leto nodded toward the exit. "His Imperial lordship didn't want the tram to halt, so it didn't. He has the access codes in his array." He tapped a finger against his brow.

Luxi's mouth fell open. "Bel really is a lord?" She reached down to collect her bag from under the bench.

"You didn't know?"

"I wasn't sure. I've never seen an Imperial lord before." She frowned. "He looked really young."

"That's because he had really good genetic engineering." Leto grinned. "He's about twice your age."

She frowned. "You never did tell me what he said, from before."

Leto bit back a smile. "He saw the way you were watching me and asked me…" He took a breath and released it. "If I thought I could seduce you."

Luxi stilled. "And then we kissed."

Leto's brow lifted. "And then *you* kissed *me*."

Luxi felt the hair stand on the back of her neck. "Then you meant to…to fuck me the whole time?"

He shrugged. "Well, yeah. That's what seduction generally means."

She sucked in a sharp breath and her cheeks flushed with heat. It had been a trick from beginning to end. "Goodbye, Leto." She turned and fled the tram.

Luxi strode across the tram station deck toward the lifts on the far wall, moving buoyantly through the low gravity as though through water. She shook her head in painful humiliation. She couldn't believe she had been tricked so easily!

"Luxi!"

Oh, glory, he's yelling for me. Luxi hurried as much as the low gravity would allow. If she could get to the lifts, it would be easy to disappear; this was a big station...

She was jerked to a halt by a hand gripping her wrist. *Shit.*

"Luxi."

She turned to look up at Leto. "What now?"

Leto caught her face in his palms and took her mouth in a swift kiss.

She hesitated, he tasted so good... She jerked her mouth from his and stepped back. "What was that for?"

Leto licked his lips and his mouth set in a hard smile. "You *do* want me."

Her cheeks heated painfully. "So? Why do you care? You already got what you were after."

Leto set his hands on his hips. "I want more."

"Too bad for you! I'm leaving, remember?" Her knuckles whitened on her bag's tow-handle.

"Not immediately, we still have time..."

"No. Absolutely not."

Leto's lips lifted in a sly smile. "I seduced you once; I can do it again."

She jabbed her finger at him. "*You* are a beast! A sneaky, conniving, lying beast!"

"You know me so well!" He grinned shamelessly.

Luxi turned on her heel and stomped into the open lift.

His laughter burned in her ears.

* * *

Luxi stepped out of the lift and into gravity, feeling exhausted. The broad green bands on the walls told her that she had finally reached the hallways in the Garden District. It took her several minutes of walking before she was used to moving in real gravity again. Sticky, sweaty, and tired, she stopped at the first fully equipped facility she found. Luckily, it was only a few minutes' walk away from the lift.

She shoved through the door with a groan of relief. The tastefully appointed, scrupulously clean facility was huge. There was an entire wall of commode stalls and another whole wall of proper water sinks. It was also completely empty. Apparently, this facility didn't see very many people. A door at the far end led to the bathing part of the facility. The long room was lined with small single-occupant vibro-shower stalls.

In one of the small private cubicles, Luxi stripped out of her clothes, leaving them draped over the low bench against the wall. With a heavy sigh, she activated the sonic projection in the stall and the antibacterial lighting winked on. She left the small stall no longer sweaty and sticky, but somehow, she just didn't feel clean. She knew she was cleaner than any water shower could get her, but she never *felt* clean without water.

She shoved her soiled clothes into her bag, stepped into fresh panties and then her dark green jumpsuit. She was going to have to find a laundry facility sometime soon. She only had three ship-suits, and the green one was her last clean one. She fastened the suit closed and pulled out her brush to do battle with the snarls in her red mane.

Everything that had happened since she woke up this morning had really taken a toll on her hair. The shuttle flight in zero-g, the tram station's low gravity, the tram—the sex... A flash of heat stirred in her belly.

Leto's handsome face suddenly filled her thoughts. His kisses had tasted so clean. His ghost had felt so warm and firm, yet oddly like velvet under her fingers. And the way it felt when he'd touched her, exciting her to the breaking point and, finally, taken her...

She was not going to see him again. Regret stabbed through her heart.

Luxi took a deep steadying breath and focused on her snarled curls. *Pay attention to what you have to do, not on what you can't have.* Still, she was glad that she had shared that with him. If she failed to find the future she was looking for, and actually reached her final destination, Leto's kisses were going to be the only brightness in a very long and lonely life.

But her talent for reading the future had led her straight to him.

She frowned. Was it possible that he was actually part of her future? She sighed heavily. She didn't see how. He was not the type that worked anywhere near an office.

The image of the cyborg in a business suit suddenly came to mind.

She smiled and shook her head. Not a chance. He was...what he was, and she was a receptionist in need of a job. It just wasn't possible that he was a part of her future.

After a long and frustrating struggle, she was finally able to twist the wavy mass up into a tight coil and fasten it with her silver clip. Neat and tidy at last, she stepped into her half-boots and closed her bag. It was time to find that kafé.

And her next appointment with the future.

Chapter Six

Luxi pushed through smoked-glass doors and came out of the green-banded corridors onto a railed walkway that bordered on a living forest. Full-sized Terran maple trees arched over the walkway. They grew from rich earth beds only one story straight down. Live birds called and flew among the branches.

She turned left, heading station south, alongside the forest, towing her bag. Forests, gardens, and fields of crops filled the station's distant, curving sides, then climbed up and over the arching ceiling, held firmly rooted by the station's spin-generated gravity. Thin streaks of cloud and passenger shuttles flew upside down across a forest four kilometers away and directly over her head.

A catwalk opened up on her right, leading right through the forest's heart. A posted sign indicated that the concourse was located at the other end. According to the station flyer, most of the kafés could be found in the concourse area.

Perfect. She smiled and headed down the catwalk through the arching trees, completely enchanted.

The concourse was like any other interstellar shopping mall, with rows of exotic shops along a thoroughfare and potted trees and decorative benches scattered everywhere. There wasn't an enormous amount of foot traffic, but what there was, was very colorful. She spotted dozens of different alien races shopping, eating, and chatting along with various human races from all over the Imperium.

Mixed among the shops were a number of crowded kafés, but according to her talent, none of them were where she was supposed to be. With a heavy sigh, Luxi kept walking.

As she reached the far end of the concourse, the station lights dimmed into station sunset, and then station night. Tall, archaic lamp posts of black iron winked on to provide lighting. Overhead, thousands of tiny lights flickered to life, acting as stars in the completely contained world.

The Pouting Mermaid Kafé sat on the very edge of the upper gallery overlooking the formal gardens two stories below. The shop itself was little more than a fancifully nautical roofed counter framed by a pair of potted dwarf-oaks.

A dozen or so small round tables were scattered by the balcony for relaxing patrons, of which there was only one. A young man in a steel-gray, floor-length informal coat lounged casually at one of the tables under the golden glow of a lamppost. He held a cup in one gloved hand and a small fiction-reader in the other.

Within her, chance entwined with opportunity. She had arrived at the right place.

Luxi approached the counter and pulled out her data card. She was simply dying for a cup of kaffa.

The young man behind the counter was busily cleaning one of the antique kaffa brewers that lined the back wall. Artistic cups and mugs perched in nooks on the side walls. He glanced up and smiled. "Hi, I'm Brett. What can I get you?" He was perfectly ordinary. Brown hair, brown eyes, and a slightly rumpled green apron covered his black shirt and trousers.

"Hi, Brett, I'm Luxi." She grinned and gave him her order.

Brett grabbed a huge green mug from the wall and started his machines. "So, Luxi, what brings you to Port Destiny?"

Luxi shook her head. "Just passing through. But I was wondering, would you mind if I borrowed one of your tables to do some fortune-telling?"

Brett glanced over at her, his eyes wide. "Fortune-telling? Here?"

Luxi's brows lifted. "Is there a rule against it?"

Brett curled his lip sourly. "No, it's just that most of the other fortune-tellers hit the kafés closer to the middle of the concourse." He poured a liberal amount of cream into the green mug then filled it with freshly brewed black kaffa. "You any good?"

Luxi grinned. "Better than most."

Brett handed her the steaming mug and lifted his brow. "Sure about that, are you?"

Luxi took the cup in both hands. The hot brew smelled heavenly. "Let's put it this way—my talent got me fired from my last job as an information leak, and I was only the receptionist."

"Whoa..." Brett blinked. "You must be a major talent."

Luxi shrugged. "I have no idea. Unlike normal psi-talents, this one doesn't show up under testing." She smiled. "Want to test it yourself?"

Brett's mouth fell open. "Me? Oh, hell yeah!"

"Pardon me."

"Huh?" Luxi turned and nearly dropped her cup. The young man in the long gray coat stood by her left elbow with his hands tucked behind him. His eyes were as green as the leaves on the trees and seemed brilliant against the deep auburn of his tightly bound hair. The long tail falling over his breast and nearly to his waist was bound in steel-gray ribbon nearly to the end, as though to hide the deep, fiery color. His face was strongly but arrestingly carved, though he seemed young. And his mouth... He had the fullest, most kissable lips Luxi had ever seen.

He quirked up a dark red brow and smiled at Luxi. "May I observe your work?"

Luxi nearly staggered from the effect. *Whoa, that smile should have a warning label.* She swallowed to get her voice back. "That's up to Brett; it's his fortune."

Brett grinned. "Sure, I don't mind. Want a refill while you're here?"

The young man turned to Brett. "That would be wonderful. And, if I may, please put the young lady's order on my tab."

Luxi felt the tiniest shiver. The young man's voice was surprisingly deep and flavored with a rich, exotic accent. He had one of those voices that could recite a grocery list and sound compelling.

He turned to Luxi. "You don't mind, do you?"

"Yes, please! I mean, no; I mean, thank you." Luxi felt her cheeks heat. It was hard to think past that lethal smile.

"You are quite welcome." He gave her a small bow. "I am Amun Verity."

She set her cup on the counter and summoned her best manners. With her hands open and correctly placed on her thighs, she gave him a slightly deeper bow in reply, acknowledging his obviously superior rank. She bit back a smile. Everyone was superior to a receptionist. "I'm honored by your acquaintance, gentle sir. I'm Luxi Emory."

Amun grinned unexpectedly. "Was I that formal?"

Luxi shrugged. "It seemed the right thing to do."

Amun shook his head and his smile shifted to something more relaxed.

"Okay…" Brett glanced from Luxi to Amun. "Can I have my fortune now?"

Luxi turned to Brett with a grin and picked up her mug. "Absolutely. What would you like to know about: a person, a place, or a situation?"

Brett frowned. "Do you need a name?"

"Nope, just a teeny clue; like, my girlfriend, my friend, my boss, work… Stuff like that."

"Oh, that's it?"

"Yep." Luxi was well aware that her smile was smug. "I told you, I'm good."

Brett leaned both elbows on the counter. "My girlfriend; we're having problems."

Luxi turned her head to stare at nothing in particular and reached for her talent. Her inner sight bloomed, allowing her to view the tangled threads of Brett's previous choices and future possibilities. Luxi nodded absently as his story formed, then turned to face him. "Okay, this is what's going on..." She began to recite what the threads told her about his situation with his girlfriend.

Luxi finally stopped to sip her kaffa.

"Oh, wow..." Brett stared at Luxi. "Dead on the money!"

"Very impressive."

Luxi started. Amun had been so still, she had forgotten that was standing right there. She darted a glance his way, and froze.

Amun's gaze was intensely focused, and his smile tight. There was a subtle edge to his expression, as though he had found something truly interesting—and edible. "That is quite a talent."

Luxi swallowed her kaffa and hoped that the heat of her embarrassment didn't show. "Thanks." She cleared her throat and tore her gaze from Amun. If she kept looking at him, she'd fall into his green gaze and forget what she needed to say. She gathered her thoughts and focused on the lines of possibility around Brett. "Okay, now that you know what happened, this is how you fix it..."

Brett refilled Luxi's kaffa and set down a plate with one of their signature desserts. "It's on me." He shook his head. "Wow."

"Thank you!" Luxi took her refilled cup and raised her brow. "I told you I was good."

Brett rolled his eyes. "'Good' does not even begin to describe what you just did."

Luxi sipped her fresh kaffa to cover her smile. It was nice to actually deliver good news, for a change. "So I can borrow a table?"

Brett gave her a wry smile. "Sure, I'll just move a few patrons out of your way." He waved his hand at the empty tables. "I honestly don't know how much money you're going to make here. Tuesday nights are usually quiet, but I'll keep you in kaffa for as long as you're here."

"Thank you." Luxi smiled. "It'll be okay. I only need to make enough for dinner."

"In that case..." Amun bowed slightly to Luxi. "For the price of dinner, I would be honored if you would be so kind as to use your talent to view a situation I find myself in a dilemma over."

Luxi grinned up at Brett. "There, you see?" She turned to Amun and returned his less formal bow. "I'd be honored to be of service." She suddenly shivered as the last thread of synchronicity suddenly fell into place. Luxi blinked up at Amun. She was only a breath away to escaping her doom. She had one more decision to make to achieve it.

And Amun was the key.

Amun's gaze sharpened. "What is it?"

Luxi felt a stillness wash through her as she gazed into his green eyes. "I felt the lines of my own fate changing." It was the absolute truth—and she wanted to swallow the words as soon as she said them.

Amun turned and gestured toward his table by the balcony with one gloved hand. "With your level of talent?" He smiled. "I don't see why not."

Luxi picked up the plate and the cup. Why the hell had she told him that? She shook her head as she walked toward his table. *Too late now.*

Amun held out a chair for her then carefully stepped back.

Luxi caught his cue and deposited her plate and cup on the table. She turned to give him a bow in thanks and sat.

Amun smiled and his brow quirked up. "You have very nice protocol for a receptionist." He gathered the long skirts of his gray coat and sat in the chair on her immediate left.

"Oh, that?" Luxi lifted her shoulder in a small shrug and turned away. He was making her blush again. "The company had a number of off-world customers, so I brushed up on their etiquette."

Amun smiled. "Were they surprised?"

Luxi raised a brow. "I thought they would be, but it was more like they expected it."

Amun nodded. "Then you did it right." He raised a finger. "The only time manners are truly noted is when they are missing."

"Oh…"

Amun leaned back in his chair and lifted his cup. "Now then, I have two parties in contention trying to come to an accord. I would dearly like to know the results of their interaction."

Luxi set down her cup and gazed over his shoulder to clear her mind and view his synchronicities. She felt her sense of perspective shift hard as his choices and decisions flooded her mind with snarl after snarl of complicated threads that raced from the past to the future. She grabbed hold of the table and sucked in a breath as she tried to find the center, the "now" that he occupied.

"Is something wrong?" His voice was soft.

Luxi squinted as she fought through tangle after tangle to find him. "Not wrong, just really complicated." She found his center and began her search for the parties he was inquiring about within the two enormous snarls connected closely to his line. Suddenly, she realized that both parties were, in fact, the snarls. "Oh, wow...big."

Slowly, and carefully, Amun took off his gloves. "Is that so?" He reached out a finger and brushed the side of her hand. "Tell me."

Luxi swallowed. "There's lot there. Do you want their immediate decisions or the possible outcomes?"

"There is only one immediate decision I'm interested in, the one connected directly to me. Find that one decision and follow it to its outcome."

Luxi found the specific thread, followed it, and spoke.

Luxi was shaking as she finished. She let the inner-vision go and reached for her kaffa. Then she noticed that Amun was holding her left hand. Her brow rose. *Okay...*

A strong shiver rocked her, and everything she had told him slipped right out of her head. She didn't think anything of it. Memory loss of her readings was normal. The information she revealed was not hers to know, so it simply slipped away. Though never quite that quickly.

Amun's gaze narrowed. "Do you remember any of what you just told me?"

Luxi stopped with her cup halfway to her lips. "Not a thing. All I remember is a really big and tangled mess. Do you need me to go back and look?"

Amun smiled gently as he released her hand. "No; no, that won't be necessary. I have everything I need."

"Good." Luxi let out a breath. "*You* are a tough read." She sipped her kaffa. It had cooled quite a bit, but it was still heavenly.

Amun leaned back quirked up a brow. "You found me difficult?"

Luxi shook her head. "Not difficult; you just had a lot more than I was used to seeing."

"I dare say…" Amun smiled and rose from his chair. "I believe I owe you dinner?"

"Thank you." Luxi rose with a smile. "But I'm afraid I don't know any of the restaurants."

Amun tilted his head and the golden lamplight gilded his handsome face with gold and shadows. "Actually, I was thinking perhaps of someplace a bit more private."

Private? Luxi felt the slightest touch of alarm slide down her spine. "What exactly do you mean by 'private'?"

Amun smiled warmly. "I find myself loath to share your company." His gaze focused on her. "You don't mind, do you?"

Luxi was caught by the arresting green of his eyes and the luscious curve of his utterly kissable mouth. Did she mind? Really?

Chapter Seven

Amun reached out to take both of Luxi's hands and gently tugged her closer. "There is a quality about you that is not found in many people. Some would find it irresistible."

Irresistible... All rational thought was suddenly consumed by a violent rush of erotic heat. Her pulse suddenly throbbed in her throat and her nipples tightened to burning points. The firestorm of searing physical need stole her breath.

"Luxi..." Amun lowered his head.

Luxi lifted her mouth toward his, consumed by the absolute hunger to taste him. Softness brushed against her lips, then pressure. She opened to his mouth, and her eyes closed. The moist touch of his tongue brushed hers, and took possession. He tasted of expensive kaffa and rich cream with a hint of spice. His hands were so warm.

"Yes," he whispered against her mouth. "Oh, yes..." He freed one of her hands and slid his arm around her waist, pulling her up against him. He angled his head and his tongue swept hers boldly, urgently, encouraging her to taste him more fully.

She moaned softly and answered his unspoken command with strong parries of her tongue against his. Her free arm went around his hips. His coat was soft under her fingers. His body was warm, lean, and hard against hers. His scent was clean and richly flavored with masculine arousal. And unbearably exciting.

He curled her captured hand between them at her heart then lifted his hand from her waist. The clip in her hair was tugged free and her mane tumbled to her waist in a riot of unbound curls. His finger slid under the heavy mass and he groaned. He grasped a handful at the base of her neck.

An illicit bolt of brutal excitement stabbed straight down and moisture dampened her panties. Luxi gasped. Her fingers clenched in his coat and she pressed eagerly against the firm ridge of his erection that rubbed enticingly against her hip.

His fingers tightened in her hair, holding her still as he lifted his lips from hers. He smiled. "You like this," he whispered. "You like being captured, being...taken."

She trembled in his firm hold. She couldn't think past the fire that throbbed in her core, not even to agree. She shifted and the erection under his loose trousers nudged between her thighs. Want and need raked though her. She could not stop herself from rubbing against him.

Amun smiled and brushed his lips lightly, teasingly against hers. "Oh, you are going to be so much fun."

"Amun, what are you doing out of your suite? It's not safe."

Amun abruptly pushed away from Luxi.

Luxi gasped as her mind suddenly returned to her in a tangle of heat and confusion. What had just happened?

Amun blushed and frowned past her shoulder in annoyance. "Your timing is utterly inconvenient."

"So I see." A tall man in a dark suit strode past Luxi, toward Amun. A long tail of distinctive silver hair fell to the center of his back. He came to a sudden stop and turned around. His silver eyes widened, then narrowed. His face was cast in deep shadows under the lamplights, but there was no mistaking who he was. "Well, hello, Luxi. Cheating on me already?"

Leto? Luxi winced and turned away in painful embarrassment. Fate and glory, it figured... The only two men she'd kissed in several cycles *would* know each other.

Amun frowned at Leto. "You know Luxi?"

"Quite well, actually." Leto's smile was thin and sharp. "We shared a tramway car."

Oh, you bastard... Her cheeks heated with a sudden rush of hot memory.

Amun peered at Luxi and his brows rose. "I...see."

Luxi scowled at the deck. There was simply no way to explain her actions. Fine, then, she wouldn't bother. She lifted her chin and held out her hand to Amun. "My hair clip, please?"

"Of course." Amun reached into his pocket and placed the clip in her palm. His fingers brushed hers and heat shimmered from his touch.

Luxi shivered just slightly and pulled her hand away. She took a wary step back from both men and began the task of coiling her hair back up.

"So, Amun, were we having fun?" Leto's voice dripped with sarcasm.

Amun lifted his chin and folded his arms across his chest. "You realize that you are embarrassing Luxi?"

"I'm trying to embarrass you!" Leto took a step closer to Amun and his mouth thinned to a hard line. "You think I don't know what you were doing?"

Amun looked away.

Leto's hands tightened to fists. "That better be guilt I'm seeing."

Luxi frowned. What was going on? From the way Leto was glaring and the way Amun refused to look at him, you would think they were lovers. "So, just how well do you two know each other?"

"Not nearly well enough." Amun shot a narrow glare at Leto.

"Amun, if you want me to play villain, you know better than most that I am very qualified for the part." Leto lowered his brows and folded his arms. "Are you ready to go back?"

Amun stared fixedly at Luxi. "I will do so when I have what I seek."

Leto's mouth curled in a tight smile. "Did you try asking?"

"This? From you?" Amun raised a sarcastic brow at Leto. "Did *you* ask?"

Leto scowled then sighed. "You have a point." His hands dropped to perch on his hips and he nodded at Luxi. "Amun is my employer."

Luxi choked. "He's your *employer?*"

Amun snorted. "However, there seems to be some doubt as to who is actually in charge."

Leto rolled his eyes. "Luxi, I need to get him back to the suite. Why don't you come with us?"

Amun started tugging on his gloves. "I would be most obliged, and I do owe you dinner."

"Go to your suite?" Luxi crossed her arms. "What? So you can both seduce me?"

Leto pursed his lips and glanced toward Amun. "Well, yes."

Luxi blinked. "You're admitting it?"

Leto shrugged. "I tell the truth on occasion."

"Don't believe a word." Amun suddenly smiled. "He's the one being in the entire Imperium that can actually lie to a professional telepath."

"You would know." Leto snorted. "Since you're one of them."

Luxi reeled in shock. *Amun is a professional-grade telepath?* She sucked in a sharp breath. So that's what had happened. Amun had used his telepathic talent to magnify her attraction to him into full-blown sexual obsession. She aimed a glare at Amun. "You rolled my mind—you sneak!"

Amun winced and turned away.

"'Sneaky' does not begin to describe him." Leto's smile broadened. "Amun has control issues."

Amun raised a brow at Leto. "You don't seem to mind my 'control issues.'"

Leto raised a sarcastic brow. "Says you."

Amun lowered his gaze. "Am I so terrible a master?"

Leto sighed. "No, you're not terrible. I've had terrible." He lowered his brows in a glare. "But then, I can resist your mind-control tricks—unlike Luxi."

Luxi lifted her chin and folded her arms. "So, why did you roll me?"

"You were already attracted to me." Amun shrugged. "And I wanted you." His chin lowered and he focused on Luxi. "I still do."

Luxi felt a touch of pull from his gaze and hastily averted her eyes. Glory and fate, he was impressively strong. She was normally resistant to telepaths. "Do you mind?"

"My apologies." Amun smiled self-deprecatingly. "And don't be impressed. Knowing exactly what someone thinks of you at all times can be very tiring."

Leto grinned. "That's why he runs around with me. He can't read a thought in my head."

Amun raised a brow. "As if you *had* a thought in your head to read?"

Luxi rolled her eyes. "Try knowing what will happen with every decision you make."

Amun tilted his head and his brows rose. "You do possess quite a talent."

Luxi raised her brow and smiled in spite of herself. "Want to trade?"

"That's not the only talent she has." Leto moved to Luxi's side and caught her wrist. "Amun, take her hand, I want to try something."

Luxi glanced at Amun and tugged at her captured hand. "Leto!"

"Relax. He's not going to roll you." Leto raised a brow at Amun. "Is he?"

Amun sighed and pulled off his gloves. "I will endeavor to restrain myself."

Luxi gave in with a heavy sigh. "Fine, whatever." It wasn't as if she had anywhere near the strength to break the cyborg's grip.

Amun closed his warm fingers around Luxi's hand. "What is it?"

Leto released Luxi's wrist and moved behind her to drop his hands on her shoulders. "Tell me what you feel."

Amun frowned. "All right…"

Luxi felt Leto's warm familiar body pressed tight against hers. She couldn't help the curl of pleasure that arose in her.

Leto set his chin on Luxi's shoulder. His breath was warm in her ear. "Missed me?"

Luxi snorted. "You wish."

Amun lifted his chin. "I'll have you know, she just lied."

Luxi ground her teeth. "Amun!"

Leto chuckled. "Oh, I know."

Luxi felt Leto's arms slide down to wrap around her waist in a snug embrace, even though his hands were still gripping her shoulders. She sucked in a breath and looked down. She could see a pair of colorless arms around her. They had only the slightest haze about them, so they appeared a little indistinct, but they felt incredibly solid. They were from his spirit—his ghost.

Amun licked his lips. "Are you perhaps holding her around the waist?"

"Yes." Leto stared hard at Amun. "You can feel that?"

"Actually, I think I can see it." Amun frowned. "Now, that *is* interesting."

Leto's arms tightened around Luxi. "Can you feel me at all?"

His frowned deepened. "Yes…yes I do, as though there are two of you, one inside the other. I can almost grasp…"

"That's my spirit—my ghost." Leto grinned. "You're a telepath, but you can't read me. Luxi is sensitive to ghosts, so we can feel each other. When you read her, you pick me up in the process."

Amun raised a dark red brow. "Fate and glory, she's a conduit!" He raised a brow at Leto, then focused on Luxi. "I'm beginning to suspect that Luxi is a major talent."

Leto's smile was predatory. "She's definitely strong enough to act as a buffer between us."

Amun froze, his wide gaze locked on Leto. "You mean you're willing to…?"

Leto smiled. "I'm more than willing if you are."

Amun's brows lowered and his smiled. "I can't wait."

Luxi frowned. "What are you two talking about?"

"Sex," both men answered as one. Abruptly, they laughed.

Luxi glanced from one to the other. "You mean you haven't…?

"Only once." Amun's hand tightened on hers. "When we first met."

Luxi raised a brow. "Once?" She didn't see how that was possible. Both of them seemed overwhelmingly determined when it came to getting laid. "Nothing since?"

Amun pinned Leto with a hard stare. "He's afraid of hurting me."

Leto glared right back. "The one time we did, I nearly killed you!"

Luxi frowned. Leto's ghost fed on the energy generated by orgasm. She had barely felt him when he fed from hers, but that was after three other people had already climaxed. How much did he need?

Amun raised his brow. "If I remember correctly, you were *trying* to kill me at the time."

Luxi blinked. "He was trying to kill you?"

Amun shrugged. "Leto's previous profession was 'assassin.'" He cleared his throat. "I seduced him."

Assassin? Luxi's mouth fell open. "He was...you *seduced* an assassin?"

"I woke up to find a very handsome man sitting right on top of me." Amun smiled. "How could I resist?"

"I don't know how he did it, but he rolled me." Leto turned away. "And then my hunger took over. I nearly drained him dry."

"I recovered." Amun's tone was very dry.

Leto ground his teeth. "After three days of almost full-body contact!"

Amun smiled. "I wasn't complaining."

Leto rolled his eyes and sighed.

Luxi frowned. "Leto, if you were trying to kill him, why didn't you?"

Leto's arms tightened around her. "I changed my mind." He shot a narrow look at Amun. "Though sometimes I seriously wonder why."

Amun nodded at Luxi. "Now he's in my employ, as my personal bodyguard."

"Bodyguard—my ass!" Leto shot a glare at Amun. "I'm more like a nanny! I leave you alone for an hour and you sneak out to a completely undefended public area!"

Amun's brows lowered and his hand tightened on Luxi's. "You could have stayed."

Leto's eyes narrowed. "You knew damned well that I needed to hunt. If I didn't, my needs would have driven me to feed on you!"

Amun focused past Luxi's shoulder. "Leto."

Leto scowled, meeting his gaze. "What?"

Amun lifted his chin. "You are not the only one with appetites."

Luxi felt a spear of heat pass right through her heart to dive straight into Leto. She gasped.

Leto stiffened. "Amun?"

The distinct ridge of a sudden and firm erection pressed against the upper swell of Luxi's butt. Leto was hard and getting harder. Her panties dampened with a spat of cream.

Amun's eyes narrowed as he smiled. "I said that I would not roll Luxi; you, on the other hand..." He stepped in close. "I intend to show no mercy."

"Amun, I already agreed." Leto swallowed hard. "You don't need to do it this way."

"Perhaps not. Let's just say that I am not in the mood to take chances on you becoming suddenly distracted." Amun's hands slid up Luxi's arms to her shoulders until he brushed Leto's hands. "I have waited long enough." His fingers tightened over Leto's, pressing both their hands into Luxi's shoulders. "I want you." He focused on Luxi. "I want you both."

Lust rolled up from Luxi's belly in a hot, thick, syrupy fog. It wasn't coming from Amun; it was her body's reaction to the scent of warm leather laced with the rich perfume of two aroused males.

Amun took that last step, closing the distance and pressing Luxi back with his hips, locking her between their warm, firm bodies and their hard cocks. Amun's hands slid down to Leto's hips, embracing them both.

Luxi could barely breathe past the heat rolling through her. Leto's cock was a thick, hot bar against the top of her butt. Amun's cock was a broad prod against her belly. Her clit throbbed with heat and her core clenched in hunger. She suddenly, desperately wanted to spread her legs a little wider, to give both their cocks room between her thighs, to give them access and let them in.

Amun's gaze narrowed on Luxi. He reached for the clip in her hair and pulled it free. Her red curls uncoiled and flowed over her left shoulder and Leto's arm. He pocketed the clip. Both men leaned down to press their noses into her unbound hair.

It was painfully erotic. She leaned her head back against Leto's shoulder, holding her breath to keep from moaning, and her eyes closed.

"Luxi."

She opened her eyes to find Amun's green gaze locked on hers. He leaned close and his lips brushed hers. She opened for him and his tongue swept in, taking her mouth in a hungry kiss. She couldn't have stopped her moan if she'd tried.

Leto drew in a deep breath and his hands tightened around her.

Amun released her mouth with a soft smile. His gaze shifted to Leto. He leaned past Luxi and brushed his mouth against Leto's.

Leto opened his mouth to receive Amun's kiss and groaned. His spirit hand slid up from Luxi's waist to cup her breast.

She sucked in a breath. She could feel the warmth of his hand caressing her bare skin as though the cloth of her suit wasn't even there.

Leto groaned into Amun's mouth and tugged on her nipple.

Erotic lightning stabbed downward to her clit. Her core throbbed hungrily and she shifted restlessly between them.

Amun's hips pressed tighter against her and he shifted, grinding the erection behind his loose trousers against her softness until it slipped downward and nudged between her thighs and up against her clit.

Behind her, Leto shifted against her butt, his cock hard and insistent, but she was pressed too tightly between them.

Amun pulled back, releasing Leto's mouth. He licked his lips, with his hooded gaze focused on Leto.

Leto gasped for breath and his body trembled as hard as Luxi's.

"Good." Amun reached up to grab the hair at Luxi's neck, and the base of Leto's silver tail. "Let's all take a walk, shall we?" He tugged, jerking them both apart to stand on either side of him. "A short walk." He pushed.

They walked.

Chapter Eight

Amun's grip on their hair was unrelenting as he guided Luxi and Leto across the balcony plaza and into a lift. They stepped within and he turned them around to face the reflective door. "Ground level."

Leto reached out and pressed the button.

Luxi took a sharp breath. What in glory had she just gotten herself into? "Amun…" The hand tightened in her hair.

"Don't. I can feel the raw lust rolling off of you."

Luxi winced. He was right. She was so aroused she was trembling, but some of that was good, healthy fear. She'd never been with two men at the same time before. "But, I've never…"

"I realize this is all very new for you." Amun's hand loosened in her hair and his smile softened. "We will not be inconsiderate." His glance shifted to Leto. "But I will not be denied."

The lift doors slid back, opening to the deep shadows of the formal gardens.

"Shall we?" Amun's voice was pleasant, and firm.

Prodded by the fingers knotted in her hair, Luxi stepped out of the lift cautiously. She couldn't see the ground. Amun's tight hold kept her head up.

Leto was silent and wide-eyed on Amun's other side.

They stepped forward into the night-enshrouded formal gardens. The flagged path was lined with tall boxed hedges, topiary trees, and small footlights. Crickets sang in the surrounding darkness. The smell of earth and living green perfumed the air. The internal sky was dotted with distant lights that shone like stars.

Amun guided them off the main walk and onto a narrow side path that ran alongside the tall hedges of the maze. He urged them into a sudden turn. They walked into a hedge-walled, enclosed alcove with small lights along the ground. A low bench of ornate white marble commanded the very center.

Amun released them. "Disrobe."

Luxi turned to face them, her pulse racing and her mouth dry.

Amun reached for the buttons on his long gray coat. It opened, revealing a long-sleeved dress shirt of charcoal silk. He tossed the coat over the bench and lifted his chin to unbutton his shirt.

Staring at Amun, Leto reached for his fastenings. His shimmering suit parted with incredible speed. Bladed weapons were drawn from hidden sheaths as if by magic. He set them under the bench then sat down to pull off his boots.

Amun slid the charcoal shirt off, revealing deceptively broad shoulders and a lightly furred chest with nipples tightened to hard points. Deep shadows played across the sleek muscles and defined a slender line of dark hair that trailed down his flat stomach. He tossed the shirt to the ground and reached for the button to his trousers.

Leto stood and pulled the suit from his shoulders, revealing ghost-pale skin.

Amun swallowed visibly, his hands frozen on the button to his trousers. "Do you have any idea how truly beautiful you are?" His voice was husky and deep.

Leto smiled. "Am I?" He stripped out of his leather in one long pull. His well-defined, arrogantly masculine body and the strong, smooth arc of his pale cock glowed in the shadows like sculpted marble.

Oh, yes... Luxi stared at Leto's incredible form and swallowed hard. *Oh, yes, he was...* He was blindingly beautiful.

Amun held Leto's gaze with eyes that were dilated to thin green bands around broad pits of darkness. "What do you think?" His smile was strained. He opened his loose trousers, letting them fall down his strong thighs. His blushing and rigid cock jutted from a discreet nest of dark curls. The graceful curve stretched upward to his navel. He reached down to collect his trousers and dug into the pocket for a small squeeze tube, then tossed his trousers over his shirt.

Luxi had to close her mouth. Glory, they were both beautiful. Okay, she was really going to do this. She swept her long mane behind her. Her shaking fingers fumbled with her suit's fastenings. She was out of her mind, but...

Leto caught Luxi's hands and tugged her close. "What is taking you so long?" He smiled as he brushed her fingers away from the fastenings.

"I was..." Luxi's breath nearly stopped. All that naked magnificence less then a hand span away. She focused on his expressive mouth in helpless fascination and raw yearning.

He focused on her face and his eyes dilated wide, the steel of his eyes barely visible around the dark pit where the shimmer of his ghost dwelled. He lowered his mouth and took her lips in a sudden, devouring kiss.

Luxi gladly parted her lips. His tongue stroked strongly against hers, hot, wet, exciting, and hungry. She moaned. His fingers raced down her suit's fastenings and her suit opened. Cool air swept across her skin.

His mouth drifted to her jaw, then lower. His warm hands slid within her suit. "Off, off..." His breath came in swift pants. His palms drifted down her back, pushing the suit from her shoulders down to her waist. His teeth scored her throat. He impatiently tugged her arms free. His mouth opened on her shoulder and he bit down with bruising force.

Luxi gasped and pushed his shoulder to shove him back. "Leto!"

Leto released her shoulder with a wince. "Sorry," he whispered hoarsely. "I'm having trouble with my control." He knelt and continued to force her suit downward. His clever tongue, soft lips, and nipping teeth explored the revealed flesh of her breasts and belly, drawing shivers and moans. He tugged impatiently until he reached her boots. He lifted her foot.

Luxi grabbed onto his shoulders for balance as her boots were tugged off and tossed. Her suit was dragged all the way down and off.

Leto's hand caught in her panties, tugging them down and off. On his knees, he stared at the ginger curls covering her mound, his eyes wide and dark. He licked his lips and leaned forward.

"Leto."

Leto stopped. He turned on his knees to glare at Amun.

"Patience." Amun, naked and magnificently hard, held out his hand. "Luxi, come here."

Leto stood in one smooth motion.

Luxi crossed her arms and moved past Leto toward Amun.

Amun smiled as he caught at Luxi's hands. "Don't." He pulled them away from her breasts. "You have nothing to be ashamed of." He led her to the white marble bench and spread out his coat. "Straddle it and lie back." He held her hands as she lifted her leg over and sat down, steadying her as she leaned back.

Luxi pulled her hair out from under her and let the red curls spill to the ground. His coat was silky against her back, but the bench beneath it was hard stone. It was also far wider than it had looked. She had to spread her legs wide to get her toes to touch the ground. She took a deep breath and glanced over at Amun.

Amun lifted his chin at Leto. "Straddle the bench facing Luxi. This time, you are my mount."

Leto raised his brows and moved toward the bench. "No foreplay?"

Amun's lips curled in a sharp smile. "Do you really want another delay?"

Leto focused on Luxi, his mouth tight and his silver eyes still wide and dark. "I see your point."

"Thought you might."

Leto lifted his leg over the bench and sat, then reached down to lift her legs over his spread thighs. He leaned down, grasping the bench on either side of her shoulders. His cock pressed against the curls of her mound as he brushed her mouth with his. "I'll try to be gentle, but I am very close to losing it," he whispered.

Luxi smiled up at him. "That's okay. I'm close to losing it, too."

"One thing more." Humor laced Amun's voice as knelt at their side and held up a gold hoop too small for a bracelet but far too large for a finger ring.

Leto sucked in a breath. "I am *not...*"

Amun's smile was predatory as he pushed Leto to sit up. "Yes, you are."

Luxi frowned. "What is that?"

Amun wrapped his hand around Leto's cock and gave it a strong pull. "This is a cock ring." He slid his hand back down and pulled again.

Leto tilted his head back. He gasped and his hips jerked. "Son of a bitch!"

"It will keep him from climaxing." Amun pressed his fingers into the ring and the metal parted to become a slightly elastic band.

Luxi blinked. The ring had to be made of mimetic metal infused with nanites that would allow it to shift between solid and elastic.

Amun wrapped the gold band around the base of Leto's thick cock, behind his balls, drawing a moan from Leto's lips. Amun glanced at Luxi. "At least until I'm ready to let him."

Leto sucked in air past his clenched teeth. "I hate those things!"

Amun raised a brow. "Really?" He picked up a small tube from where he had set it in the grass and squeezed a thick coating of gel onto his palm. "I find them quite delightful."

Leto glanced at Amun's cock, then shot him a narrow glare. "You're not wearing one."

Amun smiled. "Yet." He set down the tube and lifted another gold ring. He grasped his cock with the gel-slick palm and stroked himself. "I am in no mood to lose it the moment I have what I have waited nearly a year to get." He coated himself thoroughly with the clear gel, then opened the ring and closed the resulting band around the base of his balls. He groaned.

Luxi swallowed and felt a fine tremor run through her. She was going to do this. She was going to have sex with two men. Two of the most beautiful men she had ever seen. She could feel her excitement, her cream, gathering and sliding from her body to the coat below her. She pressed her hands over Leto's where they rested on her wide-open thighs.

Amun rose to his feet then strode around to straddle the bench behind Leto. His hands cupped Leto's pale shoulders as he leaned over him. His gaze was hot on Luxi's face. "Mount her."

Leto's eyes widened just a hair and he leaned up then over Luxi. One hand gripped the bench by her shoulder. He gave her a quick sardonic smile. "Yes, master." His cock slid back across her ginger curls, then nudged at her damp and aching flesh.

Luxi felt her breath catch and arched up on instinct alone.

Leto thrust. In a swift, voluptuous rush, he sheathed himself fully.

They both moaned.

Amun choked, his eyes widening and his fingers digging into Leto's shoulders.

Luxi rolled her hips under him, feeling the flesh and the spirit within his flesh filling her at once with heat and darkness. She caught his shoulder and pulled him down to her even as she rose from the bench to feel more of him.

Leto dropped down over her and his mouth took her breast. He sucked greedily on her engorged nipple even as one of his hands slid down to cup her ass cheek.

Luxi moaned, scorched by his mouth, his tongue, and his teeth on her excited flesh.

Abruptly, Leto stilled, his entire body tensing.

"Push out," Amun said softly.

Leto's head lifted from her breast and his eyes closed tight. A groan escaped him. He inched forward over her, arching slightly upward.

Above and behind him, Amun's eyes were narrowed to green slits as he sighed. "Yes, oh, yes…"

Below them, Luxi felt Leto's body rock with impact as Amun sheathed himself in Leto.

Leto released a gasp. "Amun, you are not a small man."

Amun groaned. "Nor are you." He thrust. His impact transferred to Leto and drove Leto's cock hard into Luxi.

Luxi gasped and Leto gasped with her.

Amun groaned. "Oh, that was a nice clear impression from both of you."

Leto snorted. "I'm glad you're enjoying your ride in our heads."

"Oh, I am." Amun smiled. "Want to join me?"

Luxi felt the curl of vibrant heat from Amun's mind flooding her with his telepathic impressions. Suddenly she could feel Amun's cock in the hot, tight grip of Leto's ass and the wet slick grip of her own cunt around Leto's cock, in addition to the thick delicious fullness of Leto's cock within her. Lust coiled tight within her, compounded by the raging need from both men threaded with the real affection they had for each other. And were beginning to have with her.

"Now that we are all in this together..." Amun grabbed hold of Leto's tailed mane, drawing Leto's head up and back, pulling him upright as he rolled Leto's tail around his fist. "Shall we fuck?"

Leto winced and caught Luxi around the hips. "Amun, I can't... Not this way."

Luxi could feel the tension in Leto's body as he strained against the fisted grip in his hair compounded with the physical need to thrust into her body

"You're not." Amun cupped Leto's hip in one hand. "I am doing the fucking." He dug his feet into the grass and pulled, causing Leto to withdraw.

Luxi moaned. Locked in the telepathic link, she could feel the tight, near-painful fullness of Amun's cock lodged in Leto's ass, along with the bite of his fingers in Leto's hip and then the delicious, slow withdrawal mixing with her own pleasure as Leto's cock slid partway from her.

Amun shoved forward, driving himself into Leto, who drove into Luxi. "I'm fucking the both of you." He pulled back, drawing Leto from Luxi, and thrust again, swifter, harder, and deeper...

Luxi lifted her hips to receive Leto's driven strokes. She groaned as each hammering thrust struck something deep and delicious within her.

The echoes of pleasure slid from mind to mind to mind. Raw animal need rolled over all three of them, bowing them with tension, heat, and coiling fire. Sweat formed and slid across heated skin as moans, gasps, and groans filled the small alcove, along with the sound of wet flesh striking wet flesh.

Grunting with effort, Amun drove the merciless thrusts that Leto delivered as Luxi writhed beneath them, feeling the building tightness of a climax all three were going to share. Whoever climaxed first would set off the cascade in the other two.

And they fucked.

Amun suddenly shoved Leto down over Luxi.

Luxi reached up to clutch at Leto, desperate to feel his skin on hers even as his mouth descended on her breasts in a greedy hunger echoed in both men. Leto's hand gripped the bench over her head as he rocked into Amun's thrusts and let the impact drive him into Luxi's hungry wet core.

And they fucked.

From the heat growing fast in her belly within the echoes of Amun's and Leto's pleasure, compounded by the nips on her breasts and the hard suckling on her nipples, Luxi strongly suspected she would climax very soon.

Amun lifted higher, forcing Leto to lie flat over Luxi, and began to power his thrusts, increasing his speed and depth.

Leto gasped and drove faster into Luxi.

Through the telepathic link, Luxi felt the burn in Amun's balls as his body tried to climax and the snug ring prevented it.

Locked into the link with them, Leto also tried to release and was prevented by his ring.

Luxi felt the sudden clench of her own body notching tighter toward climax. She writhed in vicious pleasure, balanced on the very edge even as both men were driven back from theirs.

And they fucked.

Locked in each other's minds, their shared pleasure drove them upward toward writhing, blinding madness. Their moans became gasping cries.

"Enough." Amun groaned at Leto's back. "Take off your ring."

"About fucking time!" Leto sat up and pulled from Luxi's body with a harsh groan. He grasped the ring around the base of his cock. The mimetic metal parted and he dropped it on the grass. "Damned thing!" He caught Luxi around the thighs and surged back into her.

Luxi gasped and arched. Without the ring, Leto was seated more deeply within her body.

Amun dropped his ring on the grass and had Leto lean over. He groaned.

Leto closed his eyes and sucked in a breath. His eyes opened and he focused on Luxi. "Now?"

Amun grinned at his shoulder. "Send her over."

Luxi shivered at his words.

Leto's hand slid between their bodies. He slicked his fingers in her generous cream then found her swollen clit. He rubbed, quickly and insistently. His fingers delivered lightning bolts of erotic fire that echoed through all three.

Amun's breath came in harsh pants. "Come for us. Come for us all."

Luxi bowed up under them and drew in a breath she couldn't release.

Leto bit down hard on her nipple.

Luxi released her breath on a howl. She exploded in a firestorm of ruthless and rapturous pleasure, feeling her own body's pulsing grip around Leto as she squeezed his cock, begging for his release.

Leto stilled briefly, caught in her climax, then Amun stilled, equally caught. Each man threw back his head and shouted in the ruthless grip of sudden, unstoppable release.

The white fire of backlashed ecstasy raged through Luxi's mind, violently hammering her back up and forcing her over into another rolling wave of body-shattering climax, and then another. Her screams echoed their hoarse shouts as she drowned in the liquid pleasure of both cocks pumping cum into the moist, hot, tight places they were buried. Something deep and painfully beautiful sparked between both men and arced across the link. Leto leaned back to catch hold of Amun, and kissed him. Their mouth worked as the last echoes of climax shimmered around and through them all.

Luxi's sight ran and smeared as tears spontaneously erupted and silently ran down her cheeks. She held her breath to keep from disturbing them as her heart tried to shatter in her chest.

It was love. They were very much in love.

Something she had never felt herself.

Leto abruptly released Amun to lean down over Luxi. He smiled, and kissed her, very, very gently.

Chapter Nine

Luxi wiped her eyes and panted, thoroughly worn out as she sprawled beneath Leto's gasping and heavy body. It had been the most brutally erotic thing she had ever experienced. Tremors shook her with tiny echoes of pleasure.

Amun panted and sat up, leaning his head back with his eyes closed. "Imagine if we had taken the time for foreplay?"

Leto groaned and shifted atop Luxi. "I don't think I would have survived."

Amun stroked Leto's shoulder. "There is only one way to find out." He sucked in a deep breath and leaned over to one side. "Luxi, are you all right?"

Luxi was barely able to turn her head to look at him. "I think so."

Amun smiled. "How are your administrative skills?"

Her what? Luxi blinked. "Huh?"

Amun lowered his chin and a chuckle escaped. "Do you have the training to be a personal assistant?"

"Oh..." It took two full breaths before Luxi was able to conceive of an answer, never mind verbalize it. "I have the array and I've done some assistant work."

Amun's smile was wry. "Would you consider being mine?"

Luxi went very still as synchronicity shimmered, stretched high and tight in the back of her mind. "What?"

Leto lifted his head. "He's asking if you want a job." He turned and gave Amun a crooked grin. "With us."

Luxi struggled to rise and Leto caught her by the arms to help her sit up. She focused on Amun. "Are you serious?"

Amun smiled. "Absolutely."

Leto snorted. "I hope you realize he likes to sleep with his staff?"

Luxi raised her brow at Leto. "No, really?" Her voice was very dry.

Amun's head came up. "Leto!"

Leto reached down to grab his suit. "Well, you do!"

Amun shrugged into his shirt. "Only you."

"Then you don't intend to sleep with your secretary?" Leto nodded at Luxi.

Amun sighed. "You have a point, seeing as I can't sleep with my pilot without her."

Luxi blinked at Leto. "You're a pilot, too?"

Leto shrugged as he rose from the bench. "Pilot, bodyguard..." He shot a sharp smile at Amun. "Babysitter."

Amun gave him an equally sharp smile. "Lover." He lifted his chin to catch Luxi's eye. "Think carefully. I have a very tight and varied schedule."

Leto grinned. "He means, we move around a lot and rarely see anyone but each other for long periods of time."

Luxi glanced down at the grass and then looked up at the winking lights of the distant ceiling. "I never really had much of a social life." She turned to look into Amun's green eyes and let her gaze drift over Leto's pale profile. Her choice had been made the moment she took the data card from Gentle-fem Symposia's hand. She hadn't known where it would lead, not really, but a future with these two men was definitely something she could live with. And if she was lucky, perhaps she could acquire a small corner of their hearts, too. She smiled up at Amun. "I think I'd like working for you."

Amun's gaze narrowed on her. "Then you consent to my service?"

Leto peered sharply over his shoulder. "Amun, that's..."

Amun shot him a narrow glare. "Don't interfere."

Leto turned away and stepped into his suit.

Luxi's gaze flicked from one to the other. "I consent."

Leto winced.

Amun smiled. "Then by the power I represent, I accept you into my personal attaché."

Leto sighed and smiled tiredly at Luxi. "Welcome to the insanity."

Amun rose from the bench with a groan. "As soon as we get you up to the suite, I'll have you registered and your clearances set."

Leto leaned back and rolled his shoulders. "She needs her translation programs updated, too."

Luxi winced. That was an understatement.

Amun picked up some of his discarded clothing. "I'll see to that and anything else that needs upgrading."

With much groaning and wincing, they dressed.

As they rode the lift back up to the concourse level, it seemed the most natural thing in the world for Luxi to simply lean against Amun's left side even as Leto leaned against Amun on the right. Luxi felt warm, cozy, and relaxed. More relaxed than she had ever been. She felt…safe.

Amun closed his arms about them both, his hand absently stroking Luxi's arm.

The lift doors opened.

Luxi suddenly felt probability snap into actuality with the blow of a hammer. Vincent was somewhere on the station and he was close—and getting closer with each breath. Possibilities lashed at her. According to what she was reading, Vincent was a danger to both Amun and Leto, but he didn't know them—yet. Despair washed through her. If she stayed with them, Vincent would find them, and hurt them. They would be safer if she left them immediately.

Luxi lunged out of the lift at a run. She had to find a place to hide, and fast, but she needed her bag. It was still sitting over by the kaffahouse counter where she'd left it.

"Luxi!" Leto shouted from behind her. "Where are you going?" He caught up with her before she'd made it a third of the way across the balcony, grabbing her wrist to jerk her to a halt. "Luxi, wait!"

"Leto, let go!" She turned and tugged at her wrist. "Something came up; I have to go!"

"Luxi, what's wrong?" Amun caught her by the other wrist and hissed. "Who is this man hunting you?"

Luxi flinched. Amun must have plucked the thought from her mind. "His name is Vincent." Her talent spun around her. "Amun, don't let him find you. He can hurt you."

Amun snorted. "I am more difficult to hurt than you think."

"And he'll have to go through me first." Leto grinned nastily.

Luxi stared at him. "Leto, you are in more danger than he is."

Leto's fingers tightened on her wrist. "What?"

"He calls himself a monk. He's possessed by a ghost that devours spirits." She tugged at her arm. "Amun, please, let me go…"

Leto frowned. "A monk?"

"Sounds like an Avatar." Amun frowned at Leto. "You could be in real danger."

"An Avatar?" Leto snorted. "Is that all? I've dealt with ghost-hunters before."

"Have you now?" The voice was deep and frighteningly familiar.

An icy wash of terror flowed down Luxi's spine.

Amun released her with a gasp.

Luxi turned and froze.

"I've been looking everywhere for you, girl." Vincent stepped from the deep shadows, tall and menacing in a floor-sweeping black coat. His shoulder-length sable hair gleamed with streaks of blood red, and his features seemed harsh and barbaric under the lamplight. His eyes had deep smudges from sleepless exhaustion under them, and writhing shadows within them. His smile reeked of a feral triumph that did not look natural to his face.

Leto stepped in front of Luxi and Amun. Framed in a pool of light cast by the decorative lampposts, his suit shimmered with midnight rainbows and his hair gleamed with frost. "Vincent, I presume?"

Vincent's brows lowered. "You presume correctly. I'm here for the girl."

Amun moved in front of Luxi and his narrowed his eyes at Vincent. "I'm afraid she's spoken for."

"In that, you are quite correct." Vincent's smile thinned. "I am Avatar Vincent of the Paladin Order, and I will thank you to release my legal property."

Property? Luxi's stared at Vincent's towering and shadowed form in abject horror. "That's impossible!"

Amun bared his teeth in a parody of a smile. "With all due respect, Avatar, Gentle-fem Emory is my employee."

"And I assure you, I have prior claim." Vincent's smiled frosted. "Come, Gentle-fem Emory; it's time to go home."

Luxi backed a step away. "What do you think I am— stupid?"

Vincent's smile disappeared completely. "Don't make me come get you."

Two blades appeared in Leto's hands from nowhere. "You'll have to go through me first." He smiled.

Luxi sucked in a sharp breath. Leto was impressively fast. They were going to defend her—against Vincent? No one had ever defended her from anything. It was better business to abandon the problem and not take sides.

Amun narrowed his eyes at Vincent. "There's something odd going on in Vincent's head. It's as though he is literally of two minds. He seems to be listening to someone else speaking, but I cannot make out what is being said."

Luxi glanced at Amun. "He does have two minds, if you count the ghost as one of them."

Amun frowned at Luxi. "Then according to what I am overhearing, it's the ghost that actually wants you."

"The ghost wants me?" Luxi shook her head. That didn't make any sense. "What for?"

Amun snorted. "Nothing good, I would suppose."

Vincent glared at Leto, then his gaze turned calculating. "You have a ghost. No, you *are* a ghost—housed in a robot."

"I started out as a cyborg, actually." Leto's smile gleamed in the shadows. "My body isn't biological anymore, but I actually belong here. You, on the other hand, are a living man possessed by a very dead spirit that isn't yours. It doesn't belong in you at all."

Vincent's mouth tightened. "You have no place in this world. You should return to the dead."

Leto snorted. "I can't return to where I've never been—unlike *your* other half."

Vincent's gaze chilled. "You feed on the living. You have to, to remain in that body."

"And your ghost doesn't?" Leto raised a dark silver brow. "Or does your ghost feed on *you?*"

Vincent's face flushed with rage, but his voice was quiet. "I will take great pleasure in destroying you."

"Temper, temper… So, you are feeding your ghost." Leto grinned. "And better monks than you have tried."

Vincent held out his hand. "Come, Luxi. You have caused me enough trouble already."

"No." Luxi backed away another step. "I'm not going anywhere with you."

"The way I see it, Avatar…" Amun's mouth tightened. "You seem to be the cause of all the trouble."

Vincent glared at Amun. "You know nothing." He focused on Luxi. "Come here. Do not incur more punishment than you have already earned."

"Punishment?" White-hot fury surged up Luxi's spine. "Now wait just a damned minute! Punishment for what?"

Vincent's eyes gleamed in the half-light. "For deserting your lawful master."

"Screw you!" Luxi was so angry she shook with it. "You are not my master in any way, shape, or form!"

Amun's brows shot up. He glanced at Luxi and a small smile appeared.

"Oh, but I am." Vincent's jaw tightened and took a step closer.

"That is close enough, monk." Leto pointed a serrated blade at Vincent's heart and flipped the other blade expertly in his hand. "But we can argue the *point* if you like."

Amun frowned. "He's lying, but he's not lying."

"What?" Luxi gaped at Amun in shock. "How did you…?"

"Professional-grade telepath, remember?" Amun snorted. "Vincent is projecting loud and fairly clear."

Luxi winced. "Oh…"

Vincent's black eyes focused on Leto. "Station security will have something to say about this."

"You think so?" Leto tilted his head to one side. "Ever hear the phrase 'rank has its privileges'?"

Vincent leaned back just a hair. "What?"

Leto bared his teeth in something that wasn't even close to a smile, and his voice was very soft. "Master forgot to wear his jewelry."

"Avatar." Amun's eyes narrowed. "What claim do you have on Luxi?"

Vincent frowned. "That is not your concern."

Amun sighed. "Ah. He's filed an indenture claim."

"I'm indentured?" Luxi's felt her heart stutter in her chest. She was the legal slave of this monster? How, by glory, had that happened?

"Not yet, but he has filed for it." Amun caught Luxi's shoulder and whispered. "Is your data card secure?"

Luxi touched her breast pocket. "Yes."

"Good." Amun smiled tightly. "You're safe as long as you don't give him your verbal agreement or your card."

Luxi frowned. "He can't access anything on the card."

"He can access your identity, and that's all he needs to complete enough of the process for a legal collection." Amun frowned at Vincent. "Once you're in his hands, it's a simple matter of getting a DNA sample from you, and his ownership is secured."

Luxi shuddered in icy fear. Vincent was a lot bigger than she was. Getting a verbal agreement out of her wouldn't take much force, and a single hair would carry her DNA. The only thing that really stood between her and that monster was her tiny data card.

Amun smiled at her. "Don't be afraid. I will take care of everything." He caught her gaze. "Kiss me."

Lust, heat, fire, and sincere affection rolled over Luxi's mind, emptying her thoughts of everything but an overwhelming hunger to taste him, to feel him... She pressed up against his body and kissed him with a soft moan of urgency.

Amun pulled back, releasing her mouth with a tight smile.

Luxi's mind returned in a cool rush. She jerked back. "You rolled me!"

"Just a little, to relax you." Amun said softly. "I promise, I will keep you safe. Do you believe me?"

Luxi frowned, puzzled. Somehow, she did believe him, and she did feel calmer, but... She sighed and nodded.

Amun smiled. "Good."

Luxi's talent moved in the depths of her mind. The lines of chance and potential faded into one strong line that led into the future. Her final decision had occurred, and she had somehow taken it. She was on the path to her alternate future. And she had no idea what had triggered it.

She scanned the lines of her past. Somewhere she had made a decision, done something or said something that had allowed it to happen. But for the life of her, she couldn't spot it.

Two station security guards stepped out of the lift. Their dark doublets gleamed with silver shields emblazoned with *Sojourn Corp.* over their breast pockets, and swords graced their hips. One of them nodded. "You requested security, Master Verity?"

Vincent glared at the guards then turned his glare on Leto.

Leto smiled and tapped his temple with a finger. "Told you."

Amun smiled and nodded. "I did. There seems to be a problem with my employee, Gentle-fem Emory."

Luxi's mouth popped open. Amun called security—for her?

Amun's fingers tightened on her arm. "Would you be so kind as to put Gentle-fem Emory under protective custody until a certain legal dispute has been..." He leveled a glare at Vincent. "...settled?"

Protective custody? Luxi rocked on her heels.

"Of course, Master Verity." The guard nodded at Amun, then turned to Luxi. "Gentle-fem Emory, this way please?"

Amun pushed Luxi gently toward the guards. "I will see you within the hour."

Luxi took a hesitant step toward the guards and turned back to look at Amun. "But..."

Amun leveled a stern look her way. "Go. They will keep you safe."

Vincent's brows lowered over his shadowed eyes as he glared at Amun. "This will gain you nothing."

"Leto, I need to go to my suite." Amun pulled his gloves from his pocket and slid them on, ignoring Vincent. "Immediately."

Luxi folded her arms across her chest as she was escorted by the two sword-wearing guards back across the concourse balcony to the lift she had just left. She turned toward the door to see Amun and Leto disappearing toward the opposite side of the balcony. Her bag trailed behind in Leto's grasp. She winced. Damn it, she didn't even have her hairbrush.

Vincent was a still and menacing shape that stared after her. Under the strong light of the lamp post, Vincent cast two shadows on the concourse deck. One of them was the dark bulk of Vincent's body, but the other was smaller, and a completely different shape.

Vincent's ghost was solid enough to cast a shadow.

Luxi shivered hard as the lift doors closed.

Chapter Ten

Two levels up, Luxi followed the guards out of the lift and onto a walkway that crossed one of the shuttle-ways tunneling throughout the station. Plain steel walls painted with a broad green band arched over her head. Several small four-passenger shuttles zipped up and down the roadway below.

She shoved her hands into her hip pockets and followed one guard along the walkway with the other right behind her. *Great, this is just great.* Once again, Vincent had to step in and ruin everything. She crossed her arms and gripped her elbows as she walked. She still couldn't believe that Amun and Leto were so willing to defend her. They hadn't even asked; they just…did it. She shook her head. She'd never seen anything like it. In business, you cut your losses, you didn't defend them. Not unless they were valuable.

She sighed. *I'm just a receptionist, not a whole lot of value here.*

Luxi was led around a corner and through a doorway into a small and somewhat empty steel-walled parking garage. A blocky armored security shuttle painted in Sojourn Corp.'s distinctive black and gold was parked at the bottom of the small staircase.

One of the guards opened the back passenger-side door and assisted Luxi into the back seat. The door was closed and clicked as it locked.

Luxi didn't quite conceal her flinch.

The guards climbed into the front seats without saying a single word. The hover engines whined as they powered up. In a matter of moments, the shuttle lifted on a low cushion of anti-grav and backed out of the parking space, then pulled out into the tunnels, diving into the light traffic.

Vincent... What in glory was she going to do about him? Luxi stared out the shuttle's window at the endless steel walls and tried to think. Vincent had filed for indenture, but how? She had thought that only someone legally wronged could sue for indenture. It was how businesses recovered their losses from crimes committed by employees. High debt could also result in indenture, but again, it was a monetary loss issue. She knew for a fact that all her debts had been cleared; Gentle-fem Symposia had made very sure of that.

Luxi shook her head. The only other way to be indentured was to volunteer your services. There was no way she'd ever agree to that, or turn over her data card. She lifted a hand to her breast pocket. The seal was open.

Ice water slid down Luxi's spine. She shoved her fingers into her pocket. The card was gone. That card had everything: her money, her flight plan, her identity... Panicked, she checked every pocket in her suit. Gone.

Had she left it at the counter when she'd bought her kaffa? No, she remembered picking it up. The garden; it had to be in the formal garden. Her pocket must have opened when Leto pulled her suit off to...fuck.

She eyed the passing hallways, her hands locked together in her lap to hold back the trembling. Getting back to the garden wasn't going to happen anytime soon. At this point, her only hope was that the cleaning crew would find it and notify her when it was found.

Technically, the data card was perfectly safe. The DNA encryption would not allow anyone to access anything more than a view of her identity. Her tickets and her money were inaccessible to anyone but her.

But if Vincent found a way to get his hands on her card, her identity info would be enough to get her into his custody, and then he would own her—body and soul.

She shivered slightly. Amun had said that it was the ghost that really wanted her. But that didn't make any sense at all. What would a ghost want with her?

The shuttle took a sharp left turn, ramped up into a tunnel, then drove through a security grid without bothering to slow down. They ramped up again onto a two-lane roadway marked by broad silver bands.

Luxi frowned. The Silver district was the military level. There was absolutely no way for her to leave it; she didn't have the clearance. But then, Vincent shouldn't have the clearance to enter it, either. She hoped.

They drove through another security grid and gold bands replaced the silver bands on the walls.

Luxi's brows shot up. They put people in custody in the Gold district, the high security zone? She smiled sourly. It made sense. Gold district was harder to get into or out of than Silver. It was highly doubtful that Vincent had the clearance to get near the Gold district.

The shuttle took an off-ramp that led into a small parking lot and parked. The doors opened.

Luxi climbed out of the car then checked the seat, just in case her card had fallen out in the shuttle. It hadn't.

One of the guards took her elbow to guide her. "This way, Gentle-fem Emory."

Luxi nodded and followed the guards, clenching her hands together to hold back her panic. A short walk across the parking garage led to a security door. The door opened onto a broad, richly carpeted hall painted with gold bands. Five paces into the hall, a wide doorway held a buzzing energy grid.

Luxi swallowed hard. That grid could char a living being to dust in seconds.

The guards flanked her, took her by the elbows, and marched her toward the deadly grid without pause. "Stay close to us, Gentle-fem Emory." Between one step and the next, the grid shut down, reactivating at their heels.

One of the guards smiled. "See, that wasn't so bad." She was released. "We're almost there."

Luxi sucked in a breath to get a grip on her leaping pulse. "You keep prisoners in Gold district?"

The guard grinned. "You're not under arrest, Gentle-fem Emory, just in protective custody. You'll be staying in a suite."

Luxi nearly tripped. A Gold district suite? Were they joking?

One of the guards stopped at an ornately decorated, perfectly round, shielded door. He pressed his palm to the lighted box on the right and the door rolled away to reveal a second shielded door that rolled the other way.

The hallway was arched and softly lit by decorative frosted glass sconces along the ceiling. Golden light spilled down wine-colored walls onto small, carved wooden tables holding tasteful flower arrangements and art objects. The carpet was a deep, smoke gray.

The guards stopped at a narrow door. "Here you are." The guard pressed the panel and it opened. "We'll be right outside if you need anything."

"Thank you." Luxi walked in and stopped dead.

The room was expensively decorated in gold-veined marble and cream silks. The walls were a rich, warm cream and deep gold carpeting covered the floors. Centered on the back wall, right in front of her, was a massive bed draped in cream silk and mounded with gold tasseled pillows. Gold velvet curtains cascaded from the ceiling to the floor around the bed. On the far left, a huge mirrored armoire took up most of the wall by the open door to the facility. On the far right, a marble-topped dresser with a massive oval mirror took up a large portion of that wall, with a closed door just beyond it.

This was protective custody?

Out of sheer curiosity, she went to the left and into the facility. It not only had a frosted-glass-enclosed water shower—it had a gold-flecked bathtub large enough to hold four. Thick towels and decanters of soap were laid out on the long counter next to a brush-and-comb set. A hook by the door showed a fluffy bathrobe in cream velvet and gold satin.

Luxi started pulling off her suit. She wanted to take advantage of that water shower before someone realized that she wasn't supposed to be here and made her leave.

Finally naked, Luxi tossed her clothes on the counter and selected a decanter of liquid soap scented with rich vanilla from the row of colorful squeeze bottles on the counter by the towels. Cautiously, she stepped into the roomy shower stall and turned on the water. Four strong jets sprayed decadent amounts of deliciously hot water, soothing sore muscles before spilling down her body in soul-warming sheets. Her blissful groans echoed in the room as steam curled up around her. And she didn't care.

Luxi slathered herself in soap and took great delight in scrubbing every inch of her body and her hair twice. With great reluctance, she finally turned off the water.

"You know, there's another whole bottle of that vanilla soap if you want to continue."

Luxi released a short scream and her feet slid on the slick tiles. She grabbed onto the handrail that circled the shower and whirled around.

Leto leaned against the frame of the shower's open door, grinning. His arms were folded across his marble-pale bare chest. He wore little more than knee-high dress boots and sleek velvet tights. "Having fun?"

"Leto?" She shoved wet hair from her cheeks. "How long have you been there?"

"Long enough." Leto shook his head and chuckled. "If this is what you're like in a shower, I can't wait to see what you're like in a tub."

Luxi frowned. "What are you doing here?"

Leto shook out a fluffy cream towel. "I figured I should check to see what was taking you so long."

"You knew what room I was in?" Luxi reached for the towel.

Leto dodged her hands and wrapped the towel around her, locking her in a snug embrace. "I should. You're in our suite." He dropped a quick kiss on her lips and proceeded to scrub her skin dry.

Luxi grabbed onto his shoulders to keep from being knocked over as he ruthlessly rubbed the water from her skin. "*Your* suite?"

Leto knelt as he slid the towel up her thighs. "You're in protective custody." He glanced up and grinned. "Our protective custody."

"I am?" Luxi shook her head. "No one said anything."

"Of course not." Leto grabbed a fresh towel from the counter. "We didn't want Vincent to know where you were going." He turned her around and rubbed the towel through her long, wet hair. "By the way, you have a very fine ass."

Luxi felt her cheeks heat. "Thanks."

Leto tossed the towel on the counter and walked past her to open the facility door. "Time to get dressed."

"All right." Luxi reached for her discarded green suit, vaguely disappointed that she wouldn't get to wear the robe.

Leto took two long steps back toward Luxi and snatched the green ship-suit from her hand. "Nope, not that." He tossed the suit back on the counter.

Luxi frowned. "I am not walking around naked."

Leto turned around to face her. "You could..."

"No." Luxi pointed a finger at him. "Absolutely not!"

Leto grinned and set his hands on her shoulders. "Relax. Your clothes are on the bed." He pushed her backwards toward the open facility door. "Well, what we could get for you in a hurry."

Luxi frowned up at him as she walked backwards. "You got me clothes?"

"Of course." He nodded as he pushed her out of the facility. "You can't wear a ship-suit to an Imperial diplomatic conference."

Luxi's bare feet sank into the bedroom's rich gold carpeting. "What diplomatic conference?"

Amun's voice called out from behind her. "The one I am mediating."

Luxi sucked in a breath and turned around.

Amun smiled. "Liked the shower, did you?" Formal court robes of silver and charcoal draped to his heels. A slender band of silver shimmering with rainbow hues circled his forehead.

Luxi stared in shock. Amun had an Imperial circlet? He was an Imperial lord?

Leto grinned as he pushed Luxi toward the bed. "I was convinced she was doing more than washing."

"So was I. I was beginning to feel left out." Amun lifted a shift of nearly transparent cream silk from the bed. "Hands up; we need to get you dressed so we can begin your downloads."

Too shocked to resist, Luxi stood before Amun and put her hands up. The shift was dropped over her head and a white silk robe was lifted from the bed. In very short order, Amun and Leto had folded and tied the floor-length robe around her. Between them, they arranged a heavier robe of gold-trimmed cream over the white robe, tied with a broad gold velvet sash snug under her breasts and knotted at her back. Matching velvet slippers were set on her feet.

Amun waved his hand at the deep-cream hooded robe that was still on the bed. "We'll save that for when it's time to leave." He turned her toward the open door by the dresser. "Your upgrades await you."

Luxi felt her cheeks heat. "Um, guys? How about some underwear? You know, panties?"

Leto snorted as he knelt and fussed with the folds at her back. "You won't need them."

Luxi's mouth fell open. "What!" She looked over her shoulder at Leto. "I'm a girl!"

"We had noticed that," Amun said dryly.

Leto tugged at the bows at her side. "The robes are floor-length; no one will see anything."

Luxi gripped the silk. "But I'm not... I don't... You just don't go around without underwear!"

"Are you kidding? Under heavy court robes?" Leto bit back a grin as he stood up. "It's done all the time."

Luxi almost stomped her foot. "But I don't!"

Amun covered his mouth with his hand and closed his eyes briefly. "Unless you bring attention to it, no one will be the wiser."

"You're not serious?" Luxi's fingers tightened on the robes. "No underwear?"

Amun lowered his chin. "Mind your hands, don't crease the silk."

Luxi released the robes and tucked her hands behind her. "Amun, I don't walk around without underwear!"

Amun rolled his eyes. "You'll survive an evening without panties, I promise." He caught her shoulders and turned her toward the open door by the dresser. "We have much to accomplish and not much time to accomplish it." He nudged her toward the next room. "Go."

Leto stepped into the room ahead of them, not even bothering to hide his chuckles.

The next room was enormous and done in black marble and silver with deep scarlet carpeting. The monstrous bed commanding the center of the back wall was twice the size of hers, and draped in black velvet. A massive black marble and smoked-glass desk took up one entire corner.

Leto picked up a short silk robe of deep black from the edge of the bed and shrugged into it. "Is this going to take long?"

"That depends on Luxi's download speed and how many files she needs." Amun walked to the desk and turned the black leather chair toward Luxi. "Sit here." He leaned over the desk to pick up a data-feed cord.

Luxi gathered the robes and sat carefully in the leather chair. The rich silk slid sensually against her bare rump. She scooped her long hair out of the way of her data port and leaned forward. "I really need to tie this hair up."

Amun carefully plugged the data-jack into the port at the back of her skull. "I prefer to see all those wanton, fiery curls down."

Wanton, fiery curls? Luxi rolled her eyes. "I noticed, but it gets tangled on everything."

Amun leaned over the desk to access the holographic keyboard display. "I'm sure you'll manage just fine." He turned and flashed a smile. "Let's see what you need."

Luxi felt the scan shimmering at the back of her thoughts.

"Ah, your array and interfacing are quite current, but you definitely need data files, including a number of languages." He tapped the top of her hand. "Incoming data."

Luxi closed her eyes and cleared her mind. It was better to simply let it go where it needed to be without bothering to scan through it. It saved on download time.

"Are you going to tell her?" Leto asked softly.

Luxi opened her eyes.

Amun had his back to her, facing Leto. "Of course."

Leto raised his brow at Amun as he tied a knee-length robe of deep silver over the black silk. "Now would be good." He picked up a black sash and his eyes narrowed. "Before the jewelry?"

Alarm jangled along Luxi's spine. "Am I in some kind of trouble?"

"Not at all." Amun lifted his chin but did not turn to face Luxi. "You are safe from Vincent and listed on my staff as my personal secretary."

Safe from Vincent and gainfully employed, thank glory! Luxi released a sigh. "Then Vincent's claim was false?"

Amun peered at the floor. "Not quite."

Luxi's hands tightened on the arms of the chair. "Not quite?"

"Amun…" Leto rolled his eyes. "Just say it."

Amun turned to face her, but his gaze was focused on the holographic display floating over his desk. "I'm afraid that to put you on my staff, I had to pull what is known as a dirty trick."

A dirty trick? Luxi's frown deepened. "What did you do?"

Amun pulled a shimmering card from his pocket and held it up. "I jumped Vincent's claim."

Luxi froze. A ripple of unease went through her. "Is that my data card?" The words came out breathlessly.

Amun turned to glance at her, then turned away. "Yes."

"The kiss..." Luxi's pulse pounded in her throat. He had taken the card when he kissed her. "You put in a counter claim, only you had the card."

Amun nodded. "And your verbal consent."

Luxi blinked. Fate and glory... Yes, he did. In the garden, she had formally "consented" to his service.

Leto cleared his throat. "I had your DNA." He carefully avoided looking at her as he tied his robe.

Of course he did. They had just finished sex.

"Then I'm..." Luxi's breath stopped in her throat. "I'm..." She couldn't say it. She couldn't even think it. Her heart ached as though a fist had tightened around it. "Is it done?"

Amun held her gaze. "There were no delays in the processing."

Leto shrugged into a floor-length robe of black and steel gray. "You were done before you walked into the shower."

Luxi took a small shallow breath. This was it? This was the future she had chosen? Her new future was as an indentured employee, a legal slave? She stared down at the scarlet carpet, concentrating to access her talent and scan the lines of possibility. Her line of synchronicity was broad, with few knots.

Clearly a future marked by very few decisions; a life under someone else's control. *Mother of glory...* A shiver raked her.

Amun moved to her side in a whisper of rich silk. He dropped to one knee and set his warm hand over her chilled fingers. "Luxi, I had not intended for this to happen, but it was the only way to keep you out of Vincent's hands."

Luxi stared hard at Amun. "Then why did you ask for my 'consent'?" No employer asked for consent; there were too many legal connotations. *And why, by glory, didn't I think of this before, when he asked for it?* She looked away and her cheeks heated. *Oh, that's right, I was still getting over my screaming orgasm.*

Amun dropped his chin and his cheeks flushed. "I will admit to considering it—that's why I asked—but I had already decided that it was unnecessary." He caught her gaze and his jaw tightened. "Vincent's active claim made it necessary."

Luxi bit her lip. Amun had to be telling the truth. It was too...unreal to be anything else.

Amun pressed her fingers and stood up. "I swear I will take very good care of you."

Luxi took a slow deep breath. There wasn't a whole lot she could do at this point. It was done. She was indentured. She was owned. Fate and glory, it didn't feel real at all.

"Just so you know, you're not the only one." Leto wrapped the black velvet sash around his robes at his waist.

Huh? Luxi blinked at Leto. "You're..." She still couldn't say it. "You, too?"

"Yep, only with me it *was* deliberate." Leto jerked the knot on his sash tight. "One minute, I'm a freelance contract assassin, and the next, Amun has legal rights to everything I own, including my person. He blindsided me."

Amun smiled tightly. "You should have been paying attention."

Leto snorted and started to pick up knives from the bed. "I was a little busy at the time—trying to keep you alive." He tucked small blades here and there into his sash.

Amun glanced over his shoulder at Leto. "And I was attempting to keep the Imperial guards from executing you on sight."

"Oh, that makes me feel so much better about being at the end of your leash." He smiled cynically at Luxi.

Amun leaned over the desk to check the data he was downloading into Luxi's mind. "You don't appear to be suffering."

Leto lowered his chin and peered from under his brows. "You trapped me with a legal loophole."

"I honestly didn't think it would work." Amun turned back to face Leto. "I assumed you had made provisions for it."

Luxi frowned up at Amun. "What did you do?"

Amun abruptly blushed and stared down at the carpet.

Leto scowled. "He claimed salvage rights."

"Salvage rights?" Luxi shook her head. "I don't see how?"

Amun sighed. "Leto is listed as a cyborg, but in actuality he's completely non-biological; therefore, he's technically…" He paused, biting his lip.

"Dead." Leto lifted a long black sheathed sword and belt from the bed. "I'm technically a fully functional corpse." He pulled the sword belt around his hips and buckled it. "He got a verbal consent out of me for something else, then broke into my ship's logs for the rest of the information he needed."

"I did not break in." Amun poked at the holographic display hovering over the glass desktop. "You voluntarily let me into your ship's system."

Leto frowned and picked up more blades from the bed. "Not that far."

Amun shrugged, but a smile played on his fill lips. "Was it my fault your codes were easy to guess?"

"So it was *my* fault you trapped me?" Leto knelt to tuck a blade into the top of each boot.

"You should have been prepared for the attempt."

Leto straightened and groaned. "Arguing with you is like arguing with a bulkhead!"

Amun grinned suddenly. "This comes as a surprise?"

Luxi glanced from one to the other. The argument between Amun and Leto sounded more like practiced banter than a real argument. The sarcasm was loud and clear, but it sounded more like two very close friends bickering, not like real grievances. She felt a smile creep onto her lips. They sounded like an old married couple.

Leto rolled his eyes but couldn't quite bite back his tight smile. "For someone who is serious about the truth, Amun, you have no problems changing the rules when no one's looking."

Amun's brows lowered. "I don't need to change the rules. Most people are simply unaware of how to use them properly."

Luxi raised her brow at Amun. "You sound like a lawyer."

Amun snorted. "I'm a diplomat. We're much worse."

Leto shook his head. "He's not kidding. I've seen him in action."

Luxi tilted her head to look up at Amun. "Should I be worried?"

Amun sighed dramatically. "Oh, it's far too late to worry now." He turned and smiled down at Luxi. "And that appears to be all the files you need at the moment."

"Thank glory..." Luxi leaned forward so Amun could unfasten the data jack. She only hoped that the new information was in the proper place and she could access it when she needed it.

Amun coiled the data jack and set it on the desk. He lifted his head to look over at the door. "Ah, dinner has just arrived."

"It has?" Luxi's stomach took that moment to growl.

The main entry chime sounded out in the hall.

Amun's glanced down at her, his eyes wide then smiled. "With perfect timing."

Luxi frowned toward the door. "How do you know who it is?"

Amun tapped his temple. "Our service has recognizably loud thoughts." He looked over at Leto. "Shall we go?"

"Thank the Maker, I'm starved!" Leto lunged across the room to open the door to the hall.

Luxi stood up and tugged at her hair. "Go where?"

Amun smiled. "The informal dining room."

Chapter Eleven

Across the hall, the "informal dining room" may have been small, but it certainly wasn't informal. Artistic frosted-glass fixtures spilled golden light down the deep burgundy walls. The long wall directly across from the door was commanded by a huge window with a gorgeous view of space. The round table that seated six was covered in a white cloth that looked like real Terran damask, the plates were Shido porcelain, and Luxi strongly suspected that the water tumblers were Dinarian crystal.

The food displayed in the heated silver tureens looked incredible. Luxi was pretty sure she recognized a few of the vegetables, and the sliced roast floating in steaming juice smelled like it was from an actual bovine, rather than processed.

Leto dropped into the chair on the right and started scooping food onto his plate.

Amun rolled his eyes, winked at Luxi, and walked around Leto to sit in the chair on Leto's right with his back to the window.

Luxi took the chair on Leto's left, facing the window, with her back to the door. She set her cloth napkin in her lap and served herself from each of the three steaming tureens.

Amun promptly started asking about her former duties at the last three companies she'd worked in.

Luxi replied as politically correctly as possible. She had never found it good business to mention some of her former employers' nastier habits.

Amun then posed a pile of questions on his personal schedule.

Luxi answered succinctly and smiled. Apparently, Amun was checking to see if the information he'd downloaded was filed properly. Then she realized that Amun's questions had been posed in a variety of languages. *Well, damn, looks like my translator's up to speed.* She sipped at her water to cover her smile. Her translation program had worked so smoothly she hadn't noticed.

Amun smiled. "So, you finally noticed that I was testing your translation program?"

Luxi choked, just a little. *Telepathy or a good guess?*

Amun raised a brow and smiled.

Ah, telepathy. Luxi used her napkin to cover her smile. She opened her mouth to make a comment and her inner scheduling alarm went off. Amun's appointment was in ten minutes. She rose from her chair. "The negotiations appointment! We're going to be late!"

Amun set his glass down. "Ah, the ten-minute warning."

Luxi nodded.

"Good." Amun rose from his chair and smiled. He turned to Leto. "Are we ready?"

Leto set down his fork and used his napkin hastily. "Yep." He tossed the napkin onto his plate, stood up, and headed for the door. "Let's go."

After collecting Luxi's heavy cream court robe from where they had left it on the bed, they left the guards standing by the suite door and strode deeper into the suite's apartments. In a small side alcove was a lift door. Leto pressed the call button on the side and leaned back against the alcove's wall.

Luxi blinked at the blank reflective door. "You have your own private lift?"

Amun patted her shoulder. "It is standard in diplomatic suites. For far more secure arrival at conferences."

Amun and Luxi stood at the back of the lift, facing the door while Leto applied a slide key to the menu panel on the door's right. He punched in a destination, nodded, then leaned back against the right wall. He focused on Luxi and his smile became decidedly lascivious.

Luxi's cheeks heated under Leto's stare. She scowled. "What?"

"I was just thinking..." Leto folded his arms and lifted his knee to prop one booted heel on the wall behind him. "About the panties you're not wearing."

The air exploded from Luxi's lungs. "Leto!"

Amun covered his mouth, closed his eyes briefly, and inhaled deeply. "Children, this is not the time to play."

Leto raised a brow and his smile broadened. "That never stopped you."

A small smile lifted Amun's lips. "That is entirely beside the point."

The lift door opened on a hallway painted a deep gold with autumn-red carpeting. An energy grid crackled before the door at the far end.

Leto stepped out of the lift.

Luxi took a shuddering breath. Just beyond that grid were the crowned heads of whole planetary systems. It was exciting. It was terrifying. Luxi froze. What was she doing here?

Amun took Luxi's chilled hand and folded it over his arm. "Relax. You are only required to sit still and be pleasant to anyone who addresses you." He drew her from the lift with a small tug.

"Sit still, be pleasant. Okay." Luxi tugged her mouth into a smile. "Sounds like every job I've had."

Amun grinned. "The display may be rather pretty, but I assure you, you will find the conference itself to be deadly dull in a matter of minutes."

Leto turned back to grin at her. "Do what I do—stare out the big window." He frowned and stopped, then turned to face them. "Amun, the jewelry?"

Amun jerked to a halt. "Oh, yes." He reached into his pocket, and tugged up his robes to kneel down on one knee. "Luxi, may I have your left foot?"

Luxi blinked. "My foot?"

Leto stepped closer and offered Luxi his hand. "You're putting it on her ankle?"

Luxi took Leto's hand for balance and lifted her slippered foot.

Amun took her foot in his hand and enclosed a plain iridescent ring around her ankle. "No need to announce her status."

Luxi's heart thumped in her chest. It was a binding ring, meant to control the wearer by tapping into their internal robotics, their augmentations. They were worn by indentured staff to keep track of their whereabouts and actions. She looked up at Leto.

Leto peeled back his left sleeve to show her a similar ring. He smiled and shrugged.

She frowned. He hadn't been wearing it earlier.

Amun released her foot. "There, that will take care of security's concerns."

Luxi felt a shiver in her mind and the hair lifted at the back of her neck. The ring was tapping into her internal computational.

Amun stood. "It's only temporary. Security demands that all indentured staff wear them during conferences. I'll take it off when we return to the suite." He leaned close to her ear. "I know you're not an assassin." He turned to smile at Leto.

Leto's smile soured. "Very funny." He turned and headed for the sizzling grid. The grid snapped off to let him pass, then snapped right back on. He turned around. "Come on, you two."

Luxi stopped before the grid and swallowed. That thing could kill her in seconds.

"Your clearance is already programmed." Amun pushed Luxi gently after Leto.

The grid snapped off.

Luxi lunged through the grid and plowed straight into Leto's arms.

Leto grinned down at her. "Scared?"

Luxi stepped out of Leto's arms as her cheeks heated ferociously. "Who, me?" She stepped to the side.

Amun proceeded through the grid at a far more sedate pace with an amused smile. "Luxi, you shouldn't torment Leto like that."

Luxi sucked in a breath. "Torment *him?*"

Amun shrugged as he stepped between them. "For goodness sake, woman..." He smiled slyly. "You aren't even wearing panties." He pressed his palm on a lighted grid by the door.

Luxi's mouth fell open and her temper surged in a nice, refreshing rush. "And whose idea was that?"

Amun raised his brows and his smile broadened to a grin. "Why, mine, of course."

The door opened—onto sedate pandemonium.

The assembly hall was completely circular, and smaller than Luxi had expected it to be, with triple-tiered amphitheater seating. The curving walls were a soft gold and riddled with doors framed by frosted-glass light fixtures. And uniformed security guards.

The pair of guards by their door each held up a hand-held computational. They scanned their readings, shared a glance, and nodded at Amun.

Amun proceeded down the shallow steps with Luxi and Leto behind him.

Luxi looked up, and up… The ceiling was a clear dome with an incredible view of the pink, orange, and green swirls of the nearby nebula.

Leto stepped closer. "Great view, huh?"

Luxi had to remember to breathe. "Wow."

Amun glanced back at them. "Leto used that very word, the first time he saw it."

Leto scowled. "Did not."

Amun lifted a brow and grinned as he continued down the steps. "Did so."

A long, black glass table with twelve chairs occupied the very center of the assembly hall at the lowest level. Diplomats from assorted races in jewel-toned court robes circulated around the table. Robed people of many races and descriptions milled and chatted in the auditorium seats surrounding the center.

Amun was hailed by an older gentleman with a long white braid and midnight blue robes. He smiled as he approached, and bowed. Light gleamed on the iridescent circlet he wore. He was an Imperial lord.

Amun bowed. "Senator Shodu."

Leto caught Luxi's hand. "Take a seat in the first row. We'll come get you when we're done."

Luxi tugged at Leto's sleeve. "Where are you going to be?"

Leto smiled. "Amun gets to sit in one of the big chairs; I get to stand behind him and be menacing."

Luxi raised a brow at him. "Menacing, huh?" She smiled. *Right…* "Sure you can do that?"

Leto stared down his long nose. "Is that a challenge?" His smile sharpened and shadows moved in the depth of his eyes.

Luxi shivered in spite of herself.

Leto nodded. "I thought not." He turned and strode after Amun.

Luxi sighed and sat in the red velvet fold-down seat by the aisle. "Pest."

Leto turned back. "I heard that!"

Luxi grinned. "Good!"

Amun lifted his head from his conversation to look at Luxi and then Leto, sternly.

Leto's expression was a study in innocence as he took up a position a step away from Amun's right shoulder.

Senator Shodu gestured toward the table and Amun moved to one of the chairs close to the middle.

"It is you! I thought I recognized that hair."

Luxi turned.

Bel, the violet-eyed lord from the tram, smiled at her as he stepped down the aisle. His pale cream mane was pulled back into a loose tail that fell over the shoulder of his rich gold robes. A lord's circlet graced his pale brow. "Well, hello."

His two dark-eyed fems, Orah and Faro, dressed in sleek black skin-suits, grinned from either side. Their slender hands rested comfortably on their hip-slung sword-belts.

Luxi sucked in a sharp breath. *Fate and glory, he would show up here!* She hastily rose from her seat and bowed. "Honored lord."

He gave her a formal nod and his full lips curved in a delicate smirk. "So that reprobate cyborg still has you, does he?"

Luxi winced.

Bel blinked and gave her a blinding smile. "Oh, dear, your translator is working properly."

Luxi flushed. "I had an upgrade."

Bel laughed and his cheeks flushed pink. "Please accept my apologies for my rudeness."

Luxi raised her brow and the corner of her lips lifted in half a smile. "I'll do my best."

Bel's brows shot up. "Oh, fatal strike…"

Amun arrived at Luxi's side in a rustle of silk. "Lord Belauros." He nodded and smiled. "Are you propositioning one of my employees again?"

Leto winked at Luxi from behind Amun's right shoulder.

Bel chuckled softly. "Lord Amun." He nodded toward Leto. "I'm afraid that I find both of your lovely employees a difficult temptation to resist." He raised a pale brow. "I'd be more than happy to negotiate a trade agreement; my two for your two for an evening?"

Both fems nodded vigorously, grinning broadly.

Amun glanced up at the nebula-filled ceiling, then back at Bel and smiled. "That is a very enticing offer. However, I have yet to fully explore the…range of my employees' skills." His gaze drifted to Luxi. "Especially that of my newest."

Luxi's cheeks heated under Amun's heavy-lidded and smoldering stare.

"From what I've seen so far…" Bel flashed a smile at Luxi. "…I understand perfectly why you would not be ready to…share."

Heat filled Luxi's cheeks as a visceral memory of the tram ride with Bel watching her and Leto avidly burned through her. She looked away.

Bel chuckled and moved down the steps to Amun's side. "I would also be more than interested in discussing some of *your* more esoteric talents. Perhaps privately, over coffee?"

Amun sighed. "Bel, you are incorrigible." He turned toward the gathering of lords.

Bel nodded and aimed his spectacular smile at Amun. "I do try."

"You succeed." Amun walked away, leading Bel and his fems toward the broad table. "But coffee does sound nice…"

Leto turned back to Luxi. "Be good," he said in a loud stage whisper, then turned and fell in behind Amun.

Luxi's mouth fell open. *Me?* She rolled her eyes and sat down. All around her, other robed members began taking seats in the amphitheater.

At the main negotiation table, Bel took a seat on one end of the table with the senator occupying the other end and Amun taking a chair in the center. Various other lords seated themselves around them, leaving the chair opposite Amun empty.

Luxi was surprised and pleased to discover that she could hear everything they were saying perfectly.

It seemed that Senator Shodu represented the governing republic of one world and Lord Belauros represented the royal house of another. They were discussing the disposition of a pair of colony worlds that wished to open trade, but a third world was pirating the trade routes between them. Representatives from neighboring worlds, also interested in the negotiations, were seated around the table. The representative of the third world in question had yet to appear.

According to what Luxi was overhearing, the third world was not pleased to have a professional telepath as part of the negotiation. Unfortunately, neither the senator nor Lord Bel would hold the conference without Amun to monitor the honesty of the representatives.

Luxi looked up at the brilliant nebula filling the dome overhead and felt her talent stir. Synchronicity was shifting, hard and fast. She opened her mind to her talent and reeled under a lashing hurricane of far-reaching changes that affected everyone in the room. Threads snarled and snapped with world-heavy consequences.

And beneath it, her other, smaller talent began to stir. The talent that sensed the dead.

Too occupied to worry about ghosts, Luxi gripped the chair's arms and strained to ride the cresting temporal wave of shifting potential futures. If she could find the center of the storm, the fulcrum, she could figure out what triggered this mess and perhaps sound a warning.

At the table, Amun stood, staring hard at Luxi.

Luxi caught the movement and her talent seized on him. Amun was the center of the storm. Something was about to happen to him—something fatal.

From a side aisle, a massive man in an exquisitely formal, ship captain's floor-length frock coat in deep scarlet came striding down the steps. Two well-armed cyborgs in ship's livery marched at his heels.

They were the other half of the storm. They were going to kill Amun.

Luxi lunged out of her chair. *Amun!*

Amun held up his hand and shook his head. He turned to Leto and whispered.

Luxi stood before her chair, shaking with the urgency of her vision.

Leto nodded and his gaze narrowed on the approaching trio.

Amun smiled, nodded toward Luxi. Calmly, he moved to a new seat, one closer to the senator and farther from the empty seats in the middle.

Luxi bit her lip. Amun had picked up her frantic warning. *Thank the Maker.* But the storm of change had not quite died down. Something was still going to happen. It wasn't over yet.

Chapter Twelve

The scarlet-coated ship's captain stepped up onto the dais where the representatives were gathered. His two cyborgs stopped at the bottom step directly behind him.

Lord Bel and Senator Shodu exchanged glances and rose from their chairs.

Lord Bel smiled. "I'm glad you could join us, Captain Faraday."

Captain Faraday folded his arms across his chest and lifted his chin. "I protest negotiating with a telepath present."

Senator Shodu smiled. "We understand and accept. However, negotiations will not proceed without one."

Luxi felt the lines of synchronicity shiver with tension. A decision was being made.

Captain Faraday looked around the table at the seated representatives.

Luxi's fingers dug into the arms of her chair. *He's looking for the telepath. He's looking for Amun.*

Both Lord Bel and the senator remained focused on the captain.

Lord Bel smiled. "With all due respect, would you kindly leave your exceedingly well-armed companions off the floor?"

Captain Faraday scowled. "Why? You have your guards."

Lord Bel's smile broadened. "Yes, but as you can see, they are far from marine-augmented."

Captain Faraday jerked his head toward his guards. They saluted and stepped back.

Bel lifted his hand toward the table. "Thank you. We will begin as soon as you are ready."

Captain Faraday strode around the table and took Amun's vacated chair at the back.

A shimmer of energy flashed around the dais. An energy grid had been activated. The negotiation table was sealed from entry or exit. Captain Faraday's cyborgs would not be able to step up onto the dais.

Luxi swallowed. Nor would anyone else.

Captain Faraday scowled.

Senator Shodu smiled. "A precaution against assassinations. You never know who is seated in the audience." He waved his hand to indicate the dozens of people seated in the amphitheater.

A light wave of soft laughter erupted from said audience.

Lord Bel and Senator Shodu glanced at Amun, who pretended not to notice.

Captain Faraday caught the glance and focused on Amun.

Luxi's talent howled as the synchronistic tension broke. Captain Faraday had identified Amun as the telepath.

Amun stared straight at the captain and smiled, no longer bothering to hide. At his shoulder, Leto smiled as well, and succeeded in appearing thoroughly menacing.

Bel lifted a glass to catch the captain's attention. "When you are ready, Captain Faraday."

The captain nodded and sighed as he slowly stood.

Luxi's talent screamed in warning.

Amun glanced at Luxi.

Captain Faraday flicked a knife toward Amun's heart.

Leto leaned over and caught the blade in his outstretched hand. He grinned at the captain. "Nice try."

Captain Faraday hissed. "Belmortus?"

Leto's eyes narrowed, and he smiled. "That's me."

Amun smiled thinly. "My personal bodyguard is known for his short temper. I would not try that again."

Captain Faraday clenched his jaw. "Then I won't." He vaulted onto the table toward Amun in a blur of speed, drawing his sword and dagger.

Leto launched onto the tabletop to meet him. His serrated daggers caught the captain's descending sword and turned the blade. He slashed for the captain's throat...

The entire table erupted with furious bodyguards lunging onto the table to join the fight. Papers scattered, delegates scattered, the gathered audience screamed. The captain's two heavily armored cyborgs shouted, hovering at the edges of the energy field with their blades drawn.

The guards posted at the lift doors charged down the aisles with their swords drawn. The captain's marine cyborgs turned to engage them with serrated daggers nearly as long as the guards' swords.

Two guards rushed past Luxi.

And an arm closed tight around Luxi's throat.

Luxi grabbed onto the choking arm, tugging at the sleeve, and was hauled backwards out of her chair. Her mind battered by the whirling potentials, she barely felt the under-hum of her other talent.

Leto pinned Captain Faraday facedown on the table and set the point of his serrated dagger at the base of the captain's skull. "Move and die."

Faro, Bel's fem, slapped restraints on the captain's wrists.

Luxi gasped for breath and felt the potentials shift—but not change. Amun was still in danger.

Leto lifted his head, and spotted Luxi being dragged backwards up the stairs. He leapt off the table. "Shut down the grid!"

No, you idiot! Sucking for air, Luxi screamed. "No! It's not done yet!" She twisted against her captor and dug in her heels. "Amun...!" She gasped as the arm jerked her off her feet. She stumbled backwards. "Save Amun!"

Amun joined Leto at the grid's barrier. At their feet, the guards and the marines were knotted in a vicious battle. Blood sprayed and hissed against the grid.

Amun lifted his head. "Shut down the grid!"

"No! Don't!" Her shouts were cut off by the arm around her throat. *Stupid men!* She wasn't in deadly danger—Amun was! Actually, she wasn't sure. Amun's fate was so huge, she couldn't even sense hers. But, for goodness' sake, she was only a secretary. The fate of whole worlds rested in Amun's survival. She didn't actually matter...to anybody.

Tears stung her eyes. Fate, she hated crying. She yanked at the arm that held her. She had to warn them, and this moron was interfering with her *job!* Temper flared and she dug in her heels. "Let go!" She twisted hard around to face her choker and shouted. "I'm busy!"

Her attacker caught her by the wrists. His face was exotic in shape, with pin-straight, short-cropped black hair. His almond-shaped eyes were filled with moving darkness. He smiled. "What a terrible shame." His voice was a frigid wind that sliced through her mind. "I'm afraid you simply must come with me."

What? Luxi shivered as her second talent surged within her. *Another man with a ghost?* She blinked at him; he looked...odd.

The man wore a plain, high-collared uniform of gray-green with brass buttons and scarlet trim. A short cape lined in scarlet satin fell from his shoulders to the broad red sash knotted around his waist. A plain sheathed sword and an equally plain sheathed knife as long as her forearm were shoved in his sash by his hip. His knee-high-booted feet rested a full inch above the floor.

Great glory! He didn't have a ghost—he *was* a ghost. Ice water flooded her veins. She shoved back frantically. "No!"

The ghost twisted her arms brutally behind her, swinging her around to face the lift door at the top of the stairs. "Yes."

Luxi gasped at the pain in her elbows and shoulders, never mind her wrists. *Fate, this ghost is strong!* Her arms were close to being dislocated.

"Go." He shoved her forward and up the stairs at nearly a trot.

Luxi winced as her toes slammed into the steps before she could lift her feet. "Why are you doing this?"

"You have an appointment."

"An appointment. With who?"

The ghost shoved her tight up against the silver lift door. He pulled her right arm from her back and slammed her palm against the call box. "With Vincent, my host."

"Vincent?" *Oh, shit!* She was in the hands of Vincent's ghost. Temper and terror slammed through Luxi in a potent mix. "Oh, hell no, I don't!" She bucked in his hold, furious and horrified. "I don't associate with assholes!"

The lift doors opened.

"How impolite." He shoved her into the lift.

Luxi didn't quite slam against the wall, and whirled around. "I am not going anywhere with you!" She charged for the open door.

The ghost caught her around the waist and practically threw her bodily toward the back of the lift. "Yes, you are."

That time Luxi did slam into the wall. She barely missed knocking her head, but she still had to gasp for breath.

The lift doors closed.

Luxi lunged for the closed door. It was not going to open; she didn't have the slide key to activate it. "Damn it!" She turned to face the ghost. "You can't do this!"

"It is done." The ghost smiled and walked toward her.

Luxi scooted back and away from him. "I don't have a key, I can't activate the lift."

"No need for a key." Bypassing Luxi completely, the ghost plunged his hand into the menu panel on the door's right without damaging it in any way. "Electronics respond well to me." The panel activated and the lift began to proceed. "There, no need for concern."

Luxi swallowed. *No need for concern? Yeah, right!* To everyone and everything, the ghost was exactly that—a ghost. Except to those with Luxi's strange little talent. To her, the ghost was as solid as flesh and blood. And dangerous. Those phantom blades on his hip would pass through any normal person while leaving only a cold shiver behind, but they were as deadly to her as true steel.

She knotted her hands into fists. "But I don't belong to Vincent!"

The ghost's smile broadened. "Vincent? You're not for him; you're for me. He's simply going to provide for your care."

Luxi's mouth fell open. "You? What for?"

"Those of your kind feed my kind." The ghost's eyes narrowed. "Vincent is my host, but there is not enough in him on which to dine properly. On you, I shall feed well."

Feed? Luxi shook with rage. Anger was good; anger kept the fear away. She bared her teeth at him. "Over my dead body!"

"If need be." The ghost chuckled. "But I doubt it will be necessary." He pulled his hand from the control panel.

The lift stopped and the lighting flickered. They were between floors.

The ghost unfastened his cape and dropped it. The cape fluttered briefly then disappeared altogether. He reached up to tug on the red satin tasseled cord held through his scarlet epaulette. The waist-draping loops passed under and around his right shoulder about three times. Pulled completely free, it looked about four feet long. He focused tightly on Luxi and wrapped one end of the slender satin cord loosely around his wrist, letting the other end dangle, floating around him like a serpent.

Luxi eyed the phantom rope and backed up against the opposite wall. She clenched her jaw. "I am not going to let you tie my hands."

The ghost tilted his head and snorted. "Dear child, this is not for your hands. Remove the robe."

"What?" Luxi choked. "No!"

The ghost pursed his lips and shrugged. "I can choke you to barely conscious and do this with you on the floor, right through your clothes. To me, only your skin is substantial. Or you can stay upright and awake." His smile returned. "I prefer your cooperation. Choking leaves such nasty bruises on the throat."

Luxi licked her lips. If he choked her unconscious, there was no telling what *else* he'd do. "Just the robe?"

"I need to see what you have under it."

Luxi snorted. "You could have asked! I have a dress on."

"How long?"

Luxi frowned. "To the floor."

"Ah." He nodded. "Then you will need to raise your skirts to above your waist."

Raise her skirts? Luxi reeled back against the wall. "Oh, hell no! Forget it!"

The ghost shrugged. "Very well, choking it is." He took two long steps toward her and raised his hands.

Luxi slid and then rolled away from him, but there wasn't anyplace to go in a lift. His hand caught in her hair. She jerked to a halt. "Ow! Shit!"

He caught her shoulder and spun her around to face him.

Luxi screamed and scratched for his eyes.

He sneered and turned his head away from her clawing fingers, then shoved with the flat of his hand against her breastbone, slamming her, breathless, against the wall. His hands closed around her throat high up, his thumbs pressing deep into the pulses under her jaw.

Luxi couldn't breathe, not in, not out, and her head was getting light fast. She dug her fingers into his hands.

"One last chance. Cooperate or go to sleep. If we do it this way, you will awaken with a vicious headache—if I don't squeeze too hard and kill you accidentally." His hands loosened.

Luxi gasped for breath and her pulse slammed in her ears. She glared up at him.

He raised his brow.

She held his stare, trying desperately not to give in to the fear howling for her attention. "Fine. I'll do it."

He backed away and smiled. "I am pleased."

Chapter Thirteen

Luxi turned away from the archaically uniformed ghost, unfastened her cream-and-gold court robe, and let the heavy silk slide from her arms.

The ghost tugged the robe from her fingers and tossed it to the far corner of the lift.

Luxi scowled and bent over to part the bottom half of her pale cream robe and the white silk robe beneath it, then grabbed the sheer shift.

"All of it."

Luxi lifted her head. "All of what?"

The ghost leaned back against the wall with his arms folded. "Lift *all* of your clothing and remove your undergarments."

Luxi froze. She wasn't wearing undergarments. Amun's idea, of course. The brief flash of annoyance brought back what little was left of her courage. She took in a deep breath, released it, grabbed everything and lifted. She was standing against the wall with her crotch exposed. It was humiliating. Her cheeks filled with heat and she turned away, closing her eyes.

"No undergarments, and yet, you blush. How interesting."

Luxi's eyes snapped open. He was kneeling right in front of her, looking up at her with his brow raised. She hadn't heard him move. She rolled her eyes. Of course she hadn't heard him move. *He's a ghost.* They didn't actually make sounds.

He snorted and lowered his gaze, focusing on her crotch. He reached up and caught her above the knees. "Wider. Stand wider."

Luxi shivered under his cool fingers and parted her legs.

He unwrapped the cord from his wrist and carefully folded the entire length in half. The twisted satin cord looked a lot longer this close, and about as slender as her finger.

Luxi frowned. "What are you going to do with that?"

He glanced up and a smile lifted the corner of his mouth. "Bind you." He leaned forward and passed the folded cord behind her, bringing it up to her waist, then took the tasseled ends and passed them through the loop at the other end. He brought the loose ends up, then passed them down, under the double cord around her waist, against her skin, then through the resulting loop at the bottom, and pulled the knot snug. His fingers tugged at the cords binding her waist, loosening it just a bit.

Luxi didn't get it. The cords weren't even tight around her. "You're tying my waist?"

"No." He leaned back, keeping hold of the cord's ends. "Turn around."

Luxi turned around, totally confused.

The ghost brought his hands around and passed the cords between her legs. "I am binding your cunt." He slid the ends under the cords around her waist and pulled.

Luxi gasped. The cords slid up between the plump outer lips of her pussy to press against her clit, and continued back and up the division of her ass cheeks to the cords around her waist. "But why?"

The ghost tugged the cords snug, but not tight. "I need your climax to feed." He slid two fingers along the snug cords, brushing her intimately.

She shivered in sheer revulsion. "What has that got to do with a rope?"

He set two fingers right over her clit. "The binding will stimulate a swift rise, so that you will be ready for swift release when I take you." Holding that one spot between his fingertips, he tugged the cords free. "Turn back around, slowly."

Luxi turned around and stared down at the top of the ghost's head. She seriously doubted anything would get her hot enough to enjoy anything he did to her. "You're going to rape me." It wasn't a question.

"Yes." The ghost made a knot where his fingers marked. "I feed on pleasure, terror, or death." He looked up at her. "Which would you prefer?"

Luxi turned away. *I'd prefer to be home and asleep.* But home was gone. She took a shaky breath. *I don't think Leto and Amun are going to get me out of this one.* She closed her eyes. *As long as I'm breathing, there's a way out. I just have to be ready for the opportunity when it comes.*

The ghost made a second knot about three inches further down. "Death delivers the entire essence all at once, but of course, the servant is no more. Death is wasteful in one with gifts as plentiful as yours." He set his hands on her thighs. "Turn back around."

Luxi turned around and stared at the wall. *At least I'm more valuable alive than dead.*

The ghost brought the cords to the front and passed it between her legs. "Terror delivers a scanty amount and tends to render the servant incapable of functioning independently. It eventually destroys the mind." He pushed the tasseled ends up under the cords knotted around her waist. "Pleasure's release gives the largest essence without destroying the servant's mind, or the servant."

Luxi hunched her shoulders, chilled. It was like he was reciting a menu, or something.

"However, inducing pleasure in a reluctant servant curbs the will." He drew the cord snug. "Your will could benefit from curbing. You will live longer." He tugged.

Luxi's head came up and she inhaled sharply. The small knot put pressure right on top of her clit, and the other knot pressured the sensitive spot just beyond her body's entrance, just under her anus.

The ghost slid his fingers down along the cords and under, parting her intimate curls and pressing on each of the knots.

Luxi's clit pulsed in confused interest. She shivered and the hair stood on the back of her neck.

"Perfect placement." He chuckled softly. He slid both his hands under her and gently finger-tugged the cords apart, framing her clit between them, then pressing the twin cords between her tender folds. "By the time we arrive, you will be more than ready for me."

Luxi closed her eyes tight and bit back her humiliated moan. *Glory, what a sadistic asshole!*

"When I thrust into you between the cords, I will be squeezed as though you were a virgin." He slid a finger under the cords at her tailbone, loosened it a touch and knotted the ends swiftly. "And you are bound." He stepped back. "Very nice." He sighed. "Too bad there really isn't time for other pleasures. You may drop your skirts."

Luxi hastily dropped her skirts. She had no interest in what the ghost considered "other pleasures."

The ghost strode back to the lift's panel and thrust his hand in.

The lights flickered and the lift proceeded.

Luxi bent over to tug the under-robe and shift back into order. The cords and knots shifted against her clit, drawing forth a warm curl of interest. She froze. It felt as though a pair of fingers gently squeezed her clit and rubbed it at the same time. Her nipples tingled in reaction. *Oh, shit, the stupid thing actually works!*

She had to take a breath before she could continue. If this idea had belonged to anyone other than the ghost, she might have found the binding entertaining...but there was nothing entertaining about the fate he had planned for her. *Rape and draining...*

Fate! There has to be a way out of this! Keeping her back to him, she straightened slowly and opened to her talent for viewing the possibilities. Strands of synchronicity and decision stretched within her mind's eye.

"What are you doing?"

Luxi froze. He could sense that? She took a breath and scanned down her lines as fast as she could. "I'm contemplating my future." It was the absolute truth.

He chuckled. "You future will be long, if you are obedient."

Luxi looked at the lift wall but focused on her talent. The strands showed her a juncture, a decision that shifted away from the ghost and Vincent's future. *Good.* She let her talent fall back to a soft hum that would let her know when it was time, but no more.

It was all a matter of waiting for that opportunity to arrive. She just hoped she spotted the turning point in enough time to use it. She also hoped nothing happened to close that opportunity off. Too many strands of decision and potential surrounded it. One wrong move and that option would dissolve.

That meant continuing exactly as she had been, antagonistic, but not too much. She did not want him to choke her unconscious or pull out those phantom blades. She needed to be upright and in one piece to make a good escape. It was a delicate balance. She didn't want the ghost to think she had any hope left. But she didn't want him to think she'd given in entirely, either.

She pulled back her foot and kicked, striking the wall with the ball of her foot. The impact made a nice satisfying metallic bang. She released a breath. It didn't do any good whatsoever, but it made her feel a whole lot better.

The ghost laughed.

Within her, a strand of possibility pulled away and dissolved, strengthening her path toward escape.

"Come here." The ghost's voice was chill and commanding.

Warily, Luxi approached.

"Do not fight and all will be well." He slid his hand under her hair and caught a handful at the base of her neck. He tugged for good measure.

Luxi winced. *Asshole.*

"Remember, no one can see me, but you. Walk slowly and do not look into anyone's face." He pulled his hand from the lift panel.

The lift stopped

Luxi glanced toward the pile of cream silk in the corner. "My robe!"

"No."

The doors opened onto a dark hallway.

"Go."

Luxi stepped out into darkness.

A hum echoed around her and lights flickered into being around them, revealing a filthy, disused cross hallway. To the left and to the right, the hallway continued in darkness. The walls were plain steel painted with broad bands of metallic brown. They were somewhere in the Bronze district.

Luxi trembled. No one would even think to look down here for her.

The ghost turned her toward the left. "Walk."

Luxi walked. The ghost fell into step with her, his fingers snug in her hair, but not pinching. Around them, the lights bloomed into being, only to shut down as they passed. "Are you doing that, with the lights?"

"Yes." He snorted. "I do not need light, but I have no desire to have you fall and harm yourself."

"Oh." If she wanted to go back to the lift, it would be a run in the dark—chased by a ghost that didn't need light to see. Not a good plan. Her hands bunched the sides of her robe. "Where are you taking me?"

"Someplace secure."

Luxi grimaced. That answer was *so* not helpful. She took a steadying breath. *Okay, what's down here on Bronze?* The lower-income housing and cheap motels were supposed to be in Bronze. She was pretty sure she remembered reading about some kind of shopping district, too, so sooner or later, they would come to a populated area...

Her talent shimmered within her. Luxi bit her lip to hide her smile. That was where her chance of escape was, somewhere in a populated area. Her best guess was the shopping district. Was there anything else down here? Yes, as a matter of fact—direct access to privately docked ships.

A shimmer of possibility moved through her. A ship *was* woven into her possible future, the one she was trying to avoid. That had to be where the ghost was taking her. A shudder of alarm shook her. If she got on that ship, all futures closed to one dark thread.

"Is something wrong?"

"Wrong?" A spurt of sour humor startled a choked laugh out of Luxi. "You mean besides the fact that I'm the prisoner of a sadistic ghost that's going to rape me?"

The ghost snorted. "By the time we reach our destination, it will not be rape."

Luxi ground her teeth. "Yeah, right."

A nasty chuckle echoed along her outer thoughts. "Tell me, how do you find wearing the binding?"

Luxi had been focusing on other issues for a reason: to get her mind off the knots pressing and rubbing intimately with every single step. But now *he* wanted to talk about it. She took a careful breath. "It doesn't hurt."

"This binding is not designed to be painful, merely stimulating."

Luxi rolled her eyes. *Gee, thanks.* Now that her attention was on the cords rubbing back and forth against her clit, it was hard to ignore that she was definitely feeling stimulated. The cords were getting damp, too. Her clit gave an interested throb. *Change the subject! Change the subject! Change the subject!* "Um, there are painful ones?" She winced. Not a good change in subjects.

"A great many." He chuckled. "Are you getting wet?"

"Uh…"

"It is a simple matter for me to check."

Fate no, she didn't want him to check! "Yes." *Damn it.*

"Good."

Piss… Luxi scowled and ground her teeth as she walked.

The lights flickered on directly ahead, revealing a heavy steel circular blast door. They had come to the end of the hall.

Luxi stared up at the door. "I can't open that."

"I can." The ghost tugged her close to the right wall. He plunged his hand within and rummaged. "Ah!"

A ringing, grinding noise filled the small hallway. The door screeched in protest and rolled very slowly to the left. A siren wail blasted into the hall.

Luxi winced. *Looks like somebody noticed that the door was open.*

The ghost shoved her through the widening crack and into screaming pandemonium.

Chapter Fourteen

Luxi's first impressions were big, dark, noisy, and crowded. They had come out in the middle of a busy, multilevel shopping bazaar choked with tossed-together stalls made of every conceivable material. The light was uncertain and came from a million different directions, none of which were overhead. Bodies, human and otherwise, mostly otherwise, jostled her as they fought to either get *to* the opening door, or *from* it, and everyone was shouting.

Shoved among the throng by the ghost, Luxi tripped a lot. The floors were painfully uneven with cables strewn across them. The smell of oil and aging steel was overpowering. So was the smell of too many bodies of too many descriptions. Alarms were shrieking everywhere.

Luxi flinched under the noise, then stilled. Alarms meant security was coming. Her talent shimmered with tension. It was time to escape.

Luxi let the ghost propel her forward and allowed herself to be jostled back and forth by the anxious crowd.

The ghost's hands tightened in her hair and swore viciously as he fought to hang onto her.

It was coming; the opportunity was coming...

Luxi felt a hard shove and found herself in the direct path of a rather large and fast-moving bi-pedal saurian. This was it. She froze, and braced for impact.

The saurian slammed into her with incredible force, knocking her spinning and breathless out of his path. Luxi's hair ripped as she was torn right out of the ghost's grasp. And over, and into, someone's item-filled stall.

Luxi bit back a moan and opened her eyes. She had rolled into a huge pile of mechanical odds and ends she couldn't begin to identify, and they had spilled everywhere. She shifted among the pile. Everything had corners and they were digging into every inconvenient place on her body. There were going to be some nasty bruises all over her tomorrow.

Someone was shouting obscenities very close by. She looked up. The bright blue humanoid shop owner was screaming at the massive saurian—and the saurian was barking right back. She sucked in a breath. *Time to go!*

Luxi ducked her head and rolled cautiously out from under the pile. She pulled up her skirts and crawled on her hands and knees to the open back of the shop. There wasn't much room to maneuver; the shop was right up against a steel wall. As soon as both aliens were out of view, she got up on her feet and bolted along the steel wall, scooting behind the backs of dozens of makeshift stalls. *Got to find security!*

The uneven floor and deep shadows were not at all easy to negotiate at a run. There was stuff all over the floor and her slippers just weren't up to the task. Her feet were bruised in minutes. *That's it! Boots from now on!*

Running on instinct alone, she slipped between precarious booths, ducked under narrow walkways, and darted into half-lit alleys choked with people of every kind. Her talent told her that she was on the right path, but she had no idea where that path was leading. Her talent shifted in her like whiplash.

She jolted to the side, away from the oncoming...whatever it was, and rammed her shoulder against a pair of men in dark power armor. She yelped and fell.

They caught her elbows before her knees could hit the deck plates. "Whoa, take it easy!"

Luxi looked up in fright and prepared to run. *Sojourn Corp.* gleamed on their breast badges. She had found security. She sagged in their hands. "Thank the Maker!"

One of them shoved up his visor, showing startled brown eyes. "Hey, it's that missing diplomat!"

Luxi blinked. They had been looking for her? *Wow...* She gave them a smile, then darted a look around. Her talent was still shifting, the possibilities were still moving. She needed to get out of here. "My kidnapper is not far away; can we go? Like right now?"

The man grinned. "Everything will be fine now; we have you."

Luxi smiled. "Thank you, but can we go?" She shoved at his armored side.

"Sure, we can go." The men laughed and set her between them. With a heavy armored hand on each shoulder, they guided her through the heart of the bazaar.

One of the guards chatted code into his helmet communicator. He looked down. "Okay, your people are coming to meet you."

Luxi blinked. *My people?* It took her an entire breath, and then it hit her. Leto and Amun were coming. They were her people. She had to blink back sudden tears. She'd never had *people* before. She'd had companies and employers and supervisors, but not people, as in, someone she mattered to.

"Hey, do you know who opened that big power door?"

The other guard snorted. "Like she's gonna know?"

Luxi wiped at her damp cheeks. Fate and glory, her hands were filthy… "My kidnapper did it."

"What?"

Luxi lengthened her stride to get them to walk faster. "The lift from the assembly hall took us to the hallway on the other side of the door. He opened the door; that's how I'm here."

"How did he open it? Only the station master has those codes."

Luxi shook her head. "You wouldn't believe me if I told you."

"Try us."

Luxi looked around. "I will, as soon as we get someplace safe."

The guards turned a sharp corner to the left and a lift opened up right in front of her, not two steps away.

Leto, tall, dark and very menacing, and Amun, still in his deep-silver court robes, came out of the lift surrounded by four Sojourn security guards in full armor. Their mouths were tight and they looked positively furious.

Leto and Amun stopped, staring.

Luxi stopped, unsure what to do.

Amun lunged forward and wrapped her in a tight hug. "Thank the Maker!"

Leto looked around, vibrating with tension. He held out his arm and herded everyone back. "Get back in. It's coming."

Amun turned, sweeping Luxi before him, and into the lift.

The lift doors closed.

Amun, Luxi, and Leto made a small knot in the back corner. Amun caught Luxi's shoulders "Blood and fate, you are *filthy!*"

Luxi flinched. "I had to do some crawling. I'm really sorry about the silk."

Amun smiled. "Clothing is replaceable; you are not. I'm simply glad you are all in one piece."

Not replaceable? Luxi stilled in shock. No one had ever said that to her before. She turned her head and blinked. Fate, what was with her, crying over every stupid little thing? She grabbed her elbows and took a deep breath. *Later, I'll think about it later.* She looked up at Amun. "How did you get down there so fast?"

Amun smiled. "We were already on the way."

Leto grinned. "Your ankle bracelet has a transmitter in it. We were tracking you the whole time."

Oddly, Luxi felt both reassured and annoyed. She couldn't believe she'd forgotten. On second thought, she'd never worn one before, so she had no real reason to remember. She shook her head. *Never mind, I'll think about it later!* She rubbed her grubby hands on her dirty silk robe. "I think he was taking me to a ship."

Amun looked over at Leto. "I suspected as much."

Leto wrapped his arm around her shoulders and grinned. "Yeah, but we have you now."

Luxi smiled at Leto. He was warm, solid, and smelled wonderful. Her core gave a hungry throb, and then another. She still had that rope thing on, and it was doing its job a little too well. Her thighs were wet with aggravated excitement. The guards were the only thing keeping her from begging one of them to press her up against the wall. She took a deep breath. *Think about something else!* "What happened with the captain that attacked you? Did they arrest him?"

Amun sighed. "He was not taken into custody."

Luxi sucked in a sharp breath. "What? Why not?"

Leto snorted. "Diplomatic immunity."

Amun sighed. "But he has been escorted off the station and to the jump-gate."

Luxi released a breath. "I was so worried."

"You?" Leto grabbed her shoulders and turned her to face him. "When I saw that ghost drag you off, I about leaped through the grid!"

Amun cleared his throat. "Being crisped beyond redemption would not have done anyone much good."

Leto scowled. "Not all of me is physical."

Amun set his hand on Leto's shoulder. "But some of your more interesting parts are. I'd prefer if you kept them intact." He smiled. "For me." He turned to Luxi. "However did you get away?"

Luxi grinned. "I followed my talent. There was a loophole in the possibilities, so I took it."

"Good girl." Leto looked over at Amun and clenched his jaw. "We really need to deal with Vincent..."

Luxi shook her head. "It's not Vincent we need to worry about."

Amun frowned. "No?"

Luxi's hands tightened on her elbows. "I think the ghost is really in charge."

Amun nodded. "I thought that might be the case." He turned to Leto. "We *do* need a specialist."

The lights flickered.

Luxi looked up and shivered hard. "It's the ghost. He's going to stop the lift."

Amun turned to Leto and caught his wrist. "Whatever happens, do not leave her side."

Leto scowled. "Why? Where are you going?"

"To collect our specialist." Amun smiled. "Unless you'd rather I stayed with Luxi...?"

"No." Leto scowled. "Get that specialist, and get back fast—and take the damned guards with you!"

"I intend to." Amun's smile disappeared. "Do whatever it takes to survive." He turned to Luxi. "I want you both in one piece."

Leto nodded and set his hands on his blade hilts.

Luxi looked up at him. "Leto, he's a ghost—*all* ghost. Your weapons won't have any effect on him."

Leto smiled nastily. "Oh, I know."

The lift stopped. The four guards shifted uneasily.

The commanding officer turned to the guard closest to the panel. "What the hell just happened?"

The guard peered at the lift panel. "We've stopped somewhere between Bronze and Silver."

The door opened on darkness

The guard stared at open door. "I didn't know there was a floor here?"

The commander scowled. "Neither did I."

The gray-green uniformed ghost formed in the doorway and focused on Luxi. "Enjoy your little run?"

The guards stared at the open doorway, clearly seeing nothing. "What the hell is going on?"

"I don't know!"

"Do something!"

"I am doing something! The panel's not working!"

"Then do something else!"

Luxi clenched her fists and glared at the ghost. "Go away."

The ghost smiled. "Oh, but you have something I need."

Amun took hold of Luxi's shoulder. "Luxi..." He looked toward the door and drew in a breath. "Blood and hell..."

Leto closed his hand tight on Luxi's other shoulder. "You can't have her."

The ghost focused on Leto. His eyes narrowed. "You..."

Leto bared his teeth in something that didn't even remotely resemble a smile. "Yeah, me."

The ghost tilted his head and his gaze focused on Luxi. "This lift is a rather large number of floors from ground level." He smiled. "Shall I drop it?"

The lights flickered in the lift and the floor shuddered. The guards shouted in alarm.

Luxi grabbed onto Leto to keep from falling. "No! Don't"

The ghost smiled. "Then come along, so they can get on with their...lives."

Leto's lips curled back from his teeth. "You bastard!"

The ghost grinned and his eyes narrowed. "You can come, too, if you'd like to be consumed." His gaze slid to Amun, braced next to Leto and clinging to Luxi's other shoulder. "If fact, you can bring your other companion, as well."

Amun smiled slightly. "Thank you, but I'll pass." He released Luxi's shoulder and stepped back.

Leto looked back at Amun.

Amun's mouth tightened.

The ghost shrugged. "Shall we proceed?"

Leto squeezed her shoulder.

Luxi wrapped her arms around herself and stepped toward the ghost with Leto at her side.

The ghost backed away from the doorway.

"Hey!" The guard commander moved toward them. "You can't get off here!"

Leto and Luxi stepped off.

The lift door closed with blinding speed, leaving them in utter darkness. Hollow bangs came from the other side of the door, and faded.

"Alone at last." The ghost's voice was an icy wind.

Electronics hummed and archaic lights flickered on directly overhead. Several popped and went out, but enough stayed on to show an enormous, empty oval-shaped room. Plain steel girders rose along the curved walls and arched upward. The far walls were enshrouded in darkness.

Luxi looked around. "Where are we?"

"Somewhere private." The ghost smiled. "Where I can feed without disturbance."

Luxi jerked back around to stare at the ghost. Icy shivers slid down her spine.

The ghost nodded slowly. "Oh, yes, I'm afraid it's time."

Leto casually strode toward the ghost. "Out of sheer curiosity, are you from Terra, say about the turn of the nineteenth century?"

The ghost stilled. "I am."

Leto nodded. "I thought I recognized the uniform." He smiled shook his head. "You are quite an old boy."

The ghost narrowed his eyes. "Far older than you."

Leto looked up at the girders overhead. "Well, yes and no." He turned back to the ghost. "You see, I was born at the turn of the twenty-second century, but I didn't actually lose all my biological components 'til centuries later. You've been dead longer than I have, but I was alive a lot longer than you."

The ghost scowled. "I had a living host."

Leto shook his head. "Not quite the same thing." His raised his chin. "Oh, and for the record. You are not feeding on Luxi." He grinned. "She's *my* dinner date."

The ghost unsheathed his sword and knife. "Do you honestly think you can stop me?"

"Blades?" Leto rolled his eyes dramatically while pushing Luxi back. "You're using blades? Where's your imagination?"

The ghost froze and his brows lowered, clearly at a loss.

Leto laughed. "Oh, please...! You and I have been around long enough to know that true spirit-beings don't need weapons when we fight." His body froze in place. Darkness shimmered around him, and then a black form stepped forward, out of the cyborg shell.

Leto's phantom body was shaped exactly the same, but he consisted of boiling black shadow with a gleam of scarlet flame for eyes. His long mane floated behind him in smoky tendrils. A shimmer of tiny lights, like blinking circuitry, winked throughout his form. He spread his arms wide and his fingers extended into claws as long as his forearm. "Real phantoms are weapons, all by themselves."

Luxi shivered under the impact of her talent. Leto's ghostly voice was a cool, insinuating autumn wind with a hint of smoke, compared to the ghost's dead-of-winter chill.

The ghost stepped back and his lips pulled back from his teeth. "Demon!"

Leto laughed. "You have no idea." He began to expand and reshape into a monstrous two-legged form of boiling, winking shadow that was all claws, serrated scales, and fangs. "Shall we dance?" He dropped to all fours and charged, his shape flowing into something resembling a scaled feline, complete with lashing tail.

The ghost danced out of reach and slashed out with his sword.

Leto moved under and around the blade like smoke. He laughed. "Oh, come on! You're supposed to be a bad-ass! Let's see it!"

"Impudent fool!" The ghost whirled away and sheathed his blades. "Very well…" He clapped his hands together and snarled out a phrase Luxi's interpreter couldn't translate. He shouted and spread his hands.

His form extended up and up in a serpentine column of white smoke. A narrow muzzle formed, split, and filled with teeth. Eyes of yellow flame opened. Scales and serrated fins emerged down the creature's spine. Clawed arms, legs, and wings spread from its back. A long tail lashed, and it floated.

Leto laughed. "That's better!" Clawed wings spread from his monstrous feline form and he rose into the air. "Now we can do this properly..." He lunged, a snarling, demonic creature of black smoke edged with flame.

Chapter Fifteen

Ethereal wind howled and screamed as the two monstrous ghosts entangled and lashed around each other, their battle filling the echoing room with their whirling storm of smoke. Leto's blackness flowed between shapes. Heads formed and bit from every conceivable angle. Clawed limbs formed and slashed from random places, and scarlet eyes opened everywhere.

The ghost remained solidly as a snarling and coiling white, winged serpent.

Luxi backed hard against the lift, her heart slamming painfully in her chest. The hurricane of power unleashed by the two spirits was horrifically terrifying. And yet the most fantastic thing she'd ever seen.

The lift door opened at her back.

Luxi screamed and whirled around.

Amun smiled at her. "Luxi! Where's Leto?"

Luxi pointed a shaking finger toward the center of the room.

Amun focused on Leto's abandoned cyborg body and frowned. "Why is he so still?"

Luxi had to take a breath to speak. "Because he's not in it."

Amun frowned. "What?"

"See for yourself." Luxi caught his hand, allowing him direct access to her talent.

Amun froze, staring. "Holy Mother Night!"

Someone came forward from within the lift. "May I see?"

Amun stepped from the lift and to the side, his hand nearly crushing Luxi's fingers as he stared at the battling phantoms.

A young man, about a head shorter than Amun and dressed entirely in black, stepped from the lift. His broad shoulders and narrow waist were accentuated by his understated but exceedingly well-cut ankle-length suit coat and knife-edge dress slacks. His face had a handsomely exotic cast with straight black brows. His straight black hair was pulled back into a long tail that fell to between his shoulder blades. He folded his hands behind his back. "I see." He inclined his head toward Amun then looked down at Luxi. "Which one is yours?"

Luxi stared into his shadow-filled eyes and shivered. *Great Maker, another ghost!* "Leto is the black one."

The young man's almond-shaped eyes crinkled at the corners with his smile. "You must be Gentle-fem Emory."

Amun tore his gaze from the battling phantoms. "Luxi, this is Avatar Shido from the temple of the Black Lotus."

Luxi grabbed onto Amun's wrist. "Another Avatar, like Vincent?"

Amun patted her hand. "Avatar Shido is nothing like Vincent. When I told him of your pursuer, he had no idea who Vincent was. Vincent is not an actual Avatar; he's a renegade."

"Oh, Vincent is an Avatar. He has a ghost." Shido shook his head. "However, the ghost is very much a renegade."

Amun looked back toward the phantoms and squeezed Luxi's hand. "Avatar Shido is here to collect the ghost."

Luxi looked over at Avatar Shido. "What about Vincent?"

"My associates already have him in custody." Shido sighed. "We'll see that he doesn't bother you anymore." He looked up at the battling spirits and stepped away from them. "I think this has gone on quite long enough." He pressed his palms together. "Tsuke."

A form stepped out of Avatar Shido's body and became a broad man in overlapping decorative armor.

Shido turned to him. "Tsuke, do you recognize him?"

The broad ghost folded his arms across his armored chest. "I've never seen the young black one before. However, I am fairly certain the other is Yamura Kato."

Shido's hands closed into fists. "Bind-master Kato? He's been missing since Serendipity!"

"It wears his seal." Tsuke nodded toward Shido, then focused on Luxi. "Oh, that's why he was chasing the little fem."

Shido folded his arms and raised his brow. "Pity she's claimed, yes?"

Tsuke smiled. "A very great pity."

Shido tilted his head toward the room. "Can you take Kato?"

Tsuke snorted. "In my sleep." He bowed to Shido, then grinned and bowed to Luxi, too. He turned toward the center of the room and dissolved into a snaking mist that headed straight for the combatants.

The two battling ghosts snapped apart.

Tsuke slid between Leto and the flying serpent. "Good fight, boy. I'll take over from here."

Leto coalesced into his scaled feline form. "Are you sure you can handle him alone?"

"Of course! Kato and I are old companions." Tsuke laughed. "Go, before you fall apart."

The flying serpent focused on the coiling mist. "Yoshiro Tsuke?"

The mist spread in a curtain of long fingers. "Yamura Kato. It is time to go home, binder. Your temple has missed you."

"No!" Kato screamed and attacked—and became entangled in Tsuke's web.

Tsuke's laughter boomed around the struggling serpent. "You know you cannot defeat me. Why do you try?"

Leto drifted toward his abandoned cyborg shell, his form shrinking and fading until he was once again in a man's form.

Amun and Luxi hurried to meet him.

Leto dropped to the deck and stepped into his body. The cyborg gasped and collapsed to his knees. "Damn, I'm burnt."

Amun caught one arm and helped him onto his feet. "Are you going to live?"

Leto smiled tiredly. "Very funny. Ha, ha."

Luxi lifted his other arm over her shoulder and grinned at Amun. "He'll live."

Amun steadied Leto with a hand pressed to his heart. "Are you hurt?"

Leto leaned against Amun and shook his head. "I'm all right, just really exhausted."

Shido came up behind him. "You are lucky he didn't consume you."

"I think that was his plan." Leto turned to look at Shido. "But *my* plan was to keep him too busy to try it."

Shido nodded and smiled. "A good plan."

Leto raised his brow at Amun. "The specialist?"

Amun smiled tightly. "There is only one way to catch an Avatar: with another Avatar. This is Avatar Shido—"

"Shido!" Tsuke's voice boomed around them. "Kato is missing a part. I can't hold him for long without it!"

Luxi flinched. She was wearing it. "I have it."

All three men blinked. "You?"

Luxi felt her cheeks heat. "It's… I…" She swallowed. "I'm going to need help getting it off."

Shido nodded. "Show me."

Luxi ducked behind Leto. "No! It's…" She looked at Leto and Amun. "It's someplace private."

"Ah." Shido cleared his throat, but couldn't quite conceal his amusement. "You have his cord, I assume?"

Heat scorched Luxi's cheeks. She nodded.

Amun frowned, then turned to Luxi. "A cord?"

Shido turned to Amun. "She *is* going to need help getting it off."

Leto grinned. "I think I know what's going on. Luxi, why don't you show us in the lift?"

Luxi nodded.

Within the lift, Leto crouched down against the steel wall with Amun at his shoulder. Luxi parted her filthy, battered silk robes and turned around to show them the pair of red phantom cords that wound around her waist. From a knot over her navel, a pair of cords dropped straight down to a knot directly on her clit. After the knot, the cords bisected to frame her clit and then knotted again beneath her anus before traveling back up the seam of her butt cheeks to another knot at the small of her back.

Leto chuckled. "I'll be damned..."

Amun set his hand on Luxi's shoulder and frowned. "I've never seen anything like that."

Leto raised a brow. "I have, but not for a long time. Turn around, Luxi, I'll get it off."

Luxi turned around to face the interior of the lift and looked over her shoulder. "You've seen this before?"

Amun frowned. "Why is she wearing it?"

Leto's fingers tugged at the knot in the back. "This little piece of work is something from Terra's very distant past. It's used to make the wearer very aroused, very fast." His fingers slid under and along the rope. Her cream slicked his fingers. He chuckled. "And it feels like it's doing its job pretty well, too."

Luxi flinched. "Just get it off."

Amun glanced at Luxi. "Is it uncomfortable?"

"No, it's just...um..." Luxi trembled. It was just driving her insane with lust, and Leto's inquisitive explorations were not making it any easier. She had to work to keep her breathing steady, to hide the moans that were dying to come out.

Leto gently drew the cord free of Luxi's crotch. "It's not supposed to be uncomfortable." He turned her around to work the knot from her waist. "It's supposed to be stimulating." He grinned at Amun. "Stimulating to both participants."

Amun raised a calculating brow. "You don't say?"

"The idea is to slide between the cords. The knots stimulate the wearer." Leto licked his lips. "While making the fit snug."

Amun pursed his lips. "How very interesting."

Leto tugged the cord free of her waist. "This is one wet rope."

Fine, rub it in. Luxi glared at him. "Get rid of it."

Leto laughed and tossed it. The phantom cord disappeared into thin air.

Luxi began to tug her rumpled robes back down.

Leto's slid his hands up the outside of her bare thighs. "Speaking of stimulating, I'm hungry." He looked up at Luxi with burning eyes. "How about a taste of that wet pussy?"

Luxi swallowed and clutched at her spread robes. "Right now?"

Leto licked his lips and focused on her exposed crotch. "I could really use it."

Luxi's heart hammered in her chest and her breath hitched. She could use the relief, actually. "Um…"

Leto flashed a grin. "That wasn't a 'no.' Put your hands on the wall over my head and spread for me."

Luxi released her robes, letting them fall over Leto's arms. "But Avatar Shido will be in here…"

"So?" Leto tugged on her thighs. "You've had an audience before."

Luxi tipped forward and her hands slapped against the wall as she arched over Leto's head.

Amun chuckled. "Lord Bel did mention something to that effect."

Luxi groaned. "Does everybody know?" Wet heat stroked her inflamed flesh and lightning struck. She gasped and shuddered.

"Mmm...Blood and hell, you're wet." He lapped loudly. "Close, too."

Glory, yes, she was... Luxi came up on her toes, bucking in time to his lashing tongue. Tension built to a murderous pitch with incredible speed. She threw back her head and whimpers escaped her lips.

Amun came up behind her. "Is there room for one more?" His hands closed on Luxi's shoulders.

And a telepathic connection opened between them all. Heat and hunger washed in a tidal wave across the connection.

Amun gasped. "Great Maker..." His hands slid down and into Luxi's white robe to cup her breasts. His fingers closed on her swollen nipples and tugged.

Luxi arched, pressing her breasts deeper into Amun's hands, feeling his erection pressing against her butt. She turned to look up at him.

Amun took her mouth in a swift hungry kiss.

She moaned into his mouth. Amun shifted behind her and she felt him parting his silver robes, then moving her robes to one side to expose her butt. The heat of Amun's shaft slid between her thighs and up against her wet cunt, and Leto's working mouth.

Leto moaned in interest.

Amun gasped. "Just who are you licking?"

Luxi jolted with the echo of Amun's pleasure as Leto stroked the head of his cock with his wet tongue.

Leto chuckled. "What does it feel like?" His hands shifted under Luxi.

Luxi felt the head of Amun's cock center between her folds. She could actually feel both Leto's warm grasp around Amun's cock and Amun's desperate, trembling need to thrust. She could also sense his hesitation. She took a breath. "Amun, do it."

Amun thrust.

Luxi groaned as his cock stretched and filled her with his hot, hard heat.

Leto chuckled. "Oh, yeah...fuck her." His mouth descended to where their bodies were joined, and lashed across her clit and the base of the hard cock lodged in her.

Amun groaned, withdrew, and thrust, and thrust, and thrust...

Luxi braced her feet as Amun's hips slammed against her butt with merciless strength. Leto's hands steadied her against the slapping impact and Amun's fingers tightened on her aching nipples.

Climax rose and crested with breathless speed.

Leto groaned. "Oh...shit..." He pulled one hand away from her legs but continued his frantic licking.

Luxi couldn't see it, but she heard Leto open his suit. An echo of sensation told her that he had his cock out and was stroking it hard.

Leto pulled back, breathless. "Get down," he gasped. "Both of you, on your knees. Keep her upright."

Amun caught Luxi around the hips and pulled her down to her knees with him. Her thighs splayed wide as he leaned back on his heels. "Lean back against my shoulder."

Luxi set her head back against Amun's shoulder and put her arms up around his neck.

Amun smiled. "Yes, that's it." He thrust, hard.

Leto stood and leaned back against the wall, stroking his heavy cock, his eyes gleaming with red flame. "Keep fucking; don't stop."

Amun pulled her robe open on top, baring her breasts. And thrust hard, up into her, hammering her with his strong stokes.

Luxi writhed, burning and on fire, her core clenching tight. Small gasping cries escaped her lips. She was going to come…

Leto leaned over them, setting his hand on Amun's shoulder for balance and stroking his cock with vicious haste. "Oh, Maker, she's right there." He choked. "Give me your eyes!"

They both looked up.

Lightning struck and release exploded through all three of them. The liquid fire of rapture washed through them, and over them, every release flowing through each of them in a triple wave of intense, burning pleasure. They howled, shuddered, and bucked under the torment.

Leto's eyes burned—and pulled.

A part of Amun and Luxi was pulled, fluttering, from within their hearts. They gasped.

Leto drew it in on a breath…and fed.

A stream of hot, white viscous liquid splattered across Luxi's breasts, even as she felt the pulse of Amun's cock filling her.

Leto groaned as he emptied stream after stream of hot cum. He exhaled and dropped to his knees, wrapping them both in his arms. He covered Luxi's mouth in a devouring kiss, then turned to take Amun's.

They held each other, all three locked in a mutual embrace, trembling as the last of their shared pleasure burned down to embers.

Leto leaned back on his heels and grinned. "Oh, that was a nice snack."

Luxi groaned as hot cum slithered down into her robes. "Glory, I'm covered in...!" She narrowed her eyes at one, and then the other, grinning male.

Amun choked out a laugh. "Cum. You are covered in Leto's cum." He pulled her robe back over her sticky breasts.

Leto chuckled. "And let me tell you, I was happy to put it there."

"You would be." Luxi writhed. "Bloody fate, Amun, you're getting it all over the robes!"

Leto climbed to his feet and leaned against the side of the lift and laughed. "It's all over the robes anyway; I wasn't exactly careful."

Luxi shot him a hot look. "I noticed."

Amun snorted and pushed Luxi up on her feet. "The robes were already well beyond cleaning."

Luxi stood on shaky feet and felt more cum slithering down her thighs. "Oh, icky!"

Amun chuckled climbed to his feet. "Shall I run you a bath?"

Excitement coiled up Luxi's spine. "A real one, with water, in that huge tub?"

Amun smiled, tucking his robes back around him. "I'll even add bubbles."

Leto grabbed the front of Amun's robes and tugged him closer. "What do you say we all have a nice soak in the tub and spend the rest of the night fucking?"

Amun smiled. "That sounds very…appetizing."

Chapter Sixteen

"Is it safe to come in now?" Avatar Shido's voice was distinctly amused.

Luxi groaned as her cheeks flushed with warmth.

Amun chuckled. "Yes, we are quite finished."

Shido laughed as he stepped into the lift. "I'll have you know that Tsuke is quite upset that he wasn't invited." He turned and set his palm on the lift controls.

The doors closed and the lift activated.

Leto pulled both Amun and Luxi into his embrace. He smiled, but narrowed his eyes at the Avatar. "Sorry, private party."

Shido grinned. "That's what I told him." He tilted his head. "You're nearly back up to full strength. Your two chosen must be quite talented."

Leto relaxed against the back of the lift wall, an arm around Luxi and an arm around Amun. "That's one way to put it."

Amun lifted his brow. "I am a professional-grade telepath."

Shido frowned thoughtfully. "Yes, Lord Amun, this I know, but according to my...impressions, the gentle-fem is also a major talent. In fact, her ghost-touch registers as being secondary, almost minor by comparison."

Amun gently pressed his fingers against Luxi's lips. "You are quite correct. Luxi is possessed of a major talent."

Luxi looked up at Amun in curiosity. Amun didn't want Shido to know about her fortune-telling abilities? How strange.

Shido's brows lifted. "I see." He focused on Luxi. "Should you ever be in need of employment, gentle-fem, the Temple of the Black Lotus would love to have you." He quoted a salary big enough to afford a small luxury cruiser.

Leto stilled utterly.

Amun frowned. "That is quite a *princely* sum, Avatar."

Shido smiled. "For a talent like hers? I can afford it."

Amun looked down at Luxi. "Would you prefer to go with Avatar Shido?"

Luxi frowned up at Amun. "But I thought I was...?" *Indentured, a legal slave.*

Amun smiled, a little sadly. "That can be changed; easily, in fact."

Leto brushed his fingers across her brow. "Luxi, if you don't want to stay, we're not going to make you."

Amun glanced at Leto, then looked at Luxi. "Would you like to...go?"

Luxi grabbed her elbows and blinked rapidly to control the stinging in her eyes. Didn't they want her any more? She took a deep breath. "If you don't need me...to stay..."

"What kind of question is that?" Leto frowned. "If we didn't want you, we wouldn't have offered in the first place."

Amun leaned close to catch her hand. "Actually, I'd prefer to keep you, if you don't mind?"

"You would?" Luxi's heart constricted in her chest. They wanted her?

Amun smiled. "Of course, we haven't had a chance to explore the full range of your..." He raised a red brow and gave her a thoroughly lascivious smile. "...talents, yet."

Leto glared down at her. "Yes, we want you. Is that clear enough?"

Luxi had to remember to breathe "Oh... I..." They wanted her to stay—with them. "I'd like to stay, if you don't mind."

Amun nodded and smiled broadly. "Good."

Leto's head fell back against the lift wall. "Thank the Maker!"

Luxi turned to look over at Avatar Shido. "I'm sorry, Avatar, but I'm going to have to turn your more than generous offer down."

Shido grinned and shrugged. "I understand perfectly."

Leto smiled down at her. "I was beginning to think you didn't like us any more."

"Of course I like you!" Luxi rolled over to wrap Leto in a hug. She turned and smiled at Amun. "I like you both, a lot." She rubbed her chest against Leto's silk court robe, just a little.

Leto looked down and raised a brow. "You're rubbing cum all over me."

Luxi looked up and grinned. "Why yes, I am."

Amun choked on a chuckle. "Well, since you are remaining my employee, so to speak, you realize you'll have to be punished for ruining that expensive robe he's wearing?"

Luxi's mouth fell open. "Punished?"

* * *

Luxi crossed her arms over her naked breasts and stared. The huge black-and-gold marble bathtub was filled nearly to the brim with steaming bubbles. It looked completely inviting. She scowled. "Guys, this is grossly unfair."

"Unfair?" Leto let the sleek black dressing robe slide from his bare shoulders and tossed it on the counter. "I don't think so at all!" He turned to face her. His erection was a pale, smooth column arching rigidly up to his navel. "I was all for a spanking, myself."

Luxi's core gave a hungry, wet throb. He looked good enough to eat. Then it registered as to what he'd just said. "A spanking?"

Amun smiled at Leto as he let his pale silver robe slide off. "Would you prefer a spanking?" He set his robe on the counter over Leto's.

"No, but..." Luxi dragged her gaze from Leto's ruggedly masculine body and mouthwatering cock, only to find Amun's sleek muscular form and rigid cock just as arresting. She had to take a breath and close her eyes against the sight before she could gather her thoughts enough to deliver her answer. "Look, I didn't mind taking a shower to get all the dirt off before I got in the tub, but I just got that stupid rope off..." She opened her eyes and pointed toward the cream cords bound around her waist and crotch. "And you put another one on me?"

Leto shrugged. "We had to do something to punish you."

Luxi's mouth fell open. "What?"

Amun set his hands on her shoulders and smiled from only a kiss away. "Think of it as therapy, to get past your traumatic experience."

Leto strode past them chuckling. "You two can talk; I'm getting in the tub." He climbed the three steps up and stepped over the tub's broad edge, then down into the water. He groaned. "Blood and hell, this feels good."

Amun turned Luxi toward the deep tub. "Go on."

Luxi stared longingly at the bubbles. "But the cord is going to get all wet…"

Leto grinned as he moved through the waist-deep water. "Yes, and slippery too. That's high-quality silk, you know." He turned to sit on an underwater seat and leaned against the back with a heartfelt moan.

Luxi groaned. *Oh, what the hell…* She stepped to the edge, the cords caressing and rubbing, the small knot shifting back and forth against her clit as she moved. A flare of erotic heat coiled and clenched deep in her core. Carefully, she stepped up and over, then into the foamy water up to her breasts. The warmth caressed her deliciously with just a hint of sting. A moan escaped her. It felt damned good.

Amun followed right behind her, then gently steered her toward Leto, their strides sloshing through the bubbles.

Leto lifted his arms and his smile turned distinctly lascivious. "Come sit in my lap, little girl."

Luxi raised her brow disdainfully.

"Go on." Amun gave Luxi a little push.

Luxi yelped and tipped forward, catching onto Leto's shoulders...and felt the moving darkness under his skin. Her hands opened wide, spreading her fingers to feel more of him.

"Come down here." Leto groaned, caught her around the waist, and tugged her down and across his lap.

Luxi splashed into the sudsy heat, her legs splayed over his right knee and her right arm around Leto's neck for balance. The heated water closed over her breasts in a rich, decadent blanket of scented warmth. She groaned and released his neck to fall back, arching and stretching, luxuriating in the sinful delight of a bath. Her red curls fanned out in the water.

Leto raised his arm to support her neck, keeping her face out of the water, and laughed. "I think she likes it." He grinned at Amun.

Luxi grinned. "I love water."

Amun smiled and sank into the water. "It certainly looks that way." He scooted up against Leto's right shoulder and lifted Luxi's legs over his lap. He smiled at Leto. "I am interested in just how slippery that silk is getting."

Leto raised his brow. "Then why don't you check and see?" He licked his lips.

Amun smiled and leaned closer. "Don't mind if I do." He slid his hand languorously up Luxi's inner thighs and parted them.

Luxi shivered. "Amun?"

Leto bent down and caught Luxi's chin. "Kiss me."

Luxi leaned up, opening for his kiss. Velvet softness moved against her lips. She stroked his full bottom lip with the tip of her tongue then extended her tongue to meet his. Warmth, wetness, breath, shadows...

Amun's fingers drifted higher up her thighs. He brushed against the plump outer lips and then the intimate folds of her core, drawing small shudders from her flesh.

Leto pressed closer and his tongue surged into her mouth for a thorough exploration. His hand closed on her breast and squeezed. His thumb rubbed, circling one swollen pink nipple, sending jolt after hot jolt straight to Luxi's clit.

Luxi shivered with growing anticipation.

Amun's fingers lightly brushed the cords. "This is getting quite slippery." He pressed against the silk rope framing her clit.

Lightning speared Luxi's tender clit. She moaned into Leto's mouth.

Amun slid two fingers between the silk cords and into her warmth.

Luxi broke the kiss on a gasp and rolled against Amun's fingers. "Oh...shit!" Wet heat clenched tight in her belly

"I see what you meant about 'snug.'" Amun swept his thumb over the point of her clit.

Luxi bucked hard.

"And effective." Amun smiled.

Leto grinned and tugged on Luxi's trapped nipple. "If I'd had more cord, I could have done the same to her breasts, too."

Amun licked his lips. "Ah, then we will most definitely have to invest in more silk cord."

Luxi shivered under their hands. "Haven't you done enough?" The fire in her tormented nipple and pressured clit was building a ferocious and ravenous ache in her belly. If they kept this up, she was going to come right there...

Leto grinned as he squeezed and tugged Luxi's breast and nipple. "Are you kidding? With enough silk rope, I could suspend you in any position I wanted." He looked over at Amun. "It was a hobby of mine at one time, suspending captives."

Amun raised a brow thoughtfully. "That sounds quite entertaining."

"Especially on a long voyage." Leto grinned.

Luxi groaned under the pleasurable torment of their stirring hands. Being tied up and pleasured by the both of them sounded like a very delicious idea, but she wasn't sure if it was the brightest idea in the cosmos. Glory only knew what they'd think to do with her, and to her...

Amun reached up to cup her other breast then trapped her nipple in his fingers. "How much rope would be needed for such a suspension?" He pinched the swollen point.

Luxi gasped. Erotic fire seared through her, shoving her right to the edge of a ferocious release. The climax slid back and she bucked helplessly in reaction.

Leto chuckled as Luxi thrashed in his arms. "I can give you an exact set of lengths and diameters, if you like."

Amun grinned. "I'd like."

Luxi panted and boiled, shivering under the ravages of her close brush with release. "I don't know if I want to be suspended."

Amun pulled his fingers from her core and pressed them to her lips. "Suck."

Luxi opened her mouth and took his fingers into her mouth, tasting her own cream on her tongue. She shivered. It was so...*naughty.*

Amun pressed his fingers against his tongue. "Luxi, you are the indentured employee, and I am your master. You will take your orders like a good employee. Yes?" He pulled his finger from her mouth.

Luxi stared at him in shock. "But I thought you could remove...that?"

Amun smiled. "Yes, I can. But alas, for you, I am no longer so inclined."

"What?" Luxi struggled to sit up. "Oh, you...!"

Leto held her down, grinning. "Controlling bastard?"

Amun shook his head. "Leto did warn you that I have control issues."

"I did." Leto nodded, not even bothering to hide his grin. "Luxi, I did tell you."

Luxi folded her arms over her breasts and glared at them both.

Amun blinked. "Is that a pout?"

Leto stuck out his bottom lip in imitation. "Don't you love us any more?"

Luxi opened her mouth...and couldn't say a word. *Love?* Shock rippled through her entire body and a fist squeezed around her heart, stealing her breath. Actually...she did. She did love them. *Oh, glory...* How had that happened?

Amun frowned. "Luxi, what is it?"

It took two tries before she could get enough air to breath. "I, uh..." A shudder raked her. "Actually, I think I do."

Leto stilled. "You do?"

Luxi turned away and nodded. She was in love—with both of them. And they were in love—with each other. She had to close her eyes, but it didn't stop the ache in her heart, or in her eyes. It hurt... Glory, it hurt to be on the outside.

Amun glanced at Leto and tugged Luxi's hands free of her arms. Leto released her to let Amun draw her into his arms. "Luxi, it's going to be all right."

Luxi closed her arms around Amun's neck. "I'm sorry."

"Sorry?" Leto shifted closer to Amun to catch her gaze. "For what?"

Amun stroked her back. "Luxi, we don't mind if you love us."

"Oh, hell no, we don't mind!" Leto tugged at her fingers. "Luxi, do you have any idea how hard it is to find someone that would?"

Luxi sniffed and smiled. "I didn't have any problems."

Leto grinned. "That's because you're as odd as we are."

"Odd?" Amun turned to frown at Leto. "And what do you mean by that remark?"

Leto shook his head and grinned. "Oh, come on. A telepath, a cyborg, and a fortune-teller? It sounds like the beginning of a very bad joke."

Amun gently disengaged Luxi from around his neck. "Is that so?"

Luxi shifted away, watching in interest.

Leto slid away from Amun. "Amun, what's going on in that head of yours?"

Amun smiled and his eyes narrowed. "Luxi, would you like to help me tie Leto down to the bed?"

Leto's mouth fell open. "What?"

Luxi grinned. "I think I would like that a lot."

Leto glanced at Luxi, his eyes wide. "Luxi!" He looked at Amun, and moved further away. "What about the bath?"

Amun rose from the bath seat. "It will still be here when we're done. The heaters will keep it warm." Amun smiled as he stalked toward Leto. "Luxi, fetch the towels."

Luxi grinned as she sloshed toward the edge of the tub. "Coming right up!"

Leto backed away from Amun. "Amun, you're not serious?"

"Leto, are you going to come quietly?" Amun licked his lips. "Or do I need to use the override codes on you?"

Leo stilled. "You wouldn't..."

Chapter Seventeen

"Luxi, are you done?"

Down on her knees at the foot, on the left side, of Amun's massive bed, Luxi finished tying the scarlet robe tie around the iron bed support. She tugged the half-hitch knot, making sure it was tight. It was a secure knot, but it would come free with one quick tug. "Yes, it's done!"

"Good, come on up on the bed."

Luxi shoved her long hair, still damp from the bath, back from her cheek and rose from her knees. The black-marble and silver master bedroom was softly lit by a half-dozen small frosted-glass domes scattered around the room. The black velvet drapes had been drawn all the way back to the head of the monstrous bed.

Leto was a pale sculpture of erotic masculine perfection spread out across the cream sheets in the center of the bed. His unbound silver hair gleamed as it spilled across the black brocade pillow under his head. His cock was a stiff ivory length arching above his belly. He was tied, wrist and ankle, to the four corners of the bed with every robe tie and curtain cord Amun could get his hands on.

Leto twisted his bound hands and glared at Amun, kneeling between his spread legs. "There's not a whole lot I can do from this position."

"Of course not." Amun grinned broadly, his hands resting in his naked hips. His long, deep-blood mane fell in a rich cloak down his back. "That *is* the idea, Leto."

Luxi climbed onto the bed and crawled on hands and knees toward the men. Both of them looked good enough to eat. The cords that still bound her rubbed against her tender inner lips and clit enticingly.

Amun turned to regard her with his bright green eyes then held out his hand. "Come over here, Luxi."

Luxi took his hand and rose up on her knees at his side. "What are we going to do now?"

"Now?" Amun leaned closer to brush a soft kiss on her lips. "We're going to fuck Leto."

Luxi frowned " *We* are?"

"Yes, *we* are." Amun smiled down at Leto and pointed to a white squeeze tube lying above Leto's pillow. "Hand me the gel."

Leto shifted on the bed. "Amun, what are you up to?"

Luxi leaned over to get the tube of gel, somewhat confused. The gymnastics of what Amun was saying didn't quite match up in her mind. She turned back to Amun and handed him the white tube.

"You heard me." Amun opened the gel, squeezed out a generous dollop onto his palm then rubbed his palms together.

Leto frowned. "But I thought you wanted to try Luxi's binding?"

Luxi's head came up. This was news to her.

"Oh, I do." Amun grasped his cock with both hands. "Eventually." He sighed with pleasure.

Leto groaned. "Oh, you bastard..."

Amun smiled.

Luxi raised a brow. If Amun was using gel, then Amun was probably going up somebody's butt... She winced. *I hope that isn't for me.* Amun was way too big. They both were.

Leto shifted and his ties groaned. "It's damned hard for me to get off that way if I can't move."

Amun leaned down to kiss Leto's brow. "I'll make it up to you." He closed the tube and set it down on the far side of the bed. He got up on his knees and straddled Leto's hips, his strong cock striking the side of Leto's cock. He turned and held out his hand. "Luxi, come to me."

Luxi eyed the two cocks, one slicked with lubrication gel, and one not, with grave suspicion. She reached out and grasped Amun's hand.

Amun tugged her close and turned her to face the head of the bed. He patted her thigh. "Up and over, you're riding on top."

Leto licked his lips and scowled. "Amun, I'm going to get you for this."

Luxi nibbled on her bottom lip and stood up on the mattress. She stepped over Leto's hips to straddle him.

Amun caught Luxi's hips and steadied her. "There, sit and take Leto into you."

Luxi came down on her knees and leaned forward over Leto's broad chest. She reached back between her thighs to grasp his heated shaft and stopped, staring at his pale, stiff nipples. She licked her lips.

Leto's brows shot up.

Luxi held his gaze, leaned to the right, and licked the stiff nub with the tip of her tongue. The sensation of a second nipple right under it was overpowering. She pressed her entire mouth to his nipple and licked, exploring the odd but definitely interesting sensation with her lips and tongue, then sucked. She released his nipple with a wet smack.

Leto released a long, harsh groan and shifted under her. "I changed my mind. I'll come just fine as long as Luxi keeps that up."

Amun chuckled. "Leto, you are such a little slut."

Leto lifted his head and grinned. "Hell, yeah, I'm a slut!" He focused on Luxi. "Get that cock stuffed, babe. I'm in the mood to fuck."

Get that cock stuffed? Luxi snorted. *I'll show you a stuffed cock.* She set her palm on his breast for leverage and leaned up a bit. She angled Leto's broad cockhead against the folds of her core—and encountered the cords.

"Allow me." Amun's warm thumbs parted the damp, slick silk cords. "Now."

Luxi groaned as the pressure of the cord's knot on her clit increased. She took a breath and rubbed Leto's cockhead against her slick folds, then shifted her knees back a little.

Leto closed his eyes and sucked in a breath. "Luxi, I'm dying here...do it!"

Luxi shot Leto a glare. "You'll get it; don't rush me!"

"Oh, he'll get it." Amun laughed. "Go on, Luxi."

Luxi sat back, pressing his broad head into the snug, hungry mouth of her core. Her body stretched to accommodate his girth as she progressed back and down, increment by increment.

Amun released the cords and they closed around Leto's cock.

Leto closed his eyes, sucked in a breath, and bit his lip. "Oh, that's tight."

Luxi had nearly the full length in her when she stopped for a breath, slid up just a bit, then came down hard, seating herself fully.

Leto gasped. He arched, head tipped back, his hands balled into fists and his body straining up off the mattress. "Oh...shit..." He dropped.

Luxi levered herself up and smiled. "Better."

Leto wheezed dramatically. "Much."

Amun choked out a laugh. "Good, my turn. Luxi, lean down and torture Leto's nipples for a bit."

Luxi eyed Amun suspiciously and sucked on her bottom lip. "Okay." She turned to face Leto and leaned down, pressing her body against his long, warm length. His cock moved deliciously within her.

Leto smiled. "I love it when you do that tongue thing."

Luxi grinned. "Good. How about the teeth thing?"

Leto's smile disappeared. "Teeth thing?"

Luxi pressed her mouth over his nipple to demonstrate. Her tongue flicked and licked the tender nub; then she raked her teeth across it.

Leto groaned. "Oh...the teeth thing. Yeah, I like the teeth thing. Do that some more."

Behind her, Amun pressed a hand to Luxi's back, encouraging her to lay flat. He parted the cords and his finger pressed against the rose of her anus. It was slick with gel.

Luxi froze. "Amun?"

"Push out, Luxi." His finger pressed insistently. "Push out hard."

Luxi took a deep breath and pushed out. His finger slid past her anal ring and invaded her. She groaned. "Amun, I really don't think..."

"Luxi, you are very tight. Has no one ever been here before?" His finger moved around within her, coating her interior with gel. "Keep pushing out, Luxi; it relaxes the muscles."

Luxi whimpered. "No, I've never done it before." It didn't actually hurt; in fact, it was almost enjoyable, but the sensation was a dark and very different type of pleasure.

Amun rotated his finger within her. "Oh? Good." He pulled his finger back out.

Leto's brows shot up. "You've never had it up the ass?"

Luxi flinched. "No, I haven't." Glory, he made it sound like she was still virginal.

Amun leaned over her back and his hand closed on her shoulder. "Luxi, I need you to push out as hard as you can." The heat of his cock pressed against her anus.

Luxi cowered on top of Leto and her heart beat in her throat. "Amun, you're going to be too big."

Amun's fingers bit into her shoulder. "You'll adjust. Push, because I am coming in, right now." He pressed hard.

Luxi's anus spread under the pressure and the sharp pain caught her off guard. She gasped. "It hurts!"

Amun smacked her butt. "Push out!"

Luxi whimpered, and pushed. Her anus spread with a speed she didn't expect and swallowed Amun's cockhead. She groaned. "You're too big!"

Amun pulled on her shoulder and shoved his cock harder. "Keep pushing!"

Luxi kept pushing. Amun's cock was a hot bar of steel, spreading her obscenely wide as it slid against Leto's cock, already lodged within her. She moaned.

Amun groaned at her back. "Blood and hell, you are tight, woman!"

Leto chuckled under them. "I guess that means she's going to need fairly frequent anal reaming to loosen her up."

Luxi whimpered. "Leto, you are not helping!"

"Of course not." Leto cleared his throat. "I'm tied up at the moment."

Amun's thighs brushed hers and he sighed. "There, I'm in."

Luxi released a tiny breath. "Great."

Amun leaned down over her, setting his hands on the mattress to either side. He kissed her shoulder. "Do you know how long it has been since I fucked a virgin ass?"

"I don't know and I don't care!" Luxi shifted, trying to relieve the burning ache in her ass. "You guys are freaking huge!"

Leto grinned, completely without shame. "What a nice thing to say."

Luxi scowled down at him.

Leto licked his lips. "Wait 'til it's my turn to ream your tight little butt."

"When we have her suspended from the bulkhead, there'll be plenty of opportunities." Amun groaned and began to withdraw.

Luxi gasped. The pain in her butt had transformed to something entirely different, almost pleasurable.

Leto shifted impatiently. "Amun, you're not linking us. I don't feel a thing."

Amun chuckled. "This is Luxi's first ass-fucking; are you sure you want it?"

"I like pain." Leto grinned. "Do me."

Amun stopped with only his cockhead left in Luxi's ass. "Done."

Sensation rushed over Luxi in a heavy wave of raw lust and erotic, fiery tightness. She could feel her body's wet heat tight around the both of their cocks and her own wet, ravenous hunger under it all.

Amun thrust, hard, driving Luxi forward. Leto's cock withdrew as Amun's surged in.

Sharp pain, erotic heat, brutal pleasure, fierce tightness…

They gasped.

Leto choked. "Oh, shit…"

Amun's arm closed tight around Luxi's waist. He pulled her back and down onto Leto's hard cock. His cock withdrew from her anal passage with a slow, rich decadence that made them all groan and writhe with her pleasure.

Amun thrust, pushing Luxi forward and forcing Leto's withdrawal. The cocks rubbed against each other, one going in and one coming out, with only a thin wall between them.

Luxi gasped, inundated by their extreme pleasure in her tight heat, underscored by the edge of pain from her anal reaming.

Amun's body dampened with sweat. He stopped, fully within her. "Lean down and lick his nipples."

Luxi leaned down and took Leto's nipple into her mouth. She laved it with her tongue. The echo of Leto's pleasure fired her nipples, as well.

Amun withdrew in a rich slide of dark delight.

Luxi sucked hard on Leto's nipple and bore down on Leto's cock in pure reaction.

Amun slammed into her, delivering sharp pain that mixed with the raw delight of surging into her tight, hot passage.

Luxi rose from Leto's cock and bit down on his nipple, bringing a different kind of pleasure and pain into the erotic mix.

Leto groaned and bucked under her, driven to seek more.

Amun withdrew more quickly.

Luxi surged down onto Leto's cock, filling her hungry core with his thick heat and feeling the echo of the cords rubbing and squeezing around Leto's cock. She moved to Leto's other nipple and took it into the wet heat of her mouth.

Amun surged in, bringing a rush of fire and power.

Luxi bit down on Leto's nipple, delivering a sharp spark that detonated in her nipple, her clit, and in Leto's cock, even as it slid from her body.

Burning thrust, heated withdrawal, and a hot, wet, tormenting mouth on a sensitive and tender nipple... The vicious delight of one washing into the mind of the next, and the next... The fierce, ruthless ecstasy was underscored and brightened by the slight edge of pain. Over and over, and over...

Climax surged and crested in a blast-furnace of intensity.

Leto howled under them, ravenous and demanding.

Amun and Luxi stared into Leto's burning, hungry eyes.

Release crashed through them and took them in a fire-fall of horrific glory.

Leto took—and they gave.

They screamed.

Luxi opened her eyes, her cheek pressed against the warmth of Leto's shoulder.

Leto smiled, his eyes hooded and his expression sated. "Hey, love." He kissed her brow and his arms closed around her.

She frowned, confused, but unsure why.

Alongside Leto, Amun groaned and rolled onto his back. "That was...impressive."

Leto stretched. "Maker's balls, I haven't been this sated in over a century." He closed his arms around them both, his wrists trailing the bright ribbons of ripped robe ties. "And I didn't take either of you out."

Amun rolled up onto his side to throw his arm over Leto's waist. He smiled lazily. "That's because you have two major talents in bed."

Leto turned to look over at Luxi. "I'll say."

Luxi finally figured out what had caught her attention. "You broke the ties."

"What?" Leto lifted a wrist and then his ankle, both trailing shreds of robe ties. "Well, yeah. I'm a cyborg. Unless you use cabling wire, I'm going to snap it if I'm not careful."

"Oh, I forgot." Luxi sat up and groaned. Every muscle in her body ached.

"You forgot?" Leto blinked. "How could you forget?"

"Well, yeah, I forgot. It was easy." Luxi slid to the side of the bed and stood on wobbly legs. She padded gingerly around the end of the bed.

Amun dropped his head on Leto's shoulder and laughed tiredly. "She forgot you were a cyborg."

"Luxi? How could you forget?" Leto frowned ferociously. "And where are you going?"

"I keep forgetting, because I don't see you that way." Luxi turned back to the bed and smiled. "You don't kiss like a cyborg." She padded toward the bathroom. "I'm going back to the bubble bath to soak out some of these aches."

Luxi stepped into the blissfully hot water. She submerged to her neck and the heat sank loosening fingers into her muscles. She groaned in delighted gratitude. The heaters had done their job and kept the water at the perfect temperature—just on the edge of hot.

Groans and the footfalls of bare feet announced Leto and Amun's arrival. Splashes and delighted moans followed soon after.

Leto leaned up against the side of the tub next to Luxi and sank until the water rose to his neck. He sighed. "This was a good idea."

Amun stationed himself on Luxi's other side and submerged to his neck, as well. "Why do I have the feeling that we are going to need a lot of baths?"

Luxi smiled. "Because you are a man of rare intelligence?"

Amun grinned. "Keep that up and I'll give you a raise."

Leto's brows rose. "You mean she actually gets paid?"

Amun turned and smiled at Leto. "Are you sure you want to go there?"

Leto bit back his grin. "Now that I think about it? Not really. Maybe later?"

Amun turned to Luxi. "Are you sure you want to stay with us?"

Luxi yawned. "Yup." She smiled tiredly.

Leto and Amun traded grins.

Leto lifted his arms and folded them behind his neck. "Good, because I didn't want to have to hunt you down."

Luxi frowned at him. "You wouldn't..."

Amun nodded and rolled his eyes. "Oh, yes, he would. And he'd bring you back, too." He smiled slyly. "You give in simply to stop all the begging and pleading."

Leto turned and frowned at Amun. "Hey! I did not plead!"

Luxi rolled her eyes. "You two..."

"No, Luxi." Amun caught her chin and turned her to face him. "Us, three." He pressed a gentle kiss to her lips.

Leto pressed against her side and took over where Amun's kiss left off.

~*~

Morgan Hawke

Morgan Hawke has lived in seven states of the US and spent two years in England. She has been an auto mechanic, a security guard, a waitress, a groom in a horse-stable, in the military, a copywriter, a magazine editor, a professional tarot reader, a belly-dancer and a stripper. Her personal area of expertise is the strange and unusual.

Ms. Hawke has been writing erotic fiction since 1998 and maintains a close and personal relationship with her computer and her cat. Visit Morgan on the Web at www.darkerotica.net .

Printed in the United States
98693LV00004B/44/A